His gaze sent an oddly sensual quiver through every nerve in her body.

"You've no right to be running sheep in this part of the state," she said. "This is cattle country."

A dangerous smile tugged at a corner of his mouth, underscored by the dance of lightning in the dark sky behind him. "This is open range. And only a cattleman's woman would talk like that."

Rachel had to raise her voice to be heard above the echoing thunder. "A cattleman's *daughter!*" she snapped. "And if you so much as lay a finger on me—"

His cold, bitter laughter interrupted her. "I'm aware of who your father is, Miss Tolliver. I've even heard a few tales about his spoiled, redheaded hellion of a daughter. Believe me, I'd just as soon pick up a live rattlesnake as lay a finger or anything else on you...!"

* * *

Wyoming Woman
Harlequin Historical #728—November 2004

Acclaim for Elizabeth Lane's latest books

Bride on the Run
"Enjoyable and satisfying all around, *Bride on the Run* is an excellent Western romance you won't want to miss!"
—*Romance Reviews Today (romrevtoday.com)*

Shawnee Bride
"A fascinating, realistic story."
—*Rendezvous*

Apache Fire
"Enemies, lovers, raw passion, taut sexual tension, murder and revenge—Indian romance fans are in for a treat with Elizabeth Lane's sizzling tale of forbidden love that will hook you until the last moment."
—*Romantic Times*

ELIZABETH LANE

Wyoming Woman

HARLEQUIN®

TORONTO • NEW YORK • LONDON
AMSTERDAM • PARIS • SYDNEY • HAMBURG
STOCKHOLM • ATHENS • TOKYO • MILAN • MADRID
PRAGUE • WARSAW • BUDAPEST • AUCKLAND

ISBN 0-373-29328-3

WYOMING WOMAN

Copyright © 2004 by Elizabeth Lane

This edition published by arrangement with Harlequin Books S.A.

® and TM are trademarks of the publisher. Trademarks indicated with
® are registered in the United States Patent and Trademark Office, the
Canadian Trade Marks Office and in other countries.

www.eHarlequin.com

Printed in U.S.A.

Please address questions and book requests to:
Harlequin Reader Service
U.S.: 3010 Walden Ave., P.O. Box 1325, Buffalo, NY 14269
Canadian: P.O. Box 609, Fort Erie, Ont. L2A 5X3

For Barbara

Chapter One

Wyoming, May 24, 1901

The wagon road that cut south from Sheridan was little more than a rutted cow path meandering between clumps of sage and rabbit brush, skirting boulders and dipping through gullies as it wound its way toward the horizon. Its washboard surface jarred every bone in Rachel Tolliver's body as she balanced on the seat of the buggy she had rented at the railroad depot. Her gloved hands gripped the leather reins as she struggled to slow the headstrong mule. Her trunks, bags and hat boxes bounced and rattled on the floorboards as every bump threatened to send them flying into the sagebrush.

She had been in the East too long, Rachel thought. Three years ago, she would not have given the mule, the rickety buggy or the dusty, rutted road a second thought. But her time at art school in Philadelphia had spoiled her. She had become accustomed to paved roads and well-mannered horses, and had even ridden in an automobile. Wyoming was a wild, rough, different world. But it was home, and despite the bumpy ride, her heart sang with happiness.

Slamming the wheel brake forward, she swerved to miss a jutting boulder. The buggy lurched like a drunkard, almost throwing her across the patched leather seat, but the mule, who had evidently learned that a brisk pace meant a swift return to the barn, did not even slow its careening trot.

Using her legs to grip the seat, Rachel repinned her chic straw hat atop her upswept, red-gold hair and braced herself for the next washed-out section of road. She was beginning to wish she'd wired her family at the ranch and let them know she was coming a week early. They could have met the afternoon train and given her a pleasant ride home in the big, lumbering wagon they used to haul supplies. Instead she had decided to surprise them.

What in heaven's name had she been thinking?

Rachel had traveled this road countless times by horse and wagon, and she knew every rutted, bumpy, wandering foot of it. Just ahead lay the long, steep hill that marked the halfway point between Sheridan and the sprawling cattle ranch where her family lived. Once she made it over the top, the most tedious part of the trip would be over. She would be able to fly down the switchbacks on the other side, then enjoy the level stretch that cut across the open plain.

She could just imagine her family's reaction when she drove the buggy in through the ranch gate. Her mother would be overjoyed to see her but would fuss over the fact that she'd made the long drive alone. Her half Shoshone father, a loving but undemonstrative man, would give her a restrained hug, ask her about school and return to his chores. Her twin brothers, Jacob and Josh, would be clamoring to see the presents she'd brought them—a collection of the silly little mechanical toys they loved and had never outgrown, even in their late teens. They would be racing the small wind-up automobiles up and down the upstairs hallway, laughing and whooping like young savages. The sound of that laughter, Rachel thought, would be music to her ears.

Three years at art school had fulfilled a lifelong wish for her, but time had taught her that she would never be content in the city. Her heart belonged to the windswept plains and towering peaks of Wyoming, and she wanted nothing more than to spend the rest of her life here.

A prairie chicken exploded from the roadside as Rachel settled herself for the long climb up the hill. As the road wound upward, the mule, which had been tearing along like a juggernaut, gradually slowed its pace to a plodding walk. To encourage the animal, Rachel slapped its haunches with the long reins and began to sing at the top of her lungs.

"In a cavern, in a canyon, excavating for a mine, dwelt a miner, forty-niner and his daughter, Clementine…"

Despite her encouragement, she could feel the mule begin to flag as they neared the crest. Slapping the reins down hard on its dusty rump, Rachel sang louder.

"Oh, my darling, oh, my darling, oh, my darling Clementine, thou art lost and gone forever, dreadful sorry, Clementine."

The buggy crowned the hill and began to level out. Relieved of the buggy's heavy drag, the mule broke into a determined trot once more. Suddenly Rachel found herself on the downward side, going fast. Too fast.

A knot of fear jerked tight in her stomach as she thrust the brake forward. There was a grinding sound, then the sickening sense of nothing happening. The brake was gone, and the mule, with the careening buggy pushing from behind, was not going to slow down.

Sawing helplessly on the reins, she gasped as the buggy swung around the first sharp curve with a force that slammed her across the seat and almost tipped the vehicle onto its side. Clawing her way upright, Rachel got a grip on the seat just in time for the next switchback. The buggy was rolling downhill at breakneck speed, but the steepest part of the road was behind her now. If she could hold on for the two remaining turns, the slope would level out and the buggy would slow down on its own.

Clenching her teeth, she braced herself for the next hairpin turn. The wheels plowed sideways into the loose gravel with a force that threatened to snap the axle, but, miraculously, the buggy held the road.

Hat gone, hair flying, Rachel gripped the reins and

braced her feet for the final curve. It would be all right, she told herself. The grade was already leveling off, and her speed was slowing. She and the accursed mule were going to make it. Two hours from now she would be home, regaling her family with the story of her wild ride.

She was in position for the turn when the wheels hit a sudden dip. Launched upward, the buggy became airborne for a heart-stopping instant. Then it hit the road with a jolt that Rachel felt to the roots of her teeth. The impact lifted her inches off the seat, but she clung doggedly to the reins. This wasn't her day to die! She had too much living left to do. Too many pictures to paint, too many horses to break, cattle to brand and people to love! She'd be damned if she was going to let go now!

Hanging on with every last ounce of strength, she wrestled the buggy around the last curve. The vehicle rocked dangerously, then, counterbalanced by Rachel's own weight, settled back onto four wheels. Rachel felt herself begin to breathe again. She had made it down the hill in one piece. She was going to be all right.

Then she saw them.

Sheep.

They spread like a lumpy white flood across the road, a scant seventy yards ahead of her. There were hundreds of them—ewes and rams, plump with unshorn wool, and tiny lambs scampering among their legs. She could hear their piercing bleats, hear the clanging of their bells as they ambled along with their noses in the dust, so bland and stupid that they didn't even have enough sense to get out of her way.

She was going to plow right into the herd.

Frantic, Rachel jerked the reins and shouted at the top of her lungs, but the sound that emerged from her mouth was lost amid the bleating of the sheep. The brainless creatures did not even raise their heads. What in heaven's name were they doing here anyway? Where was their herder?

She flung her weight backward in the desperate hope that the mule would stop. But the buggy kept moving, like a reaper headed into a stand of wheat. It would mow down the sheep, leaving a swath of dead and injured animals until the resistance of their bodies finally stopped its motion.

There was only one thing she could do, and, with time ticking down to a split second, Rachel did it.

Wrenching the reins to the right, she swerved off the road. The mule was ripping along in a blind panic now. There was no time to choose a good spot or even to look where she was going. The buggy lurched over clumps of sage, bounded off a saddle-sized rock and careened down the side of a wash. The mule screamed and pitched onto its side as the buggy rolled, scattering trunks and boxes and throwing Rachel forward, over the dash. Like a rag doll tossed by an uncaring child, she tumbled onto the sand, moaned and lay still.

Luke Vincente heard his dogs barking as he came over the rise. The sound put him on instant alert. The two Scotch border collies tended to work the sheep quietly, uttering soft little yips as they worried the flanks of the stragglers. The clamor he heard now could have only one meaning—something was wrong.

Luke's eyes scanned the herd as he urged the rangy buckskin gelding down the slope. The sheep were ambling along at their usual pace, showing no sign that anything was amiss. But Luke could not see either of the dogs. Maybe they'd cornered a badger or come across a den of coyote pups. Or maybe they'd even found a rattler. A snake-bit dog was the last thing he wanted.

A shallow wash, etched by spring floods, cut down the side of the hill and zigzagged across the flat. That would be where the dogs were, Luke calculated. Otherwise he'd be able to see them. Anxious now, he spurred the buckskin to a trot.

Luke had come to Wyoming seeking the peace and solitude of open spaces. But he'd had enough trouble here to last him the rest of his life, especially in the past few weeks. Just this morning Luke had found three of his best purebred merino ewes shot dead around a watering hole. The cattlemen who'd done it hadn't even bothered to hide their tracks. Why should they, when the law turned a blind eye to any crime committed against people who raised sheep?

But that wasn't the worst of it. Three nights ago, his best herder, an old Spaniard who wouldn't hurt a fly, had narrowly escaped death when masked raiders had torched the sheep wagon where he slept. When the old man had stumbled outside, the masked men had beaten him to a bloody pulp and left him for dead.

Luke had no doubt that the raiders had come from neighboring ranches whose owners wanted him, his sheep and his herders off the open range. The fact that they had every right to be there only made the cattlemen more determined to drive him off.

Luke had had a bellyful of trouble over the past week. He could only hope he wasn't about to stumble into more.

The barking grew louder as he neared the wash. Now, through the tall sage, he could see a stark, black shape jutting above the rim. Luke swore under his breath as he realized what it was. What kind of damned fool would drive a buggy fast enough to run it off the road in this country?

His heart sank as he realized he was about to find out.

Luke swung out of the saddle and looped the buckskin's reins over a dead cedar bush. As he strode down into the wash the dogs bounded out from behind the buggy to greet him, their tongues lolling, their feathery black-and-white tails wagging, as if to say, "Look what we've found!"

With a low whistle and a swift hand sign that the dogs had been trained to obey, Luke sent them back to tend the herd. As they frisked up the slope of the wash, he turned and walked cautiously toward the buggy.

Its front wheels were buried axle deep in sand. One rear wheel, tipped clear of the ground, was still spinning. Either the wind was playing tricks, or the accident had only just happened.

He looked for a horse or mule, but found only the broken traces and a set of large, shod hoofprints leading up the side of the wash. Judging from the trail it had left, the animal wasn't badly hurt. Luke hoped the driver of the buggy had been as fortunate, but as he gazed at the wreckage, he knew that wasn't likely.

The buggy had been going fast when it shot over the edge of the wash, he surmised. Fast enough, most likely, to throw the driver over the dash and break his fool neck, or maybe smash his head on a rock. Either way, he wasn't going to be a pretty sight.

Luke was a half-dozen paces from the buggy when a flicker of movement beyond the far side of it caught his eye. Something was blowing in the wind—something white and lacy that looked like a petticoat. And he could see now that the debris scattered around the wreck included two hat boxes and a trunk that had burst open on impact and bounced down the wash, spilling a trail of frilly undergarments along its sandy bed.

Luke swore out loud. It was bad enough that the driver had endangered himself. That he'd been driving like a lunatic with a woman aboard was more than stupid. It was downright criminal.

As he sprinted around the buggy, Luke caught sight of crumpled petticoats and a fluttering blue skirt. For an instant he hoped it might be a heap of clothing. But the sleek little high-button boots thrusting from beneath a ruffle of ecru lace told him otherwise.

She lay on her back, amber curls spilling like a tangled skein of silk embroidery floss over the rocky gray sand. Her eyes were closed, the lashes like the soft, dark vane of a quail's feather against ivory cheeks. Her features were as perfect as a doll's, her periwinkle-blue traveling suit so well-tailored and immaculate that she looked as if she had just been lifted out of a tissue-lined box before being flung onto the ground.

She was somebody's rich, spoiled baby, that was for sure. The same kind of rich, spoiled baby who'd cost him four precious years of his life.

Her breasts were small and taut beneath the snug-fitting jacket. Their even rise and fall confirmed that she was breathing. A touch of his fingertip to her warm throat told Luke her pulse was strong and steady. His first impulse was to lift her head and try to get some water down her. But she could have fractured bones or even a broken neck, he cautioned himself. It would be best not to move her until she could tell him what was hurting. He would give her a few minutes to awaken on her own. Meanwhile, he needed to find out what had happened to the driver.

Luke glanced around and saw no sign of another person, nor could he spot any tracks leading away from the wreckage. He scanned the buggy and the area around it, then, rising to his feet, made a hasty search of the surrounding rocks and brush. Unless the driver had been snatched directly into heaven, there was only one conclusion to be made. The damn-fool woman had been driving the buggy herself.

For the space of a long breath, Luke stood gazing at the thick black clouds that were spilling over the Big Horn Mountains to the west. The afternoon breeze smelled of rain—a welcome sign. Here on the open range where sheep and cattle competed for every bite of grass, water was more precious than gold. But mountain storms could also trigger flash floods that sent mud and water boiling down washes just like this one, drowning unwary stock and burying anything that couldn't be swept away.

As if echoing his thoughts, sheet lightning flashed above the peaks, followed by the rumbling boom of thunder. This wash was no place to be stuck in a storm, especially with an unconscious female on his hands. Injured or not, he needed to get her to safe ground.

He was turning back toward her when something caught his eye—a glittering flash of blue, lodged behind one half-buried front wheel. Drawn by curiosity, he dropped to a crouch and worked the object free. It was a small, beaded reticule, fashioned of the same fabric as the periwinkle-blue traveling suit. Luke glared down at it, where it lay clutched in his big, callused hands. The little piece of frippery had probably cost enough to feed a starving family for a month. And this pampered, pretty creature probably hadn't given the money a second's thought.

Only as he was about to toss it away in disgust did it occur to him that he should open the reticule and look inside. He might find something with a name or address on it—a letter, a calling card, even an embroidered handkerchief that might tell him her name or furnish some clue about who to contact, should she need more help than he could give her.

His fingers fumbled with the small, ornate clasp. Frustrated by its intricacy, Luke cursed under his breath. For two cents he would draw his knife and cut the damned thing open like a—

"Hold it right there, sheep man!"

The taut little voice raked Luke's senses. "Drop the bag, raise your hands and turn around slowly. No tricks, or I'll blow you to kingdom come!"

Luke's rifle was on the horse and, in any case, he knew better than to make a rash move before sizing up the situation. Cursing himself for getting into this predicament, he dropped the reticule, raised his hands and slowly turned around.

The woman lay propped on one elbow. Her striking blue-green eyes blazed with raw fury. Her free hand gripped a tiny but evil-looking derringer that was pointed straight at Luke's chest.

Chapter Two

Rachel gripped the miniature one-shot pistol she'd taken from her pocket, willing her fingers not to tremble. Her temples were throbbing, and her left shoulder felt as if it had been kicked by a mule, but there was nothing missing from her memory. The recollection of swerving off the road to miss the sheep, then careening into the wash, was crystal-clear in her mind—as clear as the image of the bastard she'd just caught trying to rob her.

"Are you sure you know how to use that little toy, lady?" He spoke with a hint of southern drawl, his voice as deep and rich as blackstrap molasses.

"You don't want to find out the hard way." She glared up at him, feeling small and helpless despite the cold weight of the gun in her hand. The derringer was cocked and loaded, the man close enough to provide an easy target. But something in the lithe, easy way he stood, hands relaxed, dark eyes narrowed like a wolf's, whispered danger. Fear crept upward into her throat—a fear that she masked with spitting fury.

"Are these your sheep?" she sputtered. She took his silence for a yes. "I could have been killed! Look at this buggy! It's ruined, and the mule's run off to heaven knows where! What were those fool animals doing in the road anyway? If I hadn't swerved, I'd have crashed right into them!"

"The last I heard, there was no law against herding stock across a road," he replied icily. "Sheep and cattle have the right-of-way in this country. If you were going too fast to make the turn, that's nobody's fault but your own. Now put that silly little gun away before somebody gets hurt."

"So you can finish going through my things? Don't waste your time. I don't have enough money in that bag to be worth your trouble."

His lip curled in a sneer of contempt, and Rachel sensed at once that she had said the wrong thing. The stranger's fierce pride showed in the erect stance of his lean, muscular body, the set of his aquiline head and the unruly spill of blue-black hair over his brow. His face was more compelling than handsome, with features that could have been hewn from raw granite. His dark, hooded eyes were as sharp and alert as a hawk's. He was a disturbing man, an unsettling man whose gaze sent an oddly sensual quiver through every nerve in her body. But Rachel's instincts told her he was too proud to steal, especially from a woman.

All the same, she would be foolish to lower her guard. Gripping the derringer's tiny stock, she glared up at him. From beyond the rim of the wash, she could hear the brassy jangle of sheep's bells and the bleating of the ewes and lambs. "You've no right to be running sheep in this part of the state," she said. "This is cattle country."

A dangerous smile tugged at a corner of his mouth, underscored by the dance of lightning in the dark sky behind him. "This is open range. And only a cattleman's woman would talk like that."

Rachel had to raise her voice to be heard above the echoing thunder. "A cattleman's *daughter!*" she snapped, throwing discretion to the winds. "My name is Rachel Tolliver. My father owns the biggest cattle ranch in this county. And if you so much as lay a finger on me—"

His laughter interrupted her—cold, bitter laughter that did nothing to settle her edginess. "I'm aware of who your father is, Miss Tolliver. I've even heard a few tales about his spoiled, redheaded hellion of a daughter. Believe me, I'd just as soon pick up a live rattlesnake as lay a finger or anything else on you. Now, if you don't mind putting that gun away, my arms are getting tired."

Rachel hesitated. She'd grown up hearing that sheep men were worse than bandits. Their wretched, woolly animals fouled the water holes and destroyed good range land by nipping off every blade of grass so short that there was nothing left for the cattle to eat. Sheepherders who worked for wages tended to be Mexicans or Spanish Basques—quaint little men who lived in their hutlike wagons and kept to themselves. But this tall, insolent stranger was clearly not of that stripe.

"What do you plan to do with me, Rachel Tolliver?" he taunted her. "Shoot me? Send me packing? Either way, you'll be out here alone with a storm coming and your buggy wrecked in a wash. Like it or not, I'm the only help you've got. You've no choice except to trust me."

"I'd just as soon trust a coyote as a sheep man!" Rachel retorted, but she was beginning to see that he was right. Like it or not, unless she wanted to walk twenty miles in the rain—

The rest of her thoughts took flight at the sound of a low growl behind her. She glanced back over her shoulder to see a middle-sized dog with a shaggy black-and-white coat crouched a half-dozen paces away. Its sharp yellow fangs were bared in a threatening snarl.

"Oh—" Caught off guard, Rachel was unprepared for what happened next. With the speed of a pouncing cat, the stranger was on her. His strong hands caught her wrist and wrenched the derringer out of her grasp. The next thing she knew, she was lying flat on her back, staring up at him where he stood over her. From the ground, with thunderheads rolling in behind him, he looked as big as a mountain.

Scowling, he released the hammer and slipped the miniature pistol into his vest. Rachel was bracing for a fight when he reached down, seized her wrists and jerked her roughly to her feet. Frightened and angry, she tried to twist away from him. He released her so abruptly that she lost her balance, stumbled backward and slammed against the side of the buggy.

"Your call, Miss Rachel Tolliver," he growled, making no further move to touch her. "You can ask for my help, or I can ride off and leave you here alone with your spilled baggage. Either way, it's up to you. I don't give a damn what you decide."

He glanced down at the dog, which had moved to stand protectively at his side. At a slight motion of its master's hand and a spoken command that was no more than a whisper, the animal wheeled and raced up the side of the wash in the direction of the sheep.

Rachel flinched as the first raindrop splashed against the end of her nose. With a clatter that began like pearls falling from a broken string and grew to a solid rush of pelting rain, the storm swept down from the mountains to engulf everything in its path. Rain peppered the sand in the wash and blasted the dust from the buggy's shiny black body. Rachel felt its weight soaking her hair, its wet chill penetrating layers of clothing to reach her skin.

"Well, which will it be?" Water streamed off the sheep man's hair and beaded on his eyebrows, but he had not moved from where he stood. "Make up your mind, Miss Tolliver. I haven't got all day."

"All right. Yes, I need your help!" Rachel had lived too long in this country not to know what would happen to anything that remained in the wash. "Please! Hurry! The important things—my paints and canvases—are in the back! And we really need to get the buggy out. Otherwise my father will have to pay Finnegan's Livery for the loss of it.''

''There's a rope on my saddle. I'll get the horse.'' He turned away and strode up the side of the wash, his boots leaving muddy gouges that swiftly filled with water and crumbled away. Rachel watched his tall figure disappear through the gray curtain of rain. Then, with no more time to spare, she turned and raced to gather her scattered, soaking possessions.

Luke left her scrambling for her things and strode back through the brush to get the horse. Morgan Tolliver's daughter. He cursed under his breath. For two cents he would ride away and leave the little hellcat to the storm. He owed no favors to cattle ranchers and their kin, nor did he expect any in return. All he really wanted was to be left alone.

The buckskin was waiting beside the cedar bush. It nickered and shook its rain-soaked hide as he freed its bridle from the dead branch. A quick glance up the slope confirmed that Mick and Shep, the two collies, were doing their job, herding the sheep into a tight circle where the lambs would be protected from the worst of the storm. The precious animals would be safe enough until he could pull the buggy out of the wash and, he hoped to heaven, get the snooty Miss Tolliver on her way. She was a wild beauty, with those sea-colored eyes, that untamed mop of red-gold curls and a figure that would tempt the devil himself. But a cattleman's daughter... Luke shook his head and

swore as he led the horse toward the wash. Her kind
of trouble was the last thing he needed.

The Tolliver Ranch was the biggest spread in the
county, and likely one of the biggest in the state of
Wyoming. A remote corner of it butted onto Luke's
modest parcel of land at the foot of the Big Horn
Mountains. Luke had only a passing acquaintance
with the ranch's owner. But a cattleman was a cattleman, and if there was anything the cattle ranchers
hated more than sheep it was the men who allowed
them to graze on public land.

Had Morgan Tolliver and his twin sons been
among the raiders that had nearly burned poor old
Miguel alive in his wagon and then beat him sense-
less? Had a Tolliver gun shot the three purebred ewes
that were the best of Luke's herd—the herd he had
labored for five miserable, backbreaking years in the
Rock Springs coal mines to buy?

The answer to those questions made no difference.
Luke had nothing that would stand as proof against
the Tollivers and their kind. Even if he were to find
such proof, there'd be nothing he could do except sell
out and run for his life. And he would die, Luke
swore, before he let the bastards drive him off his
land.

Through the pelting rain, he could see the edge of
the wash and the water-soaked heap that Morgan Tolliver's daughter had made of her rescued baggage.
Hauling the buggy out of the wash would be a tough
job. And even if they could salvage it, how was she

going to get home with no mule to pull it? He would be stuck with her.

For the space of a breath, Luke hesitated. Why should he be helping the woman at all? Rachel Tolliver had held a gun on him, accused him of thievery and, in general, behaved like the spoiled brat she was. It would serve her right, maybe even teach her a lesson, if he rode off and left her on her own. Surely she would not be alone for long. Her family was bound to miss her and come looking for her.

But no—the image of Rachel shivering in the rain like a lost puppy was more than his conscience could bear. It had been a long time since he'd considered himself a gentleman, but he had not sunk so far that he would ride away and leave a woman in a dangerous situation.

He found her hunkered beside the buggy, digging around one mired wheel with a twisted sage root. Her hair hung around her face in dripping, curly strings, and her once-elegant blue suit was soaked with muddy water. She looked up in ill-disguised relief as Luke slogged his way down the bank with a coil of rope.

"I thought you'd turned tail and left," she said, raising her voice to be heard above the rain.

Ignoring the taunt, Luke found the middle of the rope and looped it around the rear axle of the buggy to make a tight slipknot.

Still kneeling, she glared up at him. Her eyes flashed like a tiger's through the dripping tendrils of her hair. "No lectures, sheep man. Just get the buggy out of the wash. I'll see that you're paid for your time.''

Rankled, Luke shot her a contemptuous glance. "My name is Luke Vincente. And I don't want your money—or your father's.''

She scrambled to her feet, her wet jacket outlining her small, high breasts and cold-puckered nipples. "I think you're too proud for your own good,'' she said, a scowl deepening the cleft in her determined chin. "But then, since the accident was mostly your fault, I shouldn't expect to pay you for helping me.''

"My fault?'' He glared at her.

"Well the problem with the brake wasn't your fault. I suppose Mr. Finnegan at the livery should take the blame for that, since he should have fixed it. But as for the rest—''

"The brake?'' He stared at her. "You mean you were ripping down that hill with no way to stop?''

She flashed him a withering look. "I would have been fine. Everything was under control, and I was planning to coast to a stop at the bottom. Unfortunately, your stupid sheep—'' Her muddy fists clenched into knots. "Don't think you're doing me any favors, Luke Vincente. This mess is your fault, not mine. You *owe* me—''

"Then let's get this over with,'' he snapped, playing out the rope as he moved up the bank to the waiting horse. "The job's going to take both of us. You can guide the horse, or you can stay in the wash and try to free the wheels. It's up to you.''

She gazed up at the buckskin, her eyes slitted

against the driving rain. "He's your horse. You'll get more out of him than I will. I'll stay with the buggy."

"Suit yourself." Luke had hoped she would leave him to free the wheels, but he was in no mood to argue. Not with the rain coming down harder by the minute. As he mounted the bank of the wash, he saw that she had found her digging stick and was scraping away the sand that trapped the left front wheel. A cattleman's spoiled brat she might be. But Rachel Tolliver had grit. He would credit her that much.

Tying the rope to the saddle horn, he swung onto the buckskin. Lightning snaked across the sky. "Get to the front," he shouted. "When I say push, give it everything you've got."

The only reply was a shattering crack of thunder. The horse danced nervously, tossing its head.

"Rachel?" He held his breath. An eternity seemed to pass before he heard her speak.

"I'm ready when you are." Her voice sounded thin and distant.

"Then…push!" He jabbed the horse with his knees. The buckskin was a powerful animal and the buggy wasn't heavy. One good, hard pull should be enough to break it loose, he calculated as the doubled rope strained tight.

But Luke hadn't counted on the sucking grip of the sand on the front wheels. He was just beginning to feel some give when he heard Rachel scream, "Stop!"

Only then did he realize what was·happening. The

front wheels were so firmly stuck that the pull of the horse was threatening to rip them loose from the axle.

Turning, Luke saw that Rachel had fallen to her knees and was slumped against the dash, one hand massaging her left shoulder. "We'll have to dig the wheels free," she said between clenched teeth. "Don't you have a shovel?"

Did the woman think he kept a blasted tool chest on the horse? "Hold on, I'll find something," Luke muttered, sliding out of the saddle. The rain was coming down in torrents and he was getting worried about the sheep. If the skittish animals panicked, even the dogs wouldn't be able to hold them.

The ground had become a sea of spattering mud that concealed any stick or rock that might be used for digging. Luke was twisting at a dead clump of sage, try to break it loose, when he heard a distant rushing sound—so faint at first that it was barely distinguishable from the drone of the rain. Only as it neared and grew did he realize, with blood-chilling certainty, what it was.

"Flood!" he shouted, wheeling back toward the wash. "Get the hell out of there!" He raced for the bank, ready to grab her hands and help her climb the muddy slope.

"No!" she shouted, clinging stubbornly to the frame of the buggy. "Get back to your horse! The water will wash the wheels loose! If we time it right, we can pull the buggy out! It's our only chance!"

"Don't be a fool! *Come on!*" Luke plunged down the bank, seized her left arm and wrenched her toward

him. Rachel yelped in sudden agony. Only then did
he realize she was hurt.

With a muttered curse, he scooped her up in his
arms and charged for the bank—too late. The flash
flood slammed into them like a buffalo stampede.
Luke fought to keep his footing as muddy water, thick
with silt and debris, swirled chest-deep around them.

Glancing uphill, Luke saw a gnarled tree trunk
sweeping downstream at murderous speed, its sharp
roots thrusting toward them like tangled daggers. Rachel gasped as he swung her into the protecting lee
of the buggy. The tree trunk hurtled past, missing
them by inches. But their safety was short-lived.
Lifted free by the water, the buggy began to move
downstream.

From the bank of the wash, the horse screamed in
terror as the moving vehicle's momentum dragged it
toward the torrent below. Luke's heart sank as he saw
what was happening. "Hang on tight!" he shouted at
Rachel.

Her uninjured arm locked around his neck, freeing
his hand to yank the hunting knife from the sheath
that hung at his belt. With the strength of desperation,
Luke hacked at the rope. One by one the tough fibers
parted—slowly, too slowly. Weakened by the flood,
the rim of the wash was already crumbling beneath
the buckskin's rear hooves. The horse squealed as its
hindquarters went down. Then, with one last cut, the
rope separated and the animal was free. Its forefeet
found solid earth, and it wrenched itself upward to
safety.

With the last of his strength, Luke shoved Rachel clear of the moving buggy. The buggy washed away from them and went crashing downstream. It wouldn't go far, Luke knew. But by the time the flood passed, the rented vehicle would be nothing but a battered, waterlogged piece of junk.

He wondered if the fool woman knew how lucky she was to be alive.

The brunt of the storm had already passed over the mountains. Ebbing now, the floodwater gushed between the banks in a waist-high, taffy-colored stream.

Rachel groaned as Luke Vincente heaved her onto the bank and scrambled for his own foothold on the muddy, crumbling slope. Fifty yards downstream she could see the buggy. It was sharply tilted out of the water as if it had run up on some high object, perhaps a boulder.

"There it is!" she cried, pointing. "We can still get it out! Hurry!"

"No."

Rachel stared up at him. He had gained the bank, and now he loomed above her, coated with mud from head to toe. His face was an expressionless stone mask.

"No?" she asked incredulously.

"You heard me." His lip curled in a contemptuous snarl. "Hasn't anybody ever said that word to you before, Miss Rachel Tolliver? If you want the damned buggy back, get it yourself, or send some moonstruck cowboy from the ranch to fetch it for you. I've got sheep to move.''

Without another word, he turned his back and walked away from her, toward his waiting horse. Rachel glared at his arrogant back, her temper igniting like kerosene spilled on a red-hot stove.

''Come back here!'' She ground out the words between clenched teeth. ''This was *your* fault! If your blasted sheep hadn't been in the road, I'd be on my way home!''

Luke Vincente did not even glance back at her. He had set out to be a gentleman, but Rachel Tolliver had pushed him beyond his limits. She could wait for her family to come, or she could damned well walk home. Either way, he was washing his hands of her.

''I'm all alone out here!'' she stormed. ''I have nothing to eat, no shelter, no dry clothes! What's more, my shoulder hurts! You can't just walk away and leave me!''

This time he paused and looked back at her. His dark eyes glinted like chips of granite. ''I can and I will,'' he said. ''Unless, of course, you want to come with me.''

''Come where?'' Rachel struggled to her feet. ''Take me home, and I'll see that my father rewards you.''

''I told you, I don't want your father's money,'' he said coldly. ''I've got sheep to get back to my ranch for shearing. Once we're safely there, if you want to hang around, we'll see about getting you warmed up and fed. Then we'll talk about taking you home.

That's the best I can offer you, Rachel Tolliver. Take it or leave it.''

Torn, she watched him walk away. Pride demanded that she let him go. But once he left her, she would be stranded. Her family was not expecting her at the ranch for another week. No one would miss her. No one would come looking for her.

"Luke!" Her voice stopped him. It was the first time she had called him by name. Slowly he turned around.

"I'll take it," she said. "Your offer, I mean. After all, I can hardly stay out here alone."

His expression did not even flicker. "Climb aboard then," he said, indicating the horse with a nod of his head. "We've got sheep to move."

Chapter Three

Rachel sat behind the saddle, her legs straddling the buckskin's slippery rump. Her waterlogged skirts were bunched above her knees, showing mud-streaked silk stockings and soaked, misshapen kidskin boots. Her gabardine suit was stained with floodwater, and her tangled hair hung down her back like a filthy string mop.

But Rachel was long past the point of caring about appearances. What she wanted most right now was a solid meal and a steaming, gardenia-scented bath. And then she wanted the blasted buggy back on the road, loaded with the bags she had so carefully packed for her journey west.

Most of her clothes would be ruined. That in itself was a crying shame, but at least clothes could be replaced. It was her precious supply of paints, brushes and canvases that worried Rachel most. She had persuaded Luke to help her carry the trunk that contained her painting supplies into some rocks above the wash, where people passing on the road would not see it, but everything else remained stacked near the mired buggy, at the mercy of weather and thieves. Rachel could only hope it would be safe until she could send someone to bring everything safely back to the ranch.

Her arms tightened around the sheep man's ribs as the horse swerved to avoid a badger hole. At the sudden pressure, Luke's sinewy body went taut with resistance. In the hour they had been riding together, he had scarcely linked one syllable with another. His silence told her in no uncertain terms that he was not pleased to have her along. Well, fine. She wasn't exactly happy to be here, herself. By rights she should be at home with her family, sitting down to a mouthwatering banquet prepared by Chang, the Tolliver ranch's aging cook who was a true artist in the kitchen. When she closed her eyes, Rachel could almost taste the garlic-seasoned roast beef, the mashed potatoes dripping with gravy, the carrots drenched in herbed butter and the flakiest buttermilk biscuits this side of heaven. A lusty growl quivered in the pit of her stomach. She willed herself to ignore the unladylike sound. Why should she care whether Luke had heard? His opinion of her was already so low that nothing she did could make him think any worse of her!

Hungry as she was, Rachel knew better than to ask Luke when they were going to stop and eat. The wretched man did not appear to have brought any food with him; and in any case, she was not about to give him the satisfaction of hearing her complain— not about her empty belly or the chill of the spring wind through her wet clothes or the darts of pain that lanced her shoulder with every bounce of the trotting horse. The shoulder did not seem to be broken—if it were, she knew she would be in agony. But it hurt enough to tell her that something was wrong.

Struggling to ignore her discomfort, Rachel gazed across the scrub-dotted foothills, toward the place where the land sloped downward to end in a sheer cliff that dropped sixty feet to the prairie below. Years ago, her father had told her, the Cheyenne and Sioux had used this place, and others like it, for driving buffalo. It had been a brutally efficient means of hunting. The warriors had only to surround a herd, stampede the terrified animals over the cliff and butcher their broken bodies at the bottom. The meat and hides from such a slaughter could supply a band for an entire season.

The buffalo were gone now, and the children of the hunters had long since been pushed onto reservations. But now, as her eyes traced the line of the cliff, Rachel could almost see the hurtling bodies, hear the death shrieks and smell the stench of fear and blood. With a shudder, she turned her gaze away. This was not a good day for such black thoughts. Not when she had problems of her own to deal with.

With the storm rolling eastward across the prairie, the sky above the Big Horns had begun to clear. Fingers of light from the slanting, late-afternoon sun brushed the snowy peaks with a golden radiance, as if heaven itself lay just beyond the thinning veil of clouds, and all a mortal needed to do was reach out and touch it.

Heaven was far beyond her reach today, Rachel mused wryly. With the buggy wrecked, her belongings scattered, her hair and clothes a sodden mess and this dark, brooding sheep man holding her a virtual prisoner, her current predicament seemed more like the place that was heaven's opposite.

But it was no use crying over spilled milk, that's what her mother would say. Time was too valuable to waste fretting over what could no longer be helped.

Rachel missed her lively, practical mother. She missed her father's quiet strength and the high-spirited antics of the twin brothers she adored. She wanted desperately to go home. But the stubborn, irascible stranger who guided the horse had made it clear that his precious sheep came first. She would not be reunited with her family until the miserable creatures were safely in the shearing pens on his own small ranch.

The sheep, about three hundred head of them not counting the lambs, spread over the landscape like a plague of ravenous gray-white caterpillars. Rachel had never cared for the dull-witted creatures. True, the baby lambs were cute and lively, but they soon grew up to be brainless eating machines that stripped the grass from every inch of open range they crossed. Rachel despised the sight of them, the sound of them, the sour, dusty smell of them.

The dogs, however, were a different matter.

She watched in fascination as the two border collies

darted among the sheep, nipping at the flanks of the stragglers, keeping the whole herd moving along together. Sometimes Luke spoke to them in a low voice or commanded them with simple hand gestures. For the most part, however, the dogs seemed to know exactly what they were doing and needed no direction. Rachel had always liked dogs, and these two alert, intelligent animals were as fine a pair as she had ever seen.

"Your dogs are magnificent," she said, watching the darker of the two chase a straying lamb back toward its mother. "Did you train them yourself?"

"Shep and Mick came with the sheep when I bought them," Luke said tersely. "*I* was the one who had to be trained."

It was a civil enough answer, but there was a dark undertone in Luke's voice, a hidden tension in his muscular body, as if something were lurking below the surface of everything he said and did. She had held a gun on him, Rachel reminded herself. She had treated Luke Vincente with as much contempt as he had treated her. But there was more at work here, she sensed, than simple animosity. There were things she didn't know, things she needed to understand for her own safety.

Rachel held her tongue for a time, hoping Luke would volunteer more. But when he did not speak again, her impatience got the better of her.

"I've been at school in Philadelphia for the past three years," she said. "You and your sheep certainly weren't around before I left."

He sighed, as if resigning himself to a conversation he did not want to have. "I came here two years ago. My property butts onto the northwest corner of your family's ranch, where those reddish foothills jut out onto the prairie."

"In that case, I'm surprised my father hasn't tried to buy you out," Rachel said. "At a fair price, of course."

Luke shrugged. "He has. Not in person, but through that little weasel of a land agent who comes sniffing around my place every few months."

"Mr. Connell is a good man," Rachel said. "My father has been dealing with him for years, and he's never cheated us out of a penny...even though he does look a bit like a weasel." She suppressed an impish smile. "What did you tell him when he made an offer on your land?"

"That I wouldn't sell. Not even for a fair price."

The edge in his reply was not lost on Rachel. "But why not?" she demanded. "You could run sheep in Nevada, or Colorado, or New Mexico, and nobody would care a fig! Why set up a sheep ranch smack in the middle of cattle country, where three-quarters of the people you meet are going to hate you?"

"Maybe because there's no law that says I can't." He spoke in a flat voice that defied her to argue with him. "Do you play poker, Miss Rachel Tolliver?"

"Some."

"I won my land in a poker game while you were probably still in pigtails," he said. "Some rough years came and went before I was able to live on it.

But it was my own piece of the earth. Whatever happened to me, it was always there, like a beacon to get me through the bad times.''

Rachel wondered about those bad times, but she knew better than to ask too many personal questions. Luke Vincente, she sensed, was a very private man who would not show his scars to unsympathetic eyes.

How old was he? she found herself wondering. He had the flat-bellied, lean-hipped body of a man in his early thirties and his hair carried only a light touch of silver. But his creased, windburned face had a hard set to it, as if his eyes had seen more than his mind wanted to remember.

"I understand how you must feel about the land," she said.

"Do you?" he asked, clearly implying that Rachel would not know what it was like to get anything the hard way. She bridled, then willed herself to ignore the barb.

"But why raise sheep, for heaven's sake?" she continued as if he hadn't spoken. "Why not cattle, like the rest of us? Why make enemies of your neighbors?"

Luke's gaze traced the spiraling flight of a redtailed hawk against the sky. "You've never had to set up a cattle operation," he said. "It takes big money these days, usually from some rich investor. And you need a whole crew of cowboys to take care of your herd—cowboys who have to be fed and housed and paid. And even if you get your cattle through the season and to the railhead in good shape, you can still lose your shirt if the market's bad.''

Rachel gazed past his shoulder at the flowing mass of sheep and the darting figures of the two dogs. Everything Luke had said was true. Cattle raising was an expensive business. The old days, when a man could buy a cheap piece of land, drive a herd of longhorns north from Mexico and have himself a working ranch were long gone.

''Sheep, even purebreds like these, are cheaper to buy than cattle,'' Luke said. ''Sheep tend to multiply faster than cattle, and they can survive in country where cows would starve. With well-trained dogs, one or two men can handle a good-sized herd. Wool is easy to store, haul and ship, and the wool market is a hell of a lot more stable than the beef market. Does that answer your question?''

Rachel studied the dark diamond of perspiration that had soaked through the back of Luke's faded chambray work shirt, outlining the taut muscles beneath the fabric. ''I suppose it does answer my question,'' she said slowly, although, in truth, it did not. She had set out to uncover the reasons behind his blazing hostility. Instead, his answers had revealed a man of burning ambitions, fierce loyalties and buried secrets. The things he had told her only served to deepen the puzzle that was Luke Vincente.

Rachel cleared her throat. ''I still don't—''

''Ssh!'' She felt his body go rigid beneath her hands. ''Listen!''

For the space of a breath, Rachel heard nothing but

the rhythmic thud of the horse's hooves against the damp earth. Then the sound reached her ears from beyond the next rise—the plaintive, terrified cry of a small animal in pain.

One of the dogs began to bark as Luke urged the horse to a canter. They came over the top of the rise to see a lamb, so small and white that it couldn't have been more than a few days old, caught beneath a big clump of sagebrush. The little creature was dangling pitifully from one hind leg. It jerked and twisted, its eyes wild with terror. The dog hovered nearby, whining anxiously.

Luke swore as he halted the horse. Behind him, Rachel jumped to the ground, allowing him to swing out of the saddle. Reaching the lamb ahead of him, she gathered the squalling baby into her arms. That was when she saw the thin wire snare that had twisted around its hind leg. The lamb's struggles had worked the wire into its tender flesh.

"There…you're all right." Rachel felt the unexpected sting of tears as she stroked the small, velvety head. She had no love for sheep, but this one was so tiny and helpless that its pain tore at her heart.

"Hold him still." Luke had brought a pair of wire cutters. His eyes glittered with fury as he cut the lamb loose and, with gentle hands, untwisted the wire from its bleeding leg. "Damn the bastards," he muttered under his breath. "Damn them all to hell!"

Rachel's lips parted as she stared at him. Until now she'd assumed that the lamb had stumbled into a trap meant for rabbits or coyotes. But Luke's face told her another story—a story that chilled the blood in her veins.

"Does this happen often?" She choked out the words.

Luke's mouth tightened in a grim line. "This lamb was lucky. Most of them we find dead, or so far gone they have to be put out of their misery. The coyotes and eagles usually get to them before we do. I've lost more than two dozen animals to these hellish wire snares."

Rachel gripped the struggling lamb as Luke cleaned its wounds. His big, weathered hands were callused and nicked with a myriad of scars—the kind of hands that had worked, fought, loved, maybe even killed. Where had those hands been, Rachel found herself wondering. What stories would those fingers tell if they could speak?

His knuckle brushed her breast through the damp fabric of her jacket. The accidental touch triggered a freshet of sensation that puckered her nipple and sent a jolt of liquid heat shimmering downward through her body. Rachel stifled a gasp, then forced herself to speak.

"You're saying someone's setting these snares just to catch your sheep?" she asked.

Luke had opened a pocket-sized tin of salve. His fingers rubbed the greasy mixture into the deep wire cuts in the lamb's leg. He did not speak, but his grim silence was enough to answer Rachel's question.

"But that's monstrous!" she burst out. "Who would do such a thing?"

His eyes flickered toward her. Rachel felt their cold hatred as if shards of ice had penetrated her flesh. Her lips parted, but no words emerged from her dry mouth. The questions in her mind would remain unasked. She did not want to hear Luke's answers.

A frantic longing seized her—to be home, to be safe on the Tolliver Ranch, with this miserable afternoon blotted from time as if it had never happened. She wanted to forget the buggy accident. She wanted to forget the helpless pain of the injured lamb. Most of all she wanted to forget this gruff, disturbing man who, through no fault of her own, had chosen to hate her on sight.

The dog that had found the sheep hovered close, brushing against Luke with its tail and looking up at Rachel with intelligent golden eyes. "What's the matter, boy?" Rachel murmured. "Are you worried about your little lamb? He'll be all right. We'll fix him up as good as new."

Luke's stormy gaze flickered toward her, then shifted to the dog. "Go, Mick," he commanded in a soft voice. "Back to the sheep."

Tail high, the dog wheeled and bounded back down the slope in the direction of the herd. But it had only gone a few yards when, abruptly, it halted in its tracks, ears up, nose to the wind. Rachel saw the hair rise and bristle along the back of its neck. A nervous growl quivered in its throat.

Luke glanced up from doctoring the lamb, his body tense and wary. Rachel held her breath, holding the lamb close as she strained to catch the danger the dog had sensed.

Luke's expression darkened. "Get out of sight!" he hissed, shoving her up the slope toward an outcrop of boulders. "Stay behind those rocks and don't make a move until I tell you it's safe!"

Only then did Rachel hear what had alarmed the dog. Faintly at first, but growing rapidly louder, the ominous cadence of galloping hoofbeats rumbled from the far side of the hill. Whoever the riders were, they were moving fast. Seconds from now they would be in sight.

With the lamb still clasped in her arms, she plunged toward the outcrop. If the mounted men proved to be friends, she could always show herself. But until she knew who they were and what they wanted, it made more sense to stay hidden.

By the time she reached the rocks, Luke was in the saddle. He spurred the horse toward the herd. The dog shot ahead of him, a dark blur of motion against the pale green slope.

Ignoring the pain in her shoulder, Rachel pressed herself into a low spot between two jutting boulders. The lamb squirmed against her. Rachel's grip tightened around the warm little body as she edged into a spot where she could look down on what was happening.

Four mounted cowboys appeared over the crest of the hill, riding hard. Just below the ridge they halted for a moment, their attention fixed on the broad, open slope and the slowly moving sheep below. Rachel's breath caught painfully as she realized that, beneath their broad-brimmed Stetsons, their neckerchiefs were pulled up to cover the lower parts of their faces. Everything was masked except their eyes.

One of the men jerked his pistol out of its holster. "Let's get 'em, boys!" he shouted, firing into the air.

Whooping like savages, the four men charged down the hill toward Luke's herd. All of them had their pistols drawn now, and for a heart-stopping moment Rachel expected them to start firing at the sheep, or even at Luke. But that was clearly not their intent. As they fanned out, shrieking wildly and shooting into the air, she realized they meant to stampede the sheep and drive them over the ledge, as the Indians had once driven buffalo.

Their plan was working all too well. As panic swept through the herd, the frantically bleating sheep began to mill in circles. A ram wheeled and bolted in dumb terror toward the unseen ledge. Others followed, and suddenly the whole herd was plunging blindly through the scrub, headed for certain destruction.

Rachel had lost sight of Luke. Now, suddenly, she saw him, racing his buckskin horse full out along the rim of the ledge. One of the dogs dashed ahead of him. The other was already tearing along the forefront of the herd, lunging at the leaders, snapping and biting as it dodged their butting heads and flying hooves.

A man, a horse and two small dogs. Could they head off three hundred stampeding sheep and scores of lambs in time to save them? Rachel pressed forward between the rocks, almost forgetting to breathe as she strained to see what was happening.

The four masked men were keeping to the rear of the herd, aiming their shots well above the sheep. Clearly they had no wish to be recognized, nor to do anything that would force the hand of the law against them. In order to file any complaint, Luke would need proof that the stampede had not been an accident. A bullet in a sheep or dog would provide that proof. But the marauders knew better than to give him that advantage. As things stood, Luke would have nothing but his own word. And Rachel knew that would not be enough.

Not unless he could produce another reliable witness to the crime.

Catching the scent of fear, the lamb in Rachel's arms began to struggle and bleat. Rachel clasped the little creature close, stroking its quivering body and praying that the plaintive racket it made would not give her away. If the riders discovered her presence, any number of things could happen, all of them ugly.

The sheep were no more than a stone's throw from the precipice and still running full out. Rachel's heart crept into her throat as she watched Luke's frantic efforts to turn them aside. He was leaning forward, almost standing in the stirrups as his horse thundered along the top of the ledge. As he rode, he shouted and flailed the air with his hat. The dogs, saved only by their lightning quickness, darted like thrusting rapiers into the herd, snarling, nipping, retreating to attack another charging animal.

Despite her feelings about sheep and their owners, Rachel caught herself praying aloud. "Please, God…don't let them go over. Let them turn…let them turn…"

On the brink of the ledge, Luke was running out of maneuvering room. With nowhere to go, he was pressing his mount into the forefront of the stampeding herd, risking horse and sheep and man. The terrified buckskin snorted, trying to rear above the milling herd while Luke fought to keep the animal under control. If the horse lost its footing, he would be swept over the precipice with the sheep. Even now, Rachel realized, his only chance of escape lay in plowing straight back through his own herd. But that would mean abandoning the sheep to their own destruction—something, she sensed, Luke would never do. She was watching a man fight for his dream. He would defend that dream with his life.

The dogs tore in and out among the sheep, snarling and biting in a frantic effort to head the leaders away from the precipice. Rachel swallowed a scream as the buckskin reared and staggered backward. The big gelding shrieked as one rear hoof slipped over the crumbling ledge. For a breathless instant, horse and rider teetered between life and death. Then, with a desperate lunge, they regained solid ground.

Spooked, perhaps, by the rearing horse, the sheep began to turn. The leaders swung hard to the right, and the rest followed, allowing the dogs to drive them away from the edge of the cliff. Like a woolly gray-white river, they flowed down the long slope of the hill toward the plain below.

Luke had paused to rest his gasping horse. His eyes glared across the distance as the four cowboys hung back, watching. For a moment Rachel feared they would fire at Luke or try to stampede the herd again, but it seemed they'd had their fill of mischief for the day.

"We'll be back, sheep man!" the leader crowed at Luke. "Next time you won't be so lucky!"

Luke kept his proud silence, refusing to give them the satisfaction of a reply. Rachel studied the defiant set of his shoulders, wondering how many times men like these had hurt and humiliated him. No wonder he hated cattlemen. No wonder he hated *her*.

Swearing and hooting with laughter, the cowboys holstered their guns, wheeled their mounts and cantered back up the hill. Only then did Rachel realize her own danger. The four riders were headed in a direction that would take them right past the rocks where she was hiding.

By now the lamb in her arms had begun to miss its mother. It squirmed and bleated in Rachel's arms, butting its head against her breasts with a force that was so painful it made her wince. Rachel's heart sank as she realized the little creature was hungry and looking for a place to nurse. The noise it was making had been lost amid the clamor of the stampede, but now that things had quieted down, its bleating was loud enough to lead the cowhands right to her.

She should let the miserable little creature go, she

thought. But the herd was too far down the slope for the lamb to catch up easily. More than likely, the poor thing would be grabbed by one of the cowhands and end the day with its carcass roasting on a spit. Much as she disliked sheep, she could not wish such a cruel fate on this trusting, innocent baby.

But neither could she let the lamb give away her hiding place. By now, she had seen far too much for her own good; and even if the four cowhands recognized her and did her no harm, she had no wish to explain why Morgan Tolliver's daughter was hiding out with a sheep man.

In desperation, Rachel thrust her finger into the lamb's warm, wet mouth. The lamb smacked down eagerly and began to suck, its eyes closed, its tail switching like a metronome gone berserk.

Rachel allowed herself a long exhalation. All quiet for now. But the riders were galloping closer; and at any moment now, the lamb would discover there was no milk coming from her finger. Even a lamb should be smart enough to figure that out. When it did, it would start complaining again.

Wriggling deeper behind the rocks, she clutched the troublesome little creature against her chest, held her breath and waited.

The riders were coming up the hill, approaching fast. Rachel could hear the deep, chesty breathing of horses and the jingle of bridles. When she craned her neck at the right angle, she could see the men through a narrow opening between the rocks. Their faces were still hidden by their neckerchiefs, but all four of them were lithe and slender, and they sat their horses with the careless ease of youth. Had harassing the sheep man been their own idea, she wondered, or had they been set on this errand by someone with more age and power and more to gain?

By now the riders were so near that she could have hit them with the toss of a pebble. The tallest and huskiest of the four was cursing their failure to drive the sheep over the ledge. "Told you we shoulda shot those damned dogs," he growled. "That, or snuck in and poisoned the buggers first. That woulda fixed that sheep man's wagon!"

The others, still masked, were silent. Their shadows, cast long by the low western sun, fell across the rocks where Rachel crouched with the lamb's head cradled below her breasts. She remained perfectly, agonizingly motionless, scarcely daring to breathe as they reached the rocks, then turned their mounts aside to head up the hill.

The last rider to pass her hiding place was small and wiry, younger, perhaps, than the others. As he came into Rachel's full view, one mahogany brown hand tugged at his bandana, pulling it down to reveal a lean, dark, familiar face.

Rachel stifled a cry as she realized she was looking up at one of her own brothers.

Chapter Four

By the time the riders crested the ridge, the lamb had given up on sucking Rachel's finger and burst into ravenous bleating. Its piercing baby cries echoed across the rain-soaked hillside, but if the four young men had heard, they paid no attention.

Numb with shock, Rachel stared after the defiant figure of her younger brother. Had it been Jacob or Josh? In their growing-up years, she'd never had any trouble telling the twins apart—Jacob had a cowlick in his ebony hair, and Josh had a dimple in his left cheek. This time she had felt no surge of recognition. But the boys would have grown older since her last sight of them, she reminded herself. And the glimpse of that youthful, unmasked face beneath the Stetson had been so brief, the expression on the sharp young features so hardened that the shock of it had left her breathless.

The lamb struggled free and scampered away, un-heeded, as Rachel watched the riders vanish over the top of the hill. Only one of her brothers had been with them, she surmised. None of the other three had matched his wiry build. But she was hard put to imagine either of the gentle, lively boys she remembered taking part in something as brutal as the driving of three hundred sheep to their deaths.

Things had clearly changed in the time she had been away from the ranch. People, it seemed, had changed, too. It was as if she had suddenly awakened in a war zone, with land mines hidden all around her.

And right now, she was clearly on the wrong side.

"Rachel? Are you there?" Luke's voice, coming from below the rocks, startled her. Straining forward, she saw him striding toward her through the grass with the lamb clutched in his arms. The horse stood behind him, its sleek buff coat flecked with foam.

Legs quivering, Rachel rose to her feet. Relief flickered like passing sunlight across his leathery features; then his expression soured. "I thought maybe you'd taken off with your cowboy friends," he said.

"They're not my friends!" Rachel was not about to make matters worse by telling him that one of the marauders had been her brother. "But I must say I'm surprised to see you back here," she said, deliberately changing the subject. "I thought you might just ride off with your precious sheep and leave me to walk home by myself."

Luke's eyes narrowed. "I had to come back for the lamb," he said brusquely. "If you're coming with me, get down here and let's get moving. I have to get the sheep home before anything else goes wrong."

He turned away and strode to his horse without a

backward glance, leaving Rachel to scramble down the rocks alone. By the time she reached the horse, he was already in the saddle, cradling the lamb across his lap. Without a word, he reached down, caught her arm and swung her none too gently up behind him. Rachel clambered across the buckskin's rump, feeling damp and sticky and cross. She had barely regained her seat when he kneed the horse to a brisk trot. The sudden motion flung her off balance, throwing her to one side, so that she had to grab his waist to keep from sliding to the ground.

"Blast it, this isn't my fault!" she muttered, her face pressed against his sweat-soaked shirt. "Stop treating me as if I were to blame for your troubles!"

His body was like stone to the touch, his muscles tense, his spine rigid. His skin smelled of sage and leather and salty male perspiration. The odor teased at her senses, triggering an odd tingle where her knees pressed the backs of his legs. The sensation crept upward to pool at the joining of her thighs. Rachel stared past Luke's shoulder, struggling to fix her thoughts elsewhere.

"You're one of them," he said. "You told me as much the first time you opened that pretty mouth of yours. I didn't invite you to be here, Rachel Tolliver, and as far as I'm concerned, the sooner I'm rid of you the better."

"Well, at least we agree on something," she said tartly. "How often do you get social calls like the one you had this afternoon?"

"Depends on what you call a social call." His

voice was flat, guarded. "This is the first time they've tried to run the sheep over a cliff. But having animals trapped, shot, even poisoned—that's just business as usual."

Rachel waited, expecting him to go on. Instead he gathered up the lamb, twisted in the saddle and thrust the squirming baby into her arms. "We're wasting time," he muttered, spurring the horse to a canter. "Hang on."

At once the lamb, which had lain quietly across Luke's knees, began to struggle and bleat. Rachel locked one arm around the wretched little creature, bracing it against her chest. Her other arm gripped Luke's waist as she struggled to keep from bouncing off the horse's slick rump. If she made it home safely, she vowed, she would never again have anything to do with these cursed sheep or with their sullen, arrogant, mule-headed owner. If Luke Vincente wanted to pit himself against the whole civilized world, that was his problem. She'd be damned if she was about to make it hers.

The sheep milled at the foot of the slope, under the brow of the ledge where they'd come so near to their death plunge. The tireless dogs darted along the fringes of the herd, lunging and yipping to keep their charges in line.

Sensing its kind, the lamb renewed its struggles, digging its sharp hooves into Rachel's ribs and bleating like a miniature steam calliope. A fly settled on Rachel's matted hair. She shook it away, her temper growing shorter by the second.

Luke had slowed the horse to a trot as they neared the herd, but Rachel was still bouncing behind the saddle, her buttocks miserably sore and her bladder threatening to burst. When the lamb's hoof jabbed her breast hard enough to bruise, her last thread of patience snapped. "Enough!" she yelped. "Either we stop right here and let this little monster find its mother, or I start screaming loud enough to be heard across three counties!"

"Anything to please a lady." Luke's voice dripped sarcasm as he reined the horse to a halt. Shoving the wretched animal toward him, she slid off the back of the horse and dropped wearily to the ground. For a moment she glared up at him, scrambling for a comeback that would put him in his place. But nothing came to mind except the awareness that she was sore and miserable and badly in need of a bush.

"Wait right here, and keep your back turned." Rachel spun away from the horse and, with as much dignity as she could muster, stalked off toward a clump of tall sage that grew at the foot of the slope. She had spent enough time on the range that going to the bushes in the open was nothing new. But something about this disturbing man's presence made her burn with self-consciousness.

"Watch out for rattlesnakes," he said. "They're bad in these parts."

Rachel ignored the remark, but her face blazed with heat as she ducked behind the sage. Growing up alongside brothers and cowboys had given her a natural ease with the male sex. At school, the boys had flocked around her, and she'd never wanted for escorts or dancing partners. In the past year alone, she'd rejected three proposals of marriage. Once she had fancied herself in love, but even for that brief time she had kept a cautious rein on her heart so that when the infatuation passed she was able to walk away without regret.

Always, in her relationships with men, Rachel had insisted on being the one in control. So why now, of all times, did she find herself hot and flustered and blushing like a schoolgirl? Luke Vincente was not one of her conquests. He was too old, too proud, with too many shadows lurking about his tall, dark person. Worse, he was a sheep man, with a hatred for her kind that ran bone-deep in both directions.

Why in heaven's name hadn't she called out to her brother as he rode past her hiding place? Surely she could have smoothed over the awkwardness, perhaps even lessened the tension by explaining how Luke had rescued her after the accident with the buggy.

If she had played her cards more sensibly, she might be headed for the ranch right now on the back of her brother's horse. Luke would be rid of her; she would be rid of him; everybody would be happier. So why hadn't she spoken?

But Rachel knew why. The horror she had witnessed, coupled with the shock of recognizing her adored brother, had left her mute.

As she gazed back toward the hilltop where the four riders had disappeared, a sense of pervading blackness crept over her. For months she had looked forward to home—to the grand sweep of mountain peaks and prairie sky and the smell of coffee on the crisp morning air; to friends and family, to sunny days filled with hard work and laughter and love. But home had changed, Rachel realized. And something told her it would never again be the carefree place she remembered.

Luke lowered the lamb to the ground, then stood back to watch as it tottered toward its anxious mother. A ghost of a smile tugged at his lips as it butted for her teat, clamped on and lost itself in the bliss of nursing. This one, at least, would be all right for now. But how many others would be maimed by those bloody snares? How many precious animals would he lose before the summer was over? This range war was not of his making. But each day of it was chipping away at his livelihood and slowly draining his spirit. He had never asked for anything except to be left alone. Even that simple wish, it appeared, was not to be granted.

Glancing over his shoulder, he saw that Rachel had emerged from the sagebrush and was making her way down the slope toward him. Water and mud had plastered her clothes against her skin, outlining every delicious curve and hollow of her voluptuous little body. Her wind-tangled hair blazed like fire in the fading light. Filthy, disheveled and undoubtedly sore, Rachel Tolliver still walked as if the whole world were gathered at her feet, awaiting her pleasure.

For a long moment, Luke allowed his eyes to feast

on her proud beauty. Then, still reluctant, he tore his gaze away. She was a cattleman's daughter. Worse, she was a *rich* cattleman's daughter, as strong-willed and demanding as she was beautiful. He would wager that the proper Miss Tolliver believed the sun, the moon and the stars revolved around her pretty little head, and that anything she wanted could be had by batting those lush golden eyelashes at the right man.

Luke knew about such women. He knew far more than he wanted to remember. Some things, in fact, he would give almost anything to forget.

The memory of Cynthia's luscious face and lying words came back to haunt him now, just as they had haunted him for the four years he had spent in the hellhole of the Louisiana State Penitentiary.

…I'm so frightened, Luke. The way he looks at me, the way he brushes against me…my own father! He's come after me before, and he'll do it again. You have to help me, Luke. Somehow you have to stop him… Then we can be together for the rest of our lives….

Lord, what a gullible fool he had been!

"Oh, will you look at that!" Rachel had come up alongside him. Her muddy hands clasped in delight as she watched the frantically nursing lamb. She had an infectious smile that crinkled her eyes at the corners, deepened the dimples in her cheeks and showed her small, pearl-like teeth. A smile like that could get a woman anything she wanted, he thought. Anything.

"Look at his tail go!" she exclaimed, laughing. "It's whipping around like a little windmill! How on earth did you manage to find his mother?"

"They found each other. I just hung on to the lamb and followed my ears." Luke kept his voice flat, resisting the temptation to return her smile. She was one of the enemy, he reminded himself. Worse, she was everything he had grown to despise in a woman. Even for this brief time, he could not let himself warm to her.

"Will he be able to walk the rest of the way with his mother?" she asked, still watching the lamb.

"He's too weak for that. We'll need to take him on the horse again. Sorry." The last word came out sounding more like a barb than an apology. The truth was, the thought of pampered Rachel holding the muddy, squirming lamb in her arms gave him an odd feeling of pleasure.

"As long as you let him finish eating, that's fine. Since he figured out that fingers don't give milk, he's been impossible!"

She arched like a languorous cat, reaching backward to massage her weary spine. The motion strained the buttons of her form-fitting jacket, pulling the fabric tightly against her breasts, outlining her taut nipples.

Luke stifled a groan and averted his eyes. The little minx knew exactly what she was doing, he told himself. To such a woman, seductive behavior would be an instinct, as natural as breathing. No matter that the only man in sight was one she would spit on under most circumstances—a man so far below her in class as to be unworthy of notice. She would enjoy arousing him, making him want her, then walking away with a toss of her fiery little head and leaving him with the devil's own fire between his legs.

Well, let her do her worst, he thought. He would not give Miss Rachel Tolliver the satisfaction of knowing the effect she had on him. Soon their journey would be finished. He would give her a quick bite to eat, then send her off on old Henry, a horse that would return home as soon as she let it go. With luck, they would never cross paths again.

"How much longer?" She ended her stretch with a light shake of her shoulders. "I don't like the look of those clouds."

Luke followed her gaze to the west, where a bank of slate-colored clouds was spilling in over the Big Horns. He sighed, biting back a curse. He'd assumed the weather would stay clear. The last thing he'd counted on was a second storm moving in before nightfall. Anxious as he was to get rid of Rachel, he could hardly send her home in a downpour.

A scowl passed across his face as another thought struck him—one that suddenly made everything worse.

"What is it?" She was studying him, her expression so open and earnest that it caught Luke off guard.

"Your family," he said. "What will they do if you don't show up? They're bound to be out looking for you." He did not add that, from what he'd heard, any man caught trifling with Morgan Tolliver's precious daughter would do well to make his peace with heaven.

Rachel did not answer his question. Her gaze flickered away from his, then dropped to her hands, as if she were weighing the consequences of lying to him.

"Rachel?"

Still she was silent. He stared at her for the space of a long breath, then exhaled with mixed relief as the truth sank home. "They're not expecting you, are they?" he said. "You were driving that rented buggy home from Sheridan to surprise them. That's why you chose to come with me instead of waiting by the wash. You'd have been stranded if you'd stayed."

She looked up at him again, and he saw the flash of anxiety in her beautiful blue-green eyes. He was an untrusted stranger, and he had just discovered that no one would be searching for her or riding to her rescue. For better or for worse, she was at his mercy, and she knew it.

"Tell me I'm right, Rachel," he said.

Her expression hardened. Only the white-knuckled clasp of her hands betrayed her. "You're wrong," she said. "If I'm not back at the ranch before dark, there'll be two dozen armed men out looking for me, including my father and brothers. They won't rest until they know I'm safe."

The first glimpse of her vulnerability had moved him. Now it angered him. "Damn it, woman, what do you take me for?" he exploded. "Do you think I'd be crazy enough to touch one hair of your precious Tolliver head? Do you think I'd even *want* to?" He glowered at the sky, where the darkening clouds mirrored his emotions. "If you're so all-fired worried, why didn't you take your chances back there, with those four cowboy friends of yours? You could be halfway home by now.''

Without waiting for an answer, Luke swung his gaze back toward her. She looked even more frayed than she had before, her eyes too large in a face that seemed too small and pale.

"Did you know them, Rachel?" he demanded, resolving to show her no mercy. "Is that why you didn't show yourself?"

She glanced away, hesitating a second too long before she shook her head. "They were masked. I couldn't see their faces. And I didn't know what they'd do if they found me."

"So you decided you'd be safer with a sheep man." Luke made no effort to keep the edge from his voice. "Should I be flattered?"

"Stop it!" The worn thread of her patience snapped. "Can't you understand that none of this mess is my doing? I've been away at school. Except for a few days at Christmas, I haven't lived in Wyoming for almost three years!"

"That doesn't change who you are, Rachel," Luke said quietly.

. Her head went up sharply, nostrils flaring like a blooded mare's. "I'm proud of who I am," she said. "I love my family and I love this land. But today…" The words trailed off as she studied the boiling clouds. "Today I feel as if I've wandered into somebody else's nightmare and can't find my way out."

"And I'm your bogeyman." He spoke without emotion.

She shook her head. "It's not just you. It's everything. I want to wake up. I want to open my eyes and find this place the same as it was three years ago, before you came here."

"You're saying I should leave so you can have your nice, peaceful life back."

Either she'd missed the irony in his voice or she was choosing to ignore it. "My father would gladly buy you out, Luke. You could go somewhere else, with plenty of money to make a new start."

"Just like that." Luke would have laughed at her naiveté if he hadn't been choking on his own fury. "You've never had to fight for anything in your pampered little life have you, Miss Rachel Tolliver? You can't even imagine what it's like to want something so much that you'd spill your own blood to get it, and to hold onto it."

She raked her hair back from her face with restless fingers. "Maybe not," she said in a taut voice. "But I know enough to recognize a stubborn fool when I see one."

"And I know enough to recognize a woman who thinks she can rearrange the people around her like furniture, to suit her own pleasure. Anyone who's spoiling her pretty view will be shown the door. Well, this time it's not going to work."

"Especially not with a man who's bent on self-destruction!"

Without waiting for his response, she stalked down the slope to where the lamb had finished nursing and was tottering away from the ewe on uncertain legs.

Bending down, Rachel caught the small creature around its chest and scooped it into her arms. As she turned back to face him, a ray of amber sunlight slanted through the clouds to touch her windblown hair. For an instant her face was haloed by living, moving flame. Luke was no artist, but if he could have taken brush to canvas he would have chosen to paint her exactly as he saw her now—as a rescuing angel with blazing hair and a wounded lamb cradled in her arms.

But Rachel Tolliver was no angel, he reminded himself. She was a willful, self-centered minx who demanded life on her own terms and gave no quarter to anyone else's point of view. The sooner she was off his hands and back with her own kind, the better for them both.

The vision dissolved as she moved, striding back up the hill toward him. "Let's go," she said. "I've had enough rain for one day."

Luke mounted and reached down for her. She passed him the lamb, then seized his free arm and allowed him to swing her up behind him. She was light and strong, like lifting a bird, he thought as she scrambled into place on the horse's withers. Light and strong and tough. And while she'd been pushy and temperamental and annoying, not once had he heard her whine.

Passing her the lamb, he whistled to the dogs and urged the buckskin to a trot. Overhead the skies darkened and rumbled, showing a thin streak of red above the mountains, like a bed of glowing coals glimpsed through the grate of an iron stove. The sheep were moving fast now, driven by the pressing dogs and by a sense of urgency that seemed to hover in the air around them all. Luke felt it, too, and he pushed the animals harder. He had been away from the ranch too long. There was evil afoot, his instincts shrilled. He needed to get back home before it was too late.

Chapter Five

The lamb had fallen asleep, its milk-swollen belly as taut as the skin of a drum. Rachel balanced its warm weight between her breasts and the rock-solid expanse of Luke's back. Her free hand gripped Luke's belt as the tall buckskin pushed across the open flat-land behind the sheep.

"I know this country," she muttered, bracing herself as the horse lurched up the side of a wash. "The boundary of your ranch can't be more than a mile from here."

"We've already passed it. You're on my land now." There was an edge to Luke's voice. He had said little since they'd remounted, and Rachel had been too tired to start what would surely turn into another argument. But she'd felt the tension in him. She had sensed the black weight of his thoughts, and she had been torn between the need to understand more and the fervent wish to wake up in her own bed, to the happy discovery that this whole day had been a horrible dream and there was no such person as Luke Vincente.

"You won't have to hold on much longer." The strain came through in his voice. "If it's any comfort to you, there should be a hot meal ready when we get to the ranch house."

Rachel's empty stomach growled at the mention of food, but her thoughts had already darted to another matter. Hot food meant there would be someone waiting at the ranch—a wife, most likely, since Luke didn't strike her as the sort of man who would hire a cook. And if there was a wife, there could be children as well—beautiful children, she imagined, with fierce obsidian eyes like their father's. No wonder Luke was so protective of his own. No wonder he was so determined to stay and fight off all comers.

Where she gripped his belt, she felt his sinewy body shift against her hand. His aura surrounded her, setting off a shimmer of heat, as if his fingertips had brushed her bare skin. The leathery, masculine aroma, which had lain dormant in her nostrils, suddenly stirred, triggering a jolt of awareness. It had been there all along, she realized, this slumbering sense of his maleness. Why now, of all times, did it have to wake up and kick her like a mule, leaving her warm and damp and tingling?

Was it because she'd just surmised that he was married and therefore forbidden? Ridiculous, Rachel told herself. She had branded Luke Vincente as forbidden from the moment she found out he was a sheep man. It made no difference whether he was married or not. Nothing had happened between them. Nothing would happen. The whole idea was unthinkable.

Laden with the smell of rain, a chilly wind whipped Rachel's hair across her face. By now the sun was gone. Inky clouds, back-lit by flashes of sheet lightning, rumbled across the twilight sky. The sheep flowed through the hollows like patches of fog, their bells clanging eerily in the darkness. There was little need for the dogs to hurry them now. The urgency to reach home before the storm broke was driving them all.

Luke's tense silence had begun to gnaw at Rachel's nerves. "Are these all the sheep you have?" she asked, forcing herself to make conversation.

He sighed, sounding drained. "There are just under a thousand head in all, so you're only seeing about a third of them. I don't usually run so many of them together. After what happened today, you won't have to ask why. But we're...shorthanded now. There wasn't much choice."

The catch in his voice was barely perceptible, but the impact of the emotion behind it struck Rachel like a slap. Whatever was happening here, she sensed, she had barely glimpsed the surface of it. The truth was larger and uglier than she had ever imagined.

"When I was growing up, I loved the open range," she said, thinking aloud. "Even as a little girl, I could ride for miles, go anywhere I wished, and feel perfectly safe. This was a happy place, Luke Vincente...before the trouble with sheep men started."

A bolt of lightning flashed across the indigo sky. As thunder cracked behind them, she felt Luke's muscles harden beneath his damp shirt. "You're not a little girl anymore, Rachel," he said. "If you don't like what's happened here, you can go back East and make a life for yourself. Marry well. Have a family, and keep that happy place in your memory. As long as you don't come back here, it will never change."

The bitterness in his voice stung her. "I don't intend to go back East," Rachel answered crisply. "The ranch is part mine. It's my home, and I've returned to stay."

Luke made a derisive sound under his breath. "What about that fancy eastern schooling you mentioned? Why waste so much expense and trouble if all you want to do is come back here and be a cowgirl?"

"I studied painting and sculpture," she said, ignoring his sardonic undertone. "Three of my paintings are already in a gallery, and the owner is interested in doing a show based on images of life in the West. With luck and hard work, I can have a successful career right here in Wyoming."

Luke was silent for a long moment. Then he shook his head. "Images of the West!" he snorted. "I can just picture that. The chuck wagon at sunset! Buckaroos around the old corral!"

"Stop insulting me, Luke," Rachel said quietly. "I'm not the naive little fool you think I am."

"You want images, Rachel Tolliver?" he said, his vehemence swelling. "I could show you images that would burn themselves into your mind for the rest of your life! Animals shot, trapped, crippled, or lying dead around a poisoned water hole. And more—more than a fine lady like you would even want to think about.''

Rachel flinched against the leaden impact of every word he spoke. Another image flashed through her mind—a hand tugging down a crimson neckerchief to reveal a dark young face. A face she loved.

She had heard enough of Luke's bitter words to make her stomach churn. But far worse was the idea of what he had left unsaid. He had intimated, with a cutting scorn, that she was too gently reared to deal with the full truth of what was happening. But Luke didn't know the half of it. He had no idea of what she'd seen, or how the sight of her darling brother's face had left her gasping for breath like a fish flung out of its element.

She had to know. She had to know everything, even if it broke her heart to hear it.

''Tell me,'' she demanded, her fingers tightening around the worn leather strap of his belt. ''I want to hear the worst.''

''Why trouble your pretty head with such an ugly story?'' Luke's defiant question infuriated her. Only the lamb, so warm and peaceful between their bodies, kept her from shouting at him.

''This country is my home and my family's home,'' Rachel said in a level voice. ''Whatever's going on here, I need to understand it.''

Thunder filled the silence as she waited for Luke

to answer. When he outlasted her patience she pressed him again.

"We've had a few sheep in these parts since I was in pigtails," she said. "I can't say there was ever any love lost between sheep men and ranchers. But what I saw today—there was never anything like that before! What in heaven's name happened? Was it something *you* did?"

He laughed at that, a deep, bitter release that quivered through his taut body, so that she felt it more than heard it. "I'd pay good money for the answer to that question, lady. All I've ever asked of my neighbors was that they leave me alone. As long as I kept my sheep off their land, most of them, including your father, did just that—until about three months ago. That was when the raids started."

A vision of the masked riders flashed through Rachel's mind. Had it been Jacob or Josh she had seen with them? Was it possible that both of them were involved in this mess? And what about her father? Morgan Tolliver was a peaceful man, but if pushed far enough he was capable of anger. Was he capable of violence as well?

Rachel's fingers tightened around Luke's belt. She felt dizzy, as if she were spinning in space with nothing solid to support her. For months she had dreamed of coming back to the safe, secure place she called home. But the home she remembered was gone, to be replaced by a nightmare world of danger, doubt and uncertainty.

"Do you have any idea who's behind the trouble?"

she forced herself to ask. "Have you recognized anyone—any of the raiders?"

He shook his head, and she felt an unexpected surge of relief. "Most of the time I don't see them. But when they do show themselves, they always have their faces masked. The fact that they care that much about being recognized makes me think they're locals—and there's a bunch of them, more than just the ones you saw today." He whistled to direct a dog toward a straying ewe. The wind swept his raven hair back from his face.

"When I saw them up close, they struck me as very young," Rachel said, filling the pause. "Just boys, I'd guess, out to stir up some mischief."

Luke's body stiffened. "They may be young, but they're too well organized to be just boys. Somebody's behind them. Somebody with enough money to pay them or enough influence to stir them up."

Like my father, Rachel thought. She knew better than to speak the words aloud, but even the idea was terrible enough to create a dark, hollow feeling in her chest.

"As for the so-called mischief—" Luke cleared his throat, but when he spoke again, his voice was still low and gritty. "I have three herders working for me, a father and two sons. They're from Spain by way of Mexico, good men. Fine men." Luke swallowed hard. Rachel felt the strain in him, the scream of raw nerves, and she sensed that, whatever he had been holding back from her, she was about to hear it.

"Three nights ago, the old man, Miguel, was out

on the range with part of the herd. He'd bedded down
for the night in his sheep wagon when he heard riders
coming over the hill. They were making enough noise
to rouse the devil, he told us later. Probably drunk,
or making a good show of it. Miguel ordered his
dogs—the two you see here—to move the sheep out
fast. He was going to get his horse and follow them,
but he realized the riders were too close, so he ran
back to the sheep wagon and barricaded himself inside.''

"Dear heaven," Rachel whispered, bracing her
emotions for what she was about to hear.

"There were five of them, all masked," Luke said.
"Five against one old man. When Miguel wouldn't
come out of the sheep wagon, they lit a dry branch
from the campfire and threw it on the roof."

Rachel's skin was clammy beneath her mud-soaked
clothes. Her throat was paper-dry, and so tightly constricted that she could barely breathe. The lamb stirred
against her, warm and drowsy and smelling of milk,
like a creature from a world she no longer knew. A
drop of cold rain splashed her cheek. She wanted to
scream at Luke, to make him stop his story.

"The wagon went up like a torch. By the time he
got the door open, Miguel's clothes were beginning
to smolder. He staggered outside, begging for
help…''

Luke's voice broke as the rage moved inside him.
Rachel could feel it clawing at his insides, threatening
to tear him apart as he fought for enough self-control
to finish the story.

"We found him the next morning on the ground, next to the burned-out wagon. That harmless old man. Those bastards had beaten him almost to death."

The silence was so deafening that Rachel could no longer hear the wind's breath or the thunder that had trailed them across the flatland. She could no longer feel the wind on her face or the warm sleepy weight of the lamb in her arms. Her thoughts were fixed on the picture Luke's words had drawn in her mind—the blazing wagon, the balled fists that hammered the aging, battered body, the masked faces twisted with hatred. Whose fists? she wondered. Whose faces?

"How badly was he hurt?" she asked, forcing each word out of her reluctant mouth.

Luke exhaled raggedly. "Bad. Broken nose and jaw. Broken ribs. And God knows what they did to his insides. He was coughing blood when I left two days ago to bring in the sheep. He's a tough old man, and the longer he hangs on, the better his chances are. But the beating he took from those sons of—" He bit off the epithet and fell into silence, afraid, perhaps, of betraying too much emotion.

Rachel clung to his back as he pushed the horse to a lope. The rain had begun to fall around them, not hard, but gentle, like tears.

She thought of Jacob and Josh, so playful and full of innocent fun. Remembering their antics, she could not believe they had been among the raiders who'd paid a call on old Miguel. But cold reason told her otherwise. One of them had been with the marauders today. She had seen his face. If that was possible, anything was possible.

The image of her darling brothers—or, heaven forbid, her father—brutalizing a helpless old man drew the ugly knot in the pit of her stomach so tight that she wanted to retch. On top of that, another worry suddenly seized her, this one all but paralyzing her with dread.

What if they were caught? What if they were arrested and sent to prison? That would kill her mother. It would kill her father, too, whether he was involved with the others or not. Rachel fought down rising waves of panic. She had started out believing the sheep man's troubles with the ranchers were none of her concern. Only now did she realize they had the power to tear her family, and her happy, secure world, apart.

"Who have you told about this?" she asked, masking her terror with concern. "Did you send word to the authorities?"

"The authorities!" He laughed roughly. "You mean those stooges the Cattlemen's Association pays to keep the peace in these parts? Why bother to tell them? They'd only look the other way."

Rachel allowed herself to breathe, but her throat felt as if she were strangling, and the fear remained, thick and cold and heavy inside her.

"The cowards who ganged up on Miguel were masked." Luke's tone was flat with anger. "There's no way to identify them. Even if there were, what's the penalty for burning a sheep wagon and beating up an old Spaniard? Any judge who valued his job would call it boyish mischief and throw the case out of court.''

Rachel exhaled slowly and allowed the strained conversation to slip into silence. She did not trust herself to ask the question that was screaming in her mind. It was horrific enough, the acts that had been committed against a helpless sheepherder. But what if the old man were to die of his injuries? Then the crime that Luke, in his disgust, had called boyish mischief would become a crime of murder.

The rain was pouring around them now in a steady drizzle. Rachel could scarcely remember when it had begun to fall. The lamb in her arms shuddered itself awake and began to struggle, bleating for its mother. The jangle of sheep's bells echoed through the darkness.

''How much longer?'' Rachel raised her voice above the sound. She was cold and wet and sore, and she wanted nothing more than to leave this man who had opened the door into a world of nightmares. She wanted to be home, with her parents and her brothers. She wanted to hold each one of them in her arms and forget this miserable day had ever happened.

''Not much longer.'' Luke's answer, coming so long after her question, startled her. ''Look ahead. You can see the light.''

Struggling with the lamb, Rachel leaned to one side and peered around Luke's broad shoulder. Through the rainy darkness, her straining eyes caught a glimmer of light. Soon, she thought. Soon there would be food and warmth and an end to this interminable ride.

The dogs had caught the scent of home. They raced ahead, hurrying the tired sheep. Luke nudged the horse to a brisk trot, but the animal needed no urging. Mud splattered under its hooves as it surged into the darkness. Strands of wet hair whipped Rachel's face as she clung to Luke's silent back.

They passed beneath the shadow of a high gate, but Rachel could see little of the buildings that lay beyond. The light they had seen appeared to be coming from a single window in the low, dark house. Nothing moved within that small square of brightness, but as the sheep swept across the yard, the gate to a fenced pasture swung open. Rachel glimpsed a stocky figure in a woolen poncho and wide-brimmed sombrero standing at the gatepost.

When the dogs had driven the last sheep into the pasture, the man closed the gate and slipped the latch, then turned and limped toward the horse. Rain dripped off the brim of his sombrero, blurring his face as he stood in the mud, gazing up at Luke and Rachel.

"Déme el cordero, señorita." His voice was young. His hands reached upward.

Rachel hesitated, unsure of what he wanted.

"Give him the lamb, Rachel," Luke said quietly. "He'll take care of it now."

With a sigh, Rachel eased her wiggling burden into the young man's arms. Her nose tested the air for the welcoming aromas of coffee and hot food. Luke had said there would be a meal waiting, but she could smell nothing except the rain and the pungent odor of wet animals.

No womanly figure had emerged onto the porch with a lamp. No children had come tumbling out of the house to run to their father's arms. Rachel felt a bewildering surge of relief. She'd been wrong, or so it seemed, in assuming that Luke was married. But why should that make any difference to her? He was not one of her conquests. She did not even like him, let alone love him. Why should she care a fig whether he had a wife or not?

Luke and the young man were conversing in Spanish. The words meant nothing to Rachel but she found herself straining to hear every nuance of their tone and expression. Rain dripped off the wide straw brim of the young man's sombrero as he stood in the mud with the lamb cradled in his arms. A lightning flash revealed a square face with deep-set eyes and blunt features. From beneath the sombrero, straight black hair hung in lank strings. Muddy water pooled around his bare feet.

Luke's voice cracked with strain. His questions were urgent, demanding. The young man answered him quietly, his eyes dark and liquid through the misty rain. Watching them, Rachel felt invisible, like an outsider staring at a scene through a glass windowpane. This was their world—Luke's world. She was not part of it, nor did she wish to be.

They finished speaking. Cradling the lamb, the young man turned and walked back toward the house. The two dogs trotted after him like shadows.

Luke swung his weary mount toward the looming outline of the barn. Rachel waited for him to say something to her, but he had fallen silent, almost as if he had forgotten she was there, sitting behind him on the horse. Unaccustomed to being ignored, she cleared her throat and spoke.

"Luke?"

He stirred as if she had awakened him from a dream.

"What's happening?" she demanded. "What were the two of you talking about for so long?"

The whisper of the rain filled the silence between them as he guided the horse through the open door of the barn. They passed into a warm darkness, filled with the soft stirrings of animals in their stalls and the familiar smells of hay and manure.

Letting go of the saddle, Rachel slid off the horse's rump and dropped to the straw. Her legs quivered beneath her as she willed herself to stand erect and thrust her face up toward him through the deep shadows.

"I realize I don't belong here," she said. "But after all that's happened this afternoon, I believe I have a right to know what's going on."

Luke swung out of the saddle. He moved slowly, almost painfully, as if he had aged twenty years in the time since he'd last mounted the horse. Rachel could hear the sound of his harsh breathing in the darkness. His tall, craggy silhouette loomed above her as she stood waiting, holding her ground.

"The man who came out to meet us is Sebastian, Miguel's older son," he said. "He told me that just an hour ago—" Luke sucked in his breath as if gathering his strength. "An hour ago, his father died."

Chapter Six

Luke heard the sharp intake of her breath. She swayed toward him as if she were about to collapse, but when he reached out and caught her elbow to steady her, she twisted away and stumbled backward, falling against a wagon loaded with straw.

Sheet lightning glimmered through the open door of the barn, transfixing her pale face and wildly tangled hair with an eerie blue light. Her eyes were huge, as if she had just received a terrible shock and was about to burst into racking sobs.

To Luke, this show of emotion was both puzzling and disturbing. The news of Miguel's death should have evoked no more than a murmur of polite sympathy from this cattleman's pampered daughter. The old man meant nothing to her. She could not possibly understand what a crushing blow his loss would be to his sons, to the ranch and to Luke himself.

What was happening here? Could the woman know more than she had told him? Luke was too weary to even think about the possibilities.

Steadying her weight against the wagon, she pushed herself fully erect. One hand passed across her face, her small fingers raking back the sodden tangle of her hair. When she looked up at Luke again, the expression of panic was gone. Her features had re-arranged themselves into a mask of composure. Only her eyes, illuminated by the storm outside, showed traces of shock and fear.

"I'm…truly sorry for what happened," she said in a shaky voice. "Is there anything I can do?"

"Not likely." Luke bent and unfastened the cinch, then lifted the saddle off the horse and laid it over the side of a stall. "Just stay out of the way until I can see clear to get you home."

"I know the way!" She was too eager, he thought, too frantic. "Give me a fresh horse, and I'll leave now!"

Her words were lost in a violent thunderclap that shook the ground beneath their feet. The sky split open to let loose a deluge of rain. Water streamed in solid gray curtains from the eaves of the barn. She flashed Luke an anxious glance in the darkness. He shook his head. It was no secret that he would be relieved to have her gone. But no one could be turned out in such a storm.

Hands moving swiftly, he slipped off the buckskin's bridle and turned the horse into its stall. Sebastian, he noticed, had left some oats and fresh water for the hungry animal. Even in the face of tragedy and grief, there were chores to do, animals to tend. Life continued—thank heaven for that, Luke thought.

But without Miguel's humor and wisdom, life would not be the same.

"Give me a towel. I'll rub him down." Rachel's voice startled him out of his reverie. He glanced toward her, startled by her offer.

"I grew up on a ranch, remember?" she said. "I probably know more about horses than you do. Give me a towel."

He tossed her a clean cotton rag. "Here. Make yourself useful."

She caught the rag deftly, then turned away without a word. He could hear her breathing in the darkness of the stall as she began rubbing the water from the buckskin's wet coat. It was a decent thing to do, offering her help, Luke thought. Under different circumstances, he could have almost liked her for it. But he didn't want to like her. Especially not now.

"They'll be needing you in the house," she said. "Go on, do what you need to. I'll be fine here."

A protest sprang to Luke's lips, but he bit it back as he realized she was right. Sebastian and Ignacio would need his support, and Rachel's presence would only be an intrusion. For now, at least, it would be better if she remained in the barn.

"I'll be back as soon as I can," he said, turning to go.

"Take your time. I'm all right." Her voice came out of the darkness of the stall. She was not all right, Luke knew. She was cold, wet, hungry and exhausted, but right now he had even more pressing concerns.

Thrusting her from his thoughts, he strode out into

the stormy night. The single lamp, set in the kitchen window, flickered through the pouring rain as he slogged his way across the muddy yard. With each step his heart grew heavier. He ached for Sebastian and Ignacio's loss. And he ached for his own.

Luke had never known his father. His half Cherokee, half Cajun mother had been a servant in one of the great homes of Baton Rouge. When it became evident that the pretty sixteen-year-old was with child, she'd been dismissed and shunted back to her family in the bayou. "You got highborn blood in your veins, boy," Luke's mother had told him more than once. But that was all she would say about the man who had sired him.

Luke had been fifteen when his mother and grandparents had died of yellow fever. With no family to hold him, he had drifted like a piece of wreckage caught in the muddy torrent of the Mississippi. As he struggled to survive, two dubious talents had emerged—a gift for winning at games of cards and dice, and a rugged, sensual magnetism that attracted women of all classes. It was this second gift that had ultimately led to his downfall.

After the time in prison, it had taken five years of hard labor in the mines before he had enough money to buy a herd of sheep and four dogs from a Colorado rancher. Miguel and his two sons had worked for the rancher. They had hired on to help Luke move the sheep to Northern Wyoming, then stayed to become part of his ranch.

Luke had been grateful to find competent herders.

Only after months of riding behind the dogs, staying up nights for spring lambing, fighting drought, fire, coyotes, disease and cattle ranchers, did Luke realize that Miguel, Sebastian and Ignacio Montoya had become his family.

For Luke, the inhuman attack on Miguel had been like an attack on his own father. He had hoped the old man was strong enough to recover from the beating—told himself that he *was* recovering. But that was not to be. Miguel was gone. And the murdering bastards who'd killed him were as free as meadowlarks.

Bracing himself for the shock of death, he mounted the porch. The dogs—three collies and a big, surly mongrel—were huddled beneath the jutting eave. They raised their heads as Luke passed, but did not spring up to greet him as they usually did. The sensitive animals seemed to understand what had happened and, in their own quiet way, were grieving for their old friend.

The kitchen was cold and silent. The dying glow of dark-red coals glinted through the grate of the stove, casting eerie shadows on the walls and ceiling. Luke followed the dim flicker of lantern light down the hallway to the bedroom where Miguel's sons had kept their death vigil. He should have been here, too, Luke lashed himself. But someone had been needed to bring in the remaining sheep for shearing, and so he had taken two dogs and gone out onto the range. He had returned late, with an unwanted guest, at the worst of times.

Luke's throat tightened as he stepped into the bedroom. The boys had done their best. They had laid their father's body out in the plain, clean work clothes that were the best he had. They had combed his unruly bush of iron-gray hair and crossed his work-roughened hands like a saint's across his chest. But the bruises could not be hidden. Hideous blotches of blue, red and purple covered his once-handsome features like a smashed and swollen mask.

Choking on his own grief, Luke touched the rigid hands with his fingertips. At first light, while the boys dug the grave, he would build a rude coffin from the planks in the wood shed. Then they would bury the old man on the hill behind the house, where golden poppies and spires of Indian paintbrush would cover his grave in the springtime. It wasn't much of a memorial, but under the circumstances, it was the best they could do.

"I will kill them for this." Ignacio, Miguel's fiery younger son, spoke in Spanish from the shadows beyond the bed. "What they did to my father, I will do to them, one by one. I will show them no mercy. Honor demands it."

Luke gazed into the youth's blazing eyes, understanding his pain but all too aware of where such angry words could lead. "Your father would want you to live, Ignacio," he said softly. "He would never ask you to throw your life away for something that can't be changed."

"But the honor of our family—"

"There's no honor in a wasted death." Luke's voice rasped with anger too tightly reined. "We can honor your father's memory by not giving in to the bastards who killed him. That's what he would have wanted."

"And what about justice?" The young man's voice was razor-edged, his eyes like two hot coals in the darkness. "Who will give us justice? The law? *Que chiste!* I spit on the law!"

Luke gazed across Miguel's deathbed at the fiery eighteen-year-old boy who reminded him so much of himself at that age. Was Ignacio destined to make the same kind of mistakes, maybe worse? Not if he could help it, Luke vowed. It was up to him, now, to look out for Miguel's sons and keep them safe. He owed that much to his old friend.

Sebastian had come inside and was standing quietly in the bedroom doorway. Luke glanced toward him, then back at Ignacio, feeling the weight of what he was about to say.

"Listen to me, both of you," he said. "I swear to you, Sebastian and Ignacio, that if you promise to respect the law, I will find your father's murderers and bring them to justice. Whatever it takes—I swear it on my life."

"And on the grave of our father." Ignacio's voice was a hoarse whisper in the darkness.

Luke gazed down into the old man's bloodied and battered face. "On his grave," he rasped, choking back tears. "I swear it."

* * *

Rachel had finished rubbing down the horse. Now she huddled in the darkness of the barn, wet, shivering and hungry.

Luke had said he would come back. But either he had been delayed or he had simply forgotten about her. Either way, she was growing more miserable by the minute.

She should saddle a fresh horse and leave, she thought. That would be the smart thing to do. Taking her chances in the storm was a less terrifying prospect than walking into that house of mourning with no idea of how much Luke had revealed about her.

Were any members of her family tied to the old man's murder? Rachel's stomach clenched as the faces of her father and brothers flashed through her mind. Kind faces. Loving faces. She could not imagine any of them beating an old man, burning his wagon and leaving him near death. The whole idea was unthinkable.

Driven by desperation, she seized Luke's saddle. Her injured shoulder throbbed as she dragged it down from the stall where he'd left it. A pinto with the scruffy look of a wild-caught mustang, was munching hay in a nearby stall. The horse appeared strong enough to carry her through the storm. All she had to do was get the saddle on it and—

Rachel stopped herself in midmotion. Running away would resolve nothing. Dangerous as it might be, she needed to get into the house, to learn all she could about what had happened and what Luke and the old man's sons were planning to do.

To accomplish that, she would have to play sweet and innocent, to win their confidence. If such a masquerade made her feel lower than a snake's belly, so be it. She owed that much to her family.

And she owed it to her family to reserve judgment, Rachel reminded herself. There were two sides to every story, and she had heard only Luke's. The stubborn sheep man had crossed a lot of lines. She could only imagine what he might have done to bring so much anger down upon his own head.

Quivering with fatigue, she hefted the saddle back onto the side of the stall. If only things were that simple, she thought. Days, even hours ago, they might have been. But now a man had died. The hands that had battered his aging body had committed murder.

Outside, the rain fell like a beaded curtain across the open entrance to the barn. She groped in the darkness for a slicker but found nothing that could protect her. Hesitating, she sighed. What did such a small thing matter when a man was dead and the land she loved had become a battleground?

Icy pellets of water stung her skin like buckshot as she plunged into the storm and splashed her way across the yard. Through streaks of rain she could see the zigzag line of the fence and, beyond it, the pale, shifting forms of sheep.

The house lay off to the right, a low, sprawling shape with an overhanging roof. Turning, Rachel sprinted toward it. As she mounted the split log steps to the porch the four dogs that had taken shelter there raised their heads. The two that recognized her thumped their tails, but the largest animal, sensing a stranger, sprang to its feet, growling.

"Easy…it's all right, boy," Rachel whispered, soothing the dog as she edged across the porch. With every step, she prayed the door would be unlocked. When the latch yielded to the pressure of her hand, her knees all but buckled with relief. With the dog dancing toward her on stiffened legs, she made a narrow opening, stumbled into the darkness of the house and shoved the door closed behind her.

For a long moment she pressed her back against the sturdy planks. The sound of her racing heart filled her ears, like a drumbeat in the silence. Her legs quivered, threatening to collapse beneath her. Only the thought of the dog outside kept her from turning tail and fleeing back to the barn.

The room was dark, but she could see well enough to make out a wooden table and a counter where plates, bowls and cups were stacked. Against the wall stood a large iron stove, the fire in its belly burned down to coals that glimmered through the mica panes.

The kitchen and sitting area, with its massive stone fireplace, appeared to take up the front part of the house. Leading to the back was a narrow hallway. As Rachel moved cautiously toward the entrance, she could see a dim light coming from one of the rooms and hear the subdued murmur of men's voices, speaking in Spanish.

Rachel drew back, almost choking on the sudden tightness in her throat. No, she could not walk down that hallway. She could not walk into that room and face the horror and hatred she knew she would find inside. There had to be another way, a wiser way.

Heart pounding, she returned to the dark kitchen. In the wake of the old man's death, no one had tended the fire in the stove, warmed a meal or made coffee. That much, at least, she could do.

Groping in the shadows, she found the wood box. It was less than half full, but there were enough good sticks to rekindle a blaze. There was a lamp on the table and a tin of Arbuckle Coffee on the counter. With luck, once she got the fire going, she might even be able to find some bacon and eggs to cook.

Twisting back her hair and rolling up her sleeves, Rachel set to work.

There was no clock in the small bedroom, but to Luke, it was as if he could hear the seconds ticking in a slow, grim progression. They sat, the three of them, on the rough-hewn kitchen chairs at the foot of Miguel's bed, each one lost in his own private grief. Sebastian, the older and gentler of Miguel's sons, seemed most upset that his father had died without a priest to give him last rites. Ignacio, despite Luke's promise of justice, had talked of nothing except revenge and family honor.

They sat frozen in silence now, Sebastian fingering his rosary, Ignacio stirring restlessly. From where Luke sat, with his chair back against the wall, the scene appeared as a grim tableau—the narrow iron bed with its faded quilt, the rigid figure of the father, the two sons flanking the bed like figures in an old engraving from the *Lives of the Saints* book his mother had used to teach him reading.

Guilt gnawed at Luke like a living thing, boring its way into his soul. This whole tragedy was his fault. He should have realized something like this would happen and done a better job of protecting his herders. After the attack, he should have loaded Miguel on the wagon and hauled him to Sheridan, or ridden for a doctor and brought one back at gunpoint, if necessary. At the very least he should have stayed at the ranch instead of going off to get the sheep. He had thought the old man was on the mend, but given Miguel's age, he should have known better. He should never have left the boys to deal with their father's injuries alone.

Luke's thoughts scattered as a tantalizing aroma pricked his senses. Ignacio raised his head, then Sebastian. They smelled it, too. Coffee, fresh and hot, wafting from the kitchen.

Only then did Luke remember that he had left Rachel in the barn.

Muttering under his breath, Luke strode up the hallway. He stepped into the kitchen to be greeted by a flood of warmth, and the sight of Rachel standing at the counter, slicing bacon into thin strips with a butcher knife. She had lit a lamp, and hung it from the hook above the table. Its light gleamed like burnished gold on the tight, wet curls of her hair. Her mud-soaked clothes clung to her trim little body, arousing a reaction in Luke that he was in no mood to welcome.

She glanced around at him, her aquamarine eyes glinting with a rancor that caused his gaze to flicker to the knife in her hand.

"The coffee is almost ready," she said in a guarded voice. "I hope you and your friends like it black. I couldn't find cream or sugar."

"Black is the way we always have it," Luke said. "And I'm sorry for making you wait in the barn. I meant to get back to you sooner."

"You had more pressing things on your mind than a wet, tired, cranky woman." She laid the cold bacon slices in the big iron skillet and slid it onto the hot surface of the stove. "Besides, I've never waited for a man in my life. Why should I start now?"

Her eyes glittered dangerously, throwing out a challenge that intrigued him. Under different circumstances he might be interested in pursuing that challenge, Luke thought. But not tonight. And not with Morgan Tolliver's daughter.

She had set the table with the motley collection of chipped plates, mugs and cutlery she'd found on the counter. A heavenly aroma drifted from the oven. In spite of his reservations about Rachel, Luke's mouth had begun to water. Praise be, the woman had made biscuits!

Ignacio and Sebastian had come into the kitchen and were staring openly at her. Sebastian had met her briefly outside, but this was Ignacio's first sight of her. The handsome youth looked thunderstruck as he took in her sea-colored eyes, voluptuous little body and rich amber hair. For a woman who'd endured hours of mud, wind and rain, she looked damned good, Luke groused. Too good. And from what he knew of Rachel Tolliver, he would bet this meal wasn't just a neighborly gesture.

With a disarmingly tender smile on her face, she walked toward the two young men. "I'm Rachel," she said, holding out her hand, "and I want you to know how sorry I am about your father."

Stricken by shyness, Sebastian muttered a polite response in Spanish and dropped his gaze to his muddy boots. Ignacio, his handsome young face alight, caught Rachel's hand and, with a sweeping bow, pressed it to his lips. The gesture was so melodramatic that, under different circumstances, Luke might have allowed himself an amused smile. But this was not a night for amusement.

"Mucho gusto, señorita." Ignacio's long-lashed eyes were like sweet brown molasses. *"Y muchas gracias por la comida."*

His clasp on her hand lingered. Rachel shot Luke a flustered glance, as if pleading to be disentangled from a sticky situation. What would the boy do if he knew she was the daughter of the most powerful cattle baron in three counties? Luke wondered. With all Ignacio's talk of revenge, this probably wouldn't be a good time to tell him.

"Basta, hombre," Luke muttered in Spanish. *"La señorita tiene demasiados años para tí."*

Ignacio released her hand with a polite smile. Rachel spun away and bustled to the stove to tend the sizzling bacon. As she glanced toward Luke, her eyes met his. He was startled by the fear that glimmered in their blue-green depths. Only then did he realize how much grit it had taken for her to come into the house on her own.

"What did you tell him?" she whispered anxiously.

Luke took his time, studying her while the rain drummed against the windows of the house. "I said you were too old for him. I didn't think you'd mind. The boy's only eighteen."

"Then I pity the girls when he's twenty-one!" Visibly relieved, she bent to the task of turning the bacon strips and moving them to one side of the pan. Her hands worked with surprising skill, breaking the eggs on the side of the big iron skillet and slipping them into the bubbling fat so gently that not one yolk was broken. Miguel had done most of the cooking on the ranch. Since the old man's beating, no one had felt up to preparing a meal. Rachel Tolliver was giving them a greater gift than she realized.

Seizing a towel, she opened the oven door and lifted out the pan of golden biscuits. "Almost ready," she said. "You don't seem to have any butter or jam, so we'll have to eat them plain, but at least they'll be fresh."

Luke inhaled the warm aroma. "Thank you, Rachel," he said, meaning it. "I know the boys will appreciate this meal."

She glanced up, her cheeks glowing with heat from the stove. "As my mother always says, when there's trouble and there's nothing else you can do, start cooking.''

"If those biscuits taste as good as they smell, I'd say your mother must be a good teacher."

"She is." Rachel turned the eggs deftly, one by one. "But I learned to cook from Chang. He's been a part of the ranch since my grandfather hired him away from the railroad, more than forty years ago. He—'' She broke off, her face suddenly pale, as if she'd said too much. "Do your two young friends speak any English?"

"Only a few words. They wouldn't have understood what you just said, if that's what you're asking.''

She glanced nervously toward the table. Ignacio and Sebastian had brought the chairs from the back bedroom and were seated at the table, their hands and faces freshly washed, like two expectant children. Again he felt a surge of gratitude toward her—gratitude he was swift to mask.

"What have you told them about me?" A lock of hair tumbled into her face as she bent to scoop the bacon and eggs onto a tin plate.

"Nothing."

"But they're bound to ask." Her voice had dropped to a whisper. "What will you tell them?"

"That depends."

Luke saw her body stiffen as his words struck home. When she turned to face him, her eyes were wide with alarm. "What's that supposed to mean?"

She mouthed the words, her back toward the two boys at the table.

"It depends on how honest you are with me, Rachel," he said, keeping his voice low and pleasant. "I think you're hiding something. After supper, when we have time to talk, I want to know what it is."

Chapter Seven

Rachel turned away from him, her heart clenching spasmodically. The warmth she'd felt when he thanked her for the meal had fled, leaving nothing but fear and distrust in its place.

Be honest with me, Rachel, he had demanded. But how could she tell him what she had glimpsed today? How could she put the people she loved at risk when she herself knew so little of the truth?

"Let's eat." She set the plate of bacon and eggs and the pan of biscuits on the table, avoiding his eyes as she filled the four mugs with steaming black coffee. No, she thought, there was no way she could tell Luke she had seen one of her brothers today. To do so would only heighten the danger to everyone involved—her brothers, her father, herself, Luke and the two young men at the table. Rachel had always prided herself on being honest and open, but there were times when truth was better off wrapped in silence. This was one of those times.

Ignacio sprang up to pull out her chair as she took

her seat on the side of the table nearest the stove. There was a moment of awkward hesitation. Then Sebastian bowed his head and murmured a brief grace. When he had finished, Rachel picked up the plate of bacon and eggs and passed it to Ignacio, who promptly thrust it back toward her, indicating with words and dramatic gestures that she was to help herself first. He was an engaging youth, handsome almost to the point of beauty, with a reckless gleam in his liquid brown eyes. Trouble on the hoof, Rachel's mother would have said of him. But Rachel could not help liking the boy. Given the chance, she might have chosen to paint him as a fiery young cavalier with a ruffled shirt and a drawn rapier, standing on the deck of a ship with his ebony curls whipping in the wind.

And Sebastian…her gaze flickered toward him as he took a biscuit from the pan and cradled its warmth between his strong, blunt hands. Plain, shy and gentle, she would have chosen to paint him as Francis of Assisi, cradling a lamb in his arms, or maybe as Sancho Panza astride his patient little donkey.

And Luke…Rachel cast him a furtive glance over the rim of her coffee mug. She could not think of any way to portray him except as himself—a proud, stubborn man who leaned on no one. A man who had set himself apart from anything that might be read as softness or weakness, including love.

He ate with careful restraint, leaving most of the food for the two boys. Rachel studied him through the veil of her eyelashes, searching for clues about his past and the forces that had hardened his rawhide soul. There must have been a woman, she thought. A woman who had hurt him so badly that he never wanted to feel again. And she knew there were other scars as well—secrets mentioned in passing or glimpsed in the flash of his hooded eyes. Luke Vincente had the look of a man whose life had been shaped by tragedy and betrayal. A man who trusted no one.

But none of that mattered, Rachel reminded herself. She could not allow herself to care about these people, or involve herself in their lives. She was in the camp of the enemy. And she was here as a spy.

The food on her plate was getting cold. Half an hour ago she had been ravenous. Now she had to force herself to chew and swallow each bite. She should have taken the spotted horse and escaped into the storm while she had the chance. Now it was too late to run away.

"What are you going to do now?" she asked, feeling his eyes on her.

"Do?" He lifted one sardonic eyebrow.

"About the old man. About the men who beat him." *About me.*

"We'll be burying the old man in the morning." He spoke in a conversational tone that was clearly meant not to draw the attention of the two youths. "As for the rest—" He feigned a shrug. "I promised the boys that I'd find the men who murdered their father and see them brought to justice." Granite flecks glinted in his eyes. "That's where you come in."

Rachel's throat jerked so abruptly that she almost

choked on her coffee. She faked an apologetic smile for the sake of the two young men, but she knew Luke was not fooled. "Don't ask me to help you," she said. "You know I can't be part of this. And you know why."

His eyes narrowed, darkening with a hint of menace. "You do know something, don't you? Earlier I wasn't sure. Now I am."

"I know nothing about your friend's death." She forced herself to meet his gaze as she spoke. That much, at least, was true. As for the rest, no power on earth could make her admit she had seen her own brother today.

The tension between them had become almost palpable. Ignacio and Sebastian had stopped eating and were glancing from Luke to Rachel with puzzled eyes.

"Who do they think I am?" she asked softly.

"As far as they're concerned, you're just a woman I rescued from her buggy in a flood. My hot-blooded young friend would more likely have spat on your hand than kissed it if he'd known who your family was. Would you like me to tell him?"

Rachel willed herself to look calm and confident. In all her years at school, she had never yearned for home as desperately as she did now, with her family just a two-hour ride away.

"Tell them or not, that's your choice," she said, glancing away from him with pretended indifference. "It can't ease their grief or bring their father back. It can only make things worse for them, knowing a cattleman's daughter is sharing their table.''

Luke's silence told Rachel she had made her point. But she knew he was only biding his time. He would not let her off so easily.

The two youths had finished their meal and were waiting for her to rise before leaving the table. Someone, at least, had taught them proper manners. Had it been their father? Rachel caught herself wishing she'd known more about the old sheepherder.

Grateful for any excuse to move, she rose and began to clear away the dishes. Ignacio and Sebastian both sprang to help her, but she waved them away. The hour was late and both of them looked exhausted.

"Tell them, please, to get some rest," she said, glancing back at Luke. "They've had a terrible day. It's no trouble for me to finish up here."

Luke spoke a few words of Spanish, and the two young men, thanking her profusely, opened the front door and walked out onto the porch. Rising and stretching, the four dogs trotted after them, down the steps. The fast-moving storm had swept out onto the prairie, leaving patches of stars in its wake. Clouds drifted over the face of a wan crescent moon.

Luke walked to the door and bolted it shut behind them. When he turned back to face her, Rachel had the feeling she had tumbled out of the frying pan and into the fire.

"Where…do they sleep?" Her voice emerged as a nervous squeak.

"There's a bunkhouse out back. This house only

has two bedrooms, and..." he hesitated slightly. "Miguel's laid out in one of them."

He walked to the table and began clearing away the plates. "I'll take some blankets and sleep in here," he said. "You can have my bed for the night."

The color rose in her face. "Oh, but I wouldn't dream of—"

"Don't be a proper little fool, Rachel." His voice rasped with irritation. "The boys and I will be up before dawn. If you're sprawled out on the floor asleep—"

"You don't need to draw me a picture. I'll take your bed." Rachel poured heated water from the kettle into the dishpan and added some lye soap shavings, then filled a second pan with rinse water. She was too tired to be civil, but he clearly did not intend to leave her alone. Maybe she could at least steer their conversation onto safer ground.

Her gaze darted around the large room which served as kitchen, dining room and parlor. The house was small but sturdily built, with touches that showed a loving attention to detail—the log walls that had been oiled to bring out their natural golden color; the built-in shelves that flanked the fireplace, filled with dozens of well-thumbed classics; the matching leather wing chairs, worn but of good quality, that faced the unlit fireplace. On one chair a faded Navajo blanket had been flung over an arm. Its fringed corner spilled over the bare, oiled planks of the floor.

"Did you build this house?" Rachel knew her

neighborly tone would not fool him, but she had to make some effort at conversation.

"The house and most of the furniture. My grandfather was a carpenter. What little I know, he taught me." Luke set the stacked plates and mugs on the counter next to the dishpan. Relieved that he was playing along, Rachel willed herself to relax.

"I didn't just want a ranch, I wanted a home," Luke bent to take a clean flour sack towel from a basket under the counter. Picking up the first plate Rachel had washed, he began wiping it dry. "In the beginning, I didn't have much to work with, but what little I had got me this far. I always planned to build onto the place, add a wing, maybe even an upper floor, but now…" The words trailed off into a shrug, as if to say, *what for?*

"That sounds like the way my grandfather built our house—he started with a couple of good, solid rooms and added on. It's become quite a grand place." Rachel was chattering now, something she tended to do when she was nervous. "You really should go ahead with your plans. You'll need the extra space when it comes time to start a family." Turning to hand him another plate, she was struck by the smoldering frustration in his eyes. Startled, she drew back. "Did I say something wrong?"

"You saw what happened today. Even if I found a woman who could stand to live out here—and could stand *me*—" He glanced toward the back of the house, where the old man's body lay. "How could I think of exposing a wife and children to this kind of hatred?''

"But surely it won't always be like this.''

He chuckled bitterly. "Earlier today you were telling me to leave.''

"I know.'' She handed him another plate, struck, suddenly by the intimacy of the common task in the quiet, lamplit kitchen. He was standing very close to her, their fingers not quite touching as she handed him the clean dishes. His presence, so large and warm and fiercely gentle, sent a quiver of awareness through her body. "I did say you should leave.'' Her throat felt raw and husky. "But that was before I saw this ranch and realized how much of your heart you'd put into it. For you, leaving isn't a choice. You'd die on this land before you let yourself be driven off it.''

The house was so silent that Rachel could hear the small brass clock ticking on the mantel. She could hear the deep rush of Luke's breathing beside her. She dared not look up at him. To do so would be an invitation for him to touch her; and she sensed that if his fingers so much as brushed her skin, she would burst into flame like an autumn leaf in a bonfire.

"Will you tell your people that?'' His voice was gravelly, as if he needed to clear his throat.

Rachel's legs felt unsteady beneath her. A cup slipped from her fingers and tumbled into the soapy water. "Tell them what?'' she whispered.

"That I won't leave. That I'm here to stay. That all I want is to be left in peace.''

She shook her head. "You know I can't tell my

family anything. If my father knew I'd spent the night here alone with you, he'd come riding over here with a rifle and shoot you himself.''

"Then tell me what you saw today."

The saucer Rachel was holding fell from her fingers and shattered on the floor. She bent forward to snatch up the pieces, but Luke's hand caught her arm, jerking her upright. The motion whipped her against him, flattening her breasts against his chest. His eyes drilled into her like bullets.

"Tell me." His voice was flat and cold.

"I...don't know what you're talking about!" she stammered, struggling against panic.

"Yes, you do, Rachel. When those four cowboys rode away, they passed right by the place where you were hiding. When you came out from behind those rocks, you looked as if you'd seen a ghost. At the time I thought you were just scared. But there's more to the story than that, isn't there?"

"Let me go, Luke," she whispered.

"Isn't there?" His hand tightened on her arm. "You knew the bastards, didn't you?"

"They were masked. Please—"

"You knew them. And you can give me their names."

"You're wrong!" She forced herself to meet his blazing eyes. "And even if you weren't, even if I could give you their names, you'd have no proof they had anything to do with your friend's death."

"I'd have a lead. I'd have a trail to follow. That's a hell of a lot more than what I have now." He forced her upward, so that she was standing on tiptoe, her face a few perilous inches from his own. "Damn it, woman, we're not just talking about a few sheep here! We're talking about a man's life! We're talking about murder! If you have a spark of common decency in that self-centered little heart of yours—"

His words ended in a growl of frustration. Rachel's mind groped frantically for a way to end the standoff. She could swoon or pretend to be sick—but no, that would not fool him. It would only make him angrier, as would trying to fight him.

Only one thing came to mind, and before her courage had time to fail her, she did it.

"Rachel—"

Her mouth stopped his words. She kissed him hard, her free arm hooking the back of his neck so that he could not pull away. His body jerked and went rigid against her. His mouth was like carved marble, cold and resistant, but Rachel knew that breaking away now would be like jumping off the back of a tiger. Her pulse rocketed as she willed her lips to melt against his, willed her tongue to flick lightly against the taut ridge of his lower lip. He tasted of bacon and strong black coffee, and the stubble on his jaw was like rough velvet against her skin.

For the space of a long breath he stood like a wall against her. Then, with a groan, he released his arms to slide around her, molding her to him so tightly that she could feel his shirt buttons through her bodice. His response went through her like a hot blade through wax. Her heart slammed as his mouth took control of their kiss. His tongue probed deftly between her lips, brushing her tingling flesh until she ached to draw him inside her, to taste him, to feel him.

She groped for the last vestige of her self-control, then let it go. Sweet heaven, what was happening to her? Kissing boys at school had been an amusing game. She had always been the one in charge, the one who made and enforced the rules and never went too far. But she had never kissed a man like Luke Vincente.

Rachel's legs had gone liquid beneath her. Her loins seethed with molten, shimmering heat. Moisture slicked her thighs. She moaned out loud as his hands found the curve of her hips, pressing her lightly against him but stopping just short of the exquisite pressure that her body craved. The man was playing her, she suddenly realized. He was teasing her, tantalizing her with the skill of an experienced lover who knew exactly what he was doing.

He was making an utter fool of her!

Suddenly furious, Rachel wrenched herself away from him. She stumbled backward, half falling against the edge of the table before she caught her balance.

Luke's mocking eyes glittered down at her. He had won their battle of nerves, and he knew it. It had taken just one kiss to shatter her pride and reduce her to a panting, quivering mess.

The anger that welled up in Rachel was white-hot, volcanic in its fury. Her hand swung in a wild arc to strike his face. The force of the slap wrenched her sore shoulder and left a stinging red handprint on his cheek.

Luke's features did not even twitch, but when he spoke his voice was as flat and thin as a razor. "Go to bed, Rachel. The sheets are clean and you'll find everything you need in the room." His eyes narrowed dangerously. "There's a bolt on the inside of the door. See that you lock it."

Rachel half expected him to turn on his heel and walk away, but he stood his ground, forcing her to turn tail and retreat. Her spine was ramrod-stiff as she stalked down the hall to Luke's bedroom, but her legs had turned to jelly by the time she stepped across the threshold, closed the door behind her and slid the metal bolt into place with a resounding click.

The room was simply furnished. A double bed covered by a faded woolen blanket took up most of the space. Against the far wall, a wardrobe stood beside a washstand with a cracked mirror and a tin basin. Next to the bed, a small side table held a guttering candle and a stack of books.

Rachel blew out the candle. Then, surrounded by warm, dark stillness, she sank onto the edge of the bed and buried her face in her hands.

He opened his eyes to find her leaning over him, clad in nothing but a gossamer shift that skimmed her naked body like moonlight. The fabric strained against her jutting nipples, outlining the ripe, ivory globes of her breasts. Her red-gold curls framed her face like a glowing halo. But she was no angel. Lord, no. He had known that from the instant he'd held her in his arms and tasted the sweet, wild honey of her mouth.

Her scent was earth and musk, the odor of a female animal in heat. The erotic fragrance swam through his senses, awakening every cell in his body to sensations he had long since sworn to forget. Beneath the Navajo blanket, he was painfully aroused, with a need as keen as the honed edge of a knife blade.

"Rachel…" His feverish lips whispered her name as he pushed the blanket aside and drew her down beside him. Her shift vaporized beneath the heat of his hands, leaving her body naked against his aching flesh.

She was as bold as a she-cat, moaning with unbridled pleasure as he stroked her skin, exploring every curve and hollow of her. Her body rippled against him, molten, seeking as he cupped her breasts, tasting the swollen buds of her nipples, licking, sucking. Every whimper, every explosive, frantic breath begged him to take her and end the torment that threatened to turn them both to living torches.

Her fingers dug into his shoulders, gripping and clawing as he nibbled his way down her soft belly to the silken nest where her pleasure lay. She opened her thighs, arching against him as his tongue found the silken folds and the swollen nub between them. The first taste of her sent a shuddering explosion through her body. She cradled his head between her thighs, moaning softly as the storm subsided. "I want you," she whispered. "Now…please."

Unable to wait any longer, he shifted his weight and rose above her. For the space of a breath he gazed down into her beautiful, wanton face. Her wet lips parted, expectantly. Then, with a little gasp, she arched to meet him. He thrust into her hard and deep with a force that was almost brutal, taking her, filling her, again, again and again....

Luke awoke in darkness, damp, sticky and cursing like a muleskinner. Damn the dream! Damn the woman and what that searing kiss had done to him! It was a good thing he had told her to bolt the bedroom door. Otherwise he would be sorely tempted to stride down the hall and make the dream a reality.

Aching in every joint, he rolled onto his back and lay on the hard floor, staring up into the darkness. Oh, he knew why Rachel had kissed him, the little witch. He had backed her into a corner, forcing the issue of the four riders, and she had evaded him with tactics as old as Mother Eve.

He could only hope his response had startled her as much as it had him.

For a long moment he lay still, remembering the feel of her in his arms, the satiny heat of her lips and the seductive forays of her mischievous little tongue. Lord, how he had wanted her. He had deserved that slap for what he was thinking.

But her ploy was not going to work, he vowed. As soon as Rachel awoke, they would have it out. Something about her behavior wasn't right, and he could not let her go without finding out what it was.

But did he have the legal and moral right to keep

Rachel from leaving? Seething with uncertainty, Luke sat up and raked the hair out of his eyes. One brush with the law was enough. He didn't need the kind of trouble that holding her by force would bring. As an ex-convict, he wouldn't stand a chance against the law.

But he had promised Miguel's boys he would find the men who'd beaten their father to death. All his instincts told him that Rachel Tolliver was the key to keeping that promise.

But why should she help him? She was a Tolliver, a woman whose hatred of sheep and the men who raised them was bred into the very marrow of her bones. If it came to choosing sides there was no question where her loyalties would lie.

A glance toward the window showed him that the darkness was beginning to fade. It was time he woke the boys and started their painful day. He had a coffin to build. They had a grave to dig.

As for Rachel, he realized, the only hope lay in appealing to her sense of justice—if the woman had one. Only if he could convince her she was doing the right thing would she agree to help him find Miguel's killers. If he failed in that, she would lie and evade his questions until doomsday.

Sore, gritty-eyed and still damp from that cursed dream, Luke rolled out of his makeshift bed, staggered to his feet and shook himself fully awake. He was just reaching for his boots when the realization struck him.

Yesterday, when the four riders had passed close

to Rachel, she must have recognized someone from her own family—one of her brothers, most likely; maybe even both of them, or even her father.

Thunderstruck, he sank onto the edge of a chair and began the reflexive task of pulling on his boots. That would explain everything—the look of shocked disbelief on her face, the evasive answers to his questions, even the desperation with which she had kissed him. She was protecting her own flesh and blood. What a fool he'd been not to have guessed it sooner!

Now what? Luke stood up, unfastened his belt and tucked in his sleep-rumpled shirt. Appealing to her sense of justice would not be enough, he knew. Neither would a show of anger or force. He would simply have to walk into the bedroom and confront her with what he knew to be the truth. And he would have to do it now, before the boys came inside for their morning coffee and ended any chance of a private talk.

Had she bolted the bedroom door? Never mind, he would pound on the planks until she opened it. Rachel Tolliver was a stubborn woman. But she was not getting out of that room until she had told him everything he knew.

He strode down the dim hallway to find the door closed. No surprise there. Not wanting to startle her, he rapped lightly with his knuckles.

There was no answer.

He rapped harder. "Rachel, wake up! We need to talk! Now!"

When there was no reply, he tried the latch. The door yielded and swung open at his touch.

Inside the bedroom there was only silence. Through the window, a finger of gray morning light fell on the neatly made-up bed.

Rachel was gone.

Chapter Eight

Rachel yelped as her blistered toe struck a sharp rock. She'd been walking for hours, navigating by the stars as her father had taught her. The night sky had kept her from wandering in circles, but it could not protect her from badger holes, cactus spines, twisting roots, boulders and mysterious, scurrying creatures. She was bruised, scratched, bone-tired and as miserable as she had ever been in her life.

For reasons that had made perfect sense at the time, Rachel had decided against taking one of Luke's horses from the barn. The sound of a horse might have awakened Luke or his young herders, leaving her with some tall explaining to do. And she had not wanted to give Luke an excuse to track her, or to incur any further obligation to a man who was her family's sworn enemy.

All the same, Rachel had regretted her decision a hundred times over. Her dainty kidskin boots had not been made for trekking across the prairie. Already soaked by the storm, they had come unsewn and unglued as she walked. By now, every step on her bruised and blistered feet was agony. Only the fading darkness gave her the courage to keep moving. Soon it would be dawn. She would be able to see the Big Horn Mountains in the west, calculate her exact position and make a beeline for home.

As the sky lightened from pewter to opal, she forced herself to keep moving, step by painful step. When her resolve threatened to crumble, she used anger to fuel her waning strength. Luke Vincente's response to her kiss had turned her into a simpering, jelly-kneed little fool, and he had known exactly what he was doing. How had he learned to kiss like that, to touch a woman in a way that all but melted her flesh beneath his hands? How had he learned to use his lips, his tongue, like weapons of war, leaving her collapsed in defeat after the first charge? The wretched rascal must have had some expert teachers—and plenty of practice!

How far would he have gone if she hadn't pulled away? Would he have made a ruined woman of her, or would he have flung her aside and walked away laughing? The latter, more likely, she reckoned. Either way, she hated the sheep man to the depths of her burning, humiliated soul. If she never saw him again, that would suit her just fine!

The dawn sky had faded to a gleaming silver. Now, to the west, she could see the jagged outline of her beloved Big Horn Mountains. Holding up a forefinger, she took a visual measurement of the angle between two peaks—a trick she had learned years ago from Johnny Chang, the Tolliver Ranch's Chinese foreman. Her spirits lightened as she realized the ranch house was even closer than she'd hoped. If she didn't collapse on the way, she would be home in an hour.

Rachel's feet were swollen nubs of pain. Limping miserably, she forced herself to take one step, then another. She *would* make it home, she vowed, even if she had to crawl the rest of the way on her hands and knees. She had come too far to give up now. To keep up her courage, she began to sing.

"There is a tavern in the town, in the town, And there my true love sits him down, sits him down, sits him down…"

Tottering bravely ahead, she swung her arms in rhythm with the old tune. But even singing was an effort. Rachel's throat was as dry as a summer tumbleweed, and her vision had begun to blur in the morning light. Steeling herself against the pain, she broke into the chorus.

"Fare-thee-well, for I must leave thee, do not let the parting grieve thee, but remember that…"

The words died in her throat as a dark, mounted figure, still distant, emerged as a bobbing dot through the haze of her vision. Her pulse leaped as the thought flashed through her mind that it was Luke, that he'd been worried enough to come after her. But no, as the figure bobbed closer, she saw that she was wrong. The rider was approaching from the direction of the ranch. He was short and wiry, the broad-brimmed

Stetson on his head appearing almost comically large in proportion to his compact body.

Elation and relief swept over Rachel as she recognized him. "Johnny!" She waved her arms as she shouted. "Johnny Chang! Over here!"

The figure swung toward her. Johnny Chang, the son of the ranch's elderly Chinese cook, had been Morgan Tolliver's foreman for the past nineteen years; and anyone who derided him for his size or his race soon learned better. Johnny could outride, outrope and outshoot any cowhand in the state. There was no horse he couldn't break and nothing he didn't know about running the ranch. Tough, taciturn and fair, he commanded the respect of every man who knew him.

"Miss Rachel?" His homely face registered disbelief as he reined in his tall blue roan and squinted down at her. "What are you doing here?"

Rachel accepted the canteen he thrust toward her and took a long, blessed swallow of cool water. Johnny had aged since she'd last set eyes on him. The creases that marked his sun-weathered face had deepened, and his hair had begun to gray. But his narrow brown eyes were as sharp and alert as ever.

"I had trouble on the Sheridan road," Rachel said. "The buggy I'd rented wound up in a flooded wash, and I ended up walking home." That much, at least, was true. The rest of the story would have to wait. She was glad it was Johnny who had found her first. He would not grill her or lecture her. He would simply take her home.

"What are you doing out here so early in the day?" She blinked up at him through an unexpected shimmer of tears.

"Lost cow. Come on." A man of few words, as always, Johnny leaned down from the saddle and held out his hand. Rachel gripped it and, with the last of her strength, swung herself onto the horse behind him.

When she was securely seated, he nudged the smooth-gaited roan to a lope. With the sunrise behind them, they flew across the open prairie toward the heart of the Tolliver ranch. As fingers of sunlight stretched across the sage-dotted hills, Rachel felt her spirits lifting. She was home, and soon she would be with her family. That was all that mattered. Surely, given time, all the doubts and fears that had arisen yesterday would fade. Life would be as she remembered it, warm and safe, with the rhythms of the ranch, its seasons, its animals, its people, blending together like a happy song.

But no—Rachel brought herself up short. She was no longer a child, and life on the ranch had never been as idyllic as she remembered. There had been droughts, prairie fires and long, killing winters. There had been wolves and cattle rustlers, sick animals, sick people, accidents and stillborn babies. One of Johnny Chang's five sons had been killed by a runaway bull. Three years after Jacob and Josh were born, Rachel's mother had miscarried and nearly died. The doctor had told her there would be no more children.

Troubles and tragedies were part of life on the ranch. They went hand in hand with the joys. Rachel's family—the Tollivers, the Changs and the few other hardy souls who'd stayed around long enough to weave themselves into the fabric of the ranch—had endured the bad times because they cared for each other. They would endure this latest crisis as they had all the others, together. And it would take a lot more than one angry sheep man to tear them apart.

"How are things at home, Johnny?" she asked anxiously. "Is everyone all right?"

"Fine. Nobody said you were coming."

"It was meant to be a…surprise." Rachel's stomach flip-flopped as the roan sailed over a narrow wash. "I was coming down that long hill and almost ran into a herd of sheep."

"Sheep." The contempt that laced the foreman's voice left no need for more words.

"The mule bolted," Rachel said. "The buggy wound up in a wash, and then there was a flood."

"The mule?"

"It got away. The blasted animal's probably munching oats back in Sheridan by now."

"And your baggage?"

"We—I was able to get most of my things out of the wash before the flood came. Somebody will need to go and fetch them."

He was silent for a moment, and Rachel knew he had not missed her slip of the tongue. But it would not be like Johnny to probe deeper and cause her to lose face. "I will send the wagon," was all he said.

Looking past his shoulder now, Rachel caught her first glimpse of the ranch buildings—the rambling two-story log and stone house, the barn, the bunk-house, and the neat maze of sheds and corrals, all rising out of the prairie with the mountains behind them. A lump rose in her throat as she saw the smoke curling out of the massive rock chimney. She was home. Right now, that was all that mattered.

As the distance lessened, she saw her mother come out onto the porch to shake the braided rag rug that lay at the foot of the stairs. The strip of bright color rippled in the morning sunlight, then abruptly dropped to the ground as Cassandra Tolliver caught sight of the horse carrying two riders. Shading her eyes, she plunged down the steps and raced across the yard.

"Mama!" Rachel was off the back of the horse almost before Johnny had reined the animal to a halt. Pain shot through her as her blistered feet landed on the ground, but she paid no heed as she plunged toward her mother.

"Rachel!" Cassandra's hand crept to her throat. At forty-three, she was still a pretty woman, petite and energetic, her dark red curls laced with more gray than Rachel remembered. Tears glimmered in her clear blue eyes as mother and daughter stumbled into each other's arms.

Cassandra gave Rachel a long, fiercely emotional hug, then drew back to inspect her at arm's length. "Merciful heaven, we weren't expecting you for another week! And look at you! We've got to get you into the house! What on earth happened?"

Rachel told her briefly about the sheep, the wrecked buggy and the flood, leaving out any mention of Luke Vincente. "I've been walking most of the night," she said. "I was afraid that if I stopped to rest, I wouldn't get up again. If Johnny hadn't come along—"

"Hush!" Cassandra's arm tightened around her daughter's waist. "The rest of the story can wait until we get some breakfast in you. Then you'll want a hot bath and a good sleep." She glanced up at the foreman. "Johnny, go find Morgan! Tell him—" She broke off as she caught sight of her husband coming out of the barn.

Morgan Tolliver had weathered the years well, although he walked with a slight limp from a leg that had been shattered by a bucking horse. Older than his wife by more than a decade, he was still proud and erect, with the aquiline features and fierce obsidian eyes of his Shoshone ancestors.

He strode awkwardly toward them across the open ground. He was not a demonstrative man, but Rachel knew how deeply he cared for her. She rarely thought about the fact that her real father had been Jake Logan, a handsome hell-raiser who'd died in a saloon brawl before she was born. Morgan had always been there for her. He was the only father she had ever known.

Morgan stopped cold as he took in Rachel's appearance. A curse escaped his lips before he could bite it back. "What the devil happened?" were his first words to her. "Blast it, Rachel, if you'd let us know you were coming—"

"Oh, leave her be, Morgan!" Cassandra remonstrated gently. "She wrecked the buggy when she ran into a herd of sheep at the bottom of that long hill. She's been walking all night!"

"Sheep!" Morgan's scowl deepened; his tone was even more contemptuous than Johnny Chang's had been.

"Johnny said he'd send someone for my things," Rachel spoke up in an effort to change the subject. "And we'll need to get what's left of the buggy back to Sheridan. I'm afraid you may have to pay the livery stable for the damage."

Morgan swore under his breath. "That damned sheep man ought to be the one to pay for that buggy and for all the other damage those filthy range maggots have done. If you could see the grass—"

"Now, Morgan." Cassandra laid a gently restraining hand on his arm. "Rachel's only just arrived! She's been through a terrible night, and this is no time to be dumping our troubles at her feet!"

"Troubles?" Rachel met her father's stormy gaze, her interest suddenly piqued. "What troubles?"

"Never you mind, dear." Her mother steered her firmly away from him, toward the porch. "It's just the usual sort of thing. Nothing for you to worry your pretty head about. And what luck, you're just in time for breakfast! Thomas was just headed out to ring the bell."

"Thomas is doing the cooking now?" Rachel pounced on a chance to change the subject. If there was trouble with the sheep man, she would find out soon enough. Meanwhile it might be best not to appear too curious.

"Most of it." Cassandra chatted as she helped her daughter mount the steps on her throbbing feet. "Chang still does a little cooking, but the rheumatism in his bad leg has gotten so he can scarcely walk on it." She gave a melancholy little sigh. "We're all getting older, dear. Just part of life, I suppose. Can you make it upstairs to your room? You'll feel better once you're out of those miserable clothes! You can eat in your old robe and slippers while Thomas's boys heat up your bath."

"That sounds…heavenly." Rachel leaned on the banister to ease the weight on her blistered feet. Her throat tightened as she forced herself to ask "Where are Jacob and Josh?"

"They've been up since before dawn irrigating the lower hayfields. But they'll be back here for breakfast." Cassandra's arm tightened around her daughter's waist. "I can't wait to see the look on their faces. They'll be so happy to see you!"

Rachel exhaled, forcing the tension from her body. *Everything's all right,* she told herself. *Forget what you saw. Leave it be.*

But the questions sprang to her lips, burning to be heard. "How are the boys?" she asked, trying not to sound anxious. "Is everything all right with them?"

Cassandra's slight hesitation was more telling than any words. "Why…of course, dear. Is there something that would cause you to ask?"

Rachel forced herself to shrug. "They're eighteen. It's a restless age, especially for boys."

"Yes." Cassandra sighed. "Yes, it is. My, how grown up my little girl has become!" She squeezed Rachel's waist again. "But Jacob and Josh are...fine. Just fine." She repeated the word as they mounted the landing, as if to reassure herself that everything was as it should be. Rachel ached for her mother, wondering how much she knew about the activities of her precious twins.

"Your room is just as you left it." Cassandra bustled down the hallway to open the door. "I'll bring some water for the washstand and ask Thomas to set another place at the table. Then you can tell us all about your adventure over breakfast. You can't imagine how good it is to have you home, dear!"

Alone, Rachel sank wearily onto the edge of the bed she'd slept in since childhood. She had always felt so safe in this little room, with its whitewashed walls, blue gingham curtains, braided rugs, and the painted elk skin that hung on the wall opposite the bed. How many hours had she spent gazing at the mounted Cheyenne warriors, so exquisitely rendered that they seemed to flow across the creamy surface. When Rachel was eleven, her mother had replaced the medicine skin with a framed still life of pink roses and a violin, which she'd thought more suitable for a young lady. Rachel had stormed and pouted until the painted hide was returned to its rightful spot on her bedroom wall. Her family had spoiled her, she realized. But they had done so with such unwavering love that she had always felt happy and secure. Only now, as she gazed around her with a woman's eyes, did she understand how fragile that safe, happy world had been.

The buttonholes of her jacket were stiff with mud. As she fumbled with the buttons, the memory of Luke Vincente's searing kiss washed over her, arousing sensations so hot and strong that her nipples puckered beneath the damp lace of her camisole. She remembered the heat of his hands, the maddening restraint with which he had held her, playing with her emotions, making her almost scream for more…

Had he been surprised to find her gone? Had he made any attempt to find her? Rachel knew that her footprints would have been easy to follow over the muddy ground. But reason told her that Luke would not have tracked her very far. He had a friend to bury and two orphaned boys who needed him. And he had a thousand head of sheep to shear. Why should he waste a moment's thought on a cattleman's spoiled daughter?

But that question was not even worth asking, Rachel told herself. The things that had happened while she was with Luke were best forgotten. If she could blot out the memory of yesterday and last night, maybe her life would be whole again. She would no longer have these doubts, these worries, or these damnable, aching hungers.

The clanging of the big iron triangle that hung outside the kitchen shattered Rachel's reverie. That familiar sound had called the Tolliver family to meals for as long as she could remember. It was one more reminder of ties and loyalties that separated her from the sheep man and his kind. It was time to stop fretting about him and rejoin her own family.

Hurrying, she stripped off her ruined underclothes and rummaged to find an old flannel nightgown in the bottom drawer of the dresser. The worn fabric was soft and warm against her skin, pure bliss after the damp, chafing travel suit. Likewise, the scuffed woolen slippers she had left behind on the floor of the wardrobe cradled her feet like two gentle old friends. Rachel finger-combed her hopelessly tangled hair back from her forehead. Then with the fresh water her mother had left, she splashed her face and washed her hands. The mirror above the washstand showed wildly bloodshot eyes set in a face that was gray with exhaustion. She looked as if she'd just escaped from a sanitarium, she thought as she reached for her faded blue robe. But her family would not care. They would only be happy that she'd come home.

Rachel had been eager to try her wings at art school, and she had done well enough; but not a day had gone by when she had not gazed at the cluttered city skyline and ached to ride across the hills with the sweet prairie wind in her hair. Now she was back on the land she loved, this time to stay.

Years ago, in the belief that she was his own blood granddaughter, the dying Jacob Tolliver had left Rachel one-fifth of the ranch. It was a tribute to Morgan's generosity that he had never challenged his father's will. Rachel's share of the family's vast holdings was enough to make her one of the wealthiest women in the state. But to Rachel, it was not owning the land that counted. It was that the land owned *her*. She had been born on the ranch, and she was as much a part of this place as the coyotes and pronghorns and prairie dogs that had lived here.

She had been away too long, Rachel thought as she descended the stairs.

Her parents were seated at the table when she came into the dining room, but there was no sign of Jacob and Josh. Only after Rachel had seated herself in her traditional place and Thomas Chang was bringing in the platters of bacon, ham, fried potatoes and airy scrambled eggs did the twins burst into the dining room, their hair and faces still damp from a quick splashing at the pump.

Catching sight of Rachel they whooped with joy and fell on her like two half-grown pups. Rachel reached up and hugged both her brothers close, her heart aching. Maybe she'd been mistaken yesterday. Maybe it was someone else's features she'd glimpsed so briefly as the red bandana fell away. She gazed into their open, boyish faces, wanting desperately to be wrong.

"For heaven's sake, you two, sit down and let your sister eat!" Cassandra was trying not to laugh. "She had a very bad time on the road. She needs to eat and rest, not be bowled over by you two young ragamuffins!"

Still grinning, the two boys slipped into their places

on the opposite side of the table and bowed their heads for Cassandra's grace. They had grown taller and filled out since Rachel had last seen them, but Jacob's ebony hair still had the cowlick, and Josh's shy smile still showed the dimple in his cheek. Neither of them, she noticed, was wearing a red bandana.

Looking at them, loving them, Rachel ached to forget all the things she had seen and heard yesterday. There had to be some mistake, she told herself. They were so innocent, so open. Neither of them was capable of driving animals to their death, let alone beating the life out of a helpless old man.

"Can Slade eat with us, Ma?" Jacob asked, glancing toward the open doorway of the dining room.

Rachel glanced up from her second forkful of scrambled eggs to see a young man leaning against the open frame of the doorway. He was dressed in work clothes, but something in the posture of his lean, sinewy body suggested the indolence of a basking reptile. His eyes were narrow, glittering slits, his mouth too large, too sensual for his narrow face. He looked to be a year or two older than the twins, perhaps, but something about the way his gaze slid over her made the eggs turn cold and greasy in Rachel's mouth.

"Slade's been helping us irrigate," Josh put in. "He wants to take us grouse hunting after the chores are done. Is that all right, Pa?"

Morgan scowled up at the young man. "Is it all right with your uncle? I heard Lem say last week that he needed to fence off some pasture to keep the sheep out.''

''Uncle Lem's got plenty of help with the fence, sir,'' Slade replied in a tone that stopped just short of mockery. ''He said I could come over here 'long as I didn't get in the way.''

Rachel forced herself to chew her eggs and wash them down with a gulp of hot coffee. She'd surmised from the conversation that Slade must be the nephew of their neighbor, Lemuel Carmody. But it was the mention of sheep that caught her like a gut punch. She'd told herself she could forget what she'd seen yesterday. Now she knew that would be impossible.

''Sit down, Slade,'' Cassandra said with a weary sigh that betrayed her feelings toward the visitor. ''I'll ask Thomas to bring you in a plate.''

''Right kind of you, ma'am.'' He gave her a polite nod as he pulled out the chair next to Jacob, but his eyes remained on Rachel. The tip of his tongue glided along his lower lip in a way that made her flesh crawl.

Had Slade been one of the masked men she'd seen yesterday? Rachel had no way of knowing. But seeing his bold manner and the obvious influence he had over her brothers, she would have bet her life on it.

Had he been one of the old man's attackers as well? Again, she had no proof, no answers. She could not say whether it was cruelty that gleamed in those slitted young eyes or just bravado. It was not her right to judge him, or anyone, without proof. She could only curse the fate that had dumped her into the middle of this mess when all she wanted was to enjoy being with her family.

Morgan paused in the act of buttering a biscuit. "Rachel, you said you'd tell us what happened with the buggy yesterday. We're all waiting to hear your story."

Rachel felt everyone's eyes on her. This was the moment she'd been dreading, when she would have to lie to the people she loved. She had always detested lies and liars. But bringing Luke into the story would only add fuel to a fire that was already burning out of control.

"Your mother said you wrecked the buggy on your way home from Sheridan," Morgan prompted. "Something about running into a herd of sheep."

"Sheep?" Slade stiffened, leaning forward in his chair. "You ran into sheep on the road?"

"Right at the bottom of the hill," Rachel said. "They seemed to be everywhere, and I couldn't stop the mule. The next thing I knew I was in the wash, with rain falling and a flood coming, and the mule hotfooting it back to Sheridan. It was all I could do to rescue what I could and get out of the wash in time." She was already lying. If Luke had not been there to help her, she and all her things would have been swept away.

"And you walked home? On the road?" Slade's tone had become so demanding that Cassandra shot him a startled glance. But Rachel willed herself to maintain an icy calm. Slade had just given her a piece of the puzzle she was so desperate to solve.

You were there, Slade, she thought, studying him, *and you had one of my brothers with you. Now you're wondering why you didn't see me on the road. You're wondering where I was and how much I know.*

Deliberately Rachel lowered her gaze to her plate for a moment. Glancing up again, she caught him staring at her with a perplexed expression on his face.

Rachel returned his gaze, letting her silence speak her thoughts. *I don't know everything, but I can promise you this. If you've put either of my brothers in harm's way, I'll see you pay for it, you little weasel. I'll see you pay the full price!*

Chapter Nine

After breakfast Rachel took a steaming soak in the family's big copper tub. Then she eased her tortured body into bed for what she hoped would be a deep, healing sleep.

But sleep would not come. Restless and too warm, she lay between the flannel sheets, gazing at a beam of sunlight that crept between the closed curtains. Outside she could hear the familiar sounds of the ranch—the breathy nickering of horses, the crow of a rooster, the echoing clang of a hammer from the forge, and the staccato tirade of Chang, the patriarch of his growing clan, scolding an errant grandchild in the yard below. She had come home where she belonged, to the place where she wanted to bring her husband and raise her children someday—the place where she wanted to pass the years and seasons of her life.

If only she could hold it safe and protect it from the tragedy that loomed like a thundercloud. That would be her mission now. And if she failed, home would never be the same again.

Rachel stretched out on her back, staring at the ceiling as she recalled the conversation at breakfast. She had managed to give a credible account of her escape from the flood and her long trek home without mentioning Luke. Jacob and Josh had not questioned her story, but the flicker of cunning in Slade's eye had told her he was less trusting than her gently reared brothers. She would have to watch her step with him until she learned more.

But what did she expect to learn? That her sweet young brothers had been led astray? That they had become vandals and raiders, and maybe even killers? Could she face the truth if it had the power to destroy her family?

Abandoning all pretense of sleep, Rachel swung her legs over the edge of the bed and brushed back her damp hair. Ten minutes later, dressed in a faded plaid shirt and well-worn denims, she was padding barefoot down the stairs to the open parlor, where her mother sat with a basket of mending on the rug beside her rocker.

Cassandra glanced up from her work. "I was hoping you'd be able to get some sleep, dear."

"I'm too tired to sleep. And too excited about being home." Rachel sank onto the ottoman, where she had so often sat for conversations with her mother. "But I'm not too tired to listen. I want you to catch me up on what's happened to everything and everyone on the ranch!"

Cassandra's cornflower eyes crinkled at the corners. "It's not as if you'd been out of touch, Rachel. Every time I knew someone was going to town, I wrote you a letter and sent it along."

"I know," Rachel said. "I must have read every one of your letters at least six times. But it's not the same as talking."

"Precisely what I was thinking." Cassandra reached out and squeezed her daughter's hands. "To tell you the truth, I've been counting the minutes until we could have some time alone. Where would you like me to start?"

"How are Chang and Mei Li?" Rachel took a roundabout approach to what she really wanted to know.

"Getting older," Cassandra answered with a sigh. "Mei Li looks as if a strong breath could blow her away, but her will is like iron. She tells me she's vowed to see her first great-grandchild born before her spirit departs."

"Will that be anytime soon?" Rachel asked, concerned. She could not imagine the ranch without the presence of Chang's venerable, doll-like wife, who tottered about on tiny bound feet. "Are any of her grandchildren married?"

"They're a bit young for that. But she's already fretting about finding wives and husbands for them. They can hardly marry their own cousins—double cousins at that, since Thomas and Johnny married sisters. So Mei Li has been writing letters to a marriage broker in San Francisco, very expensive, she says, but very well connected.''

Rachel could not help smiling. ''Matchmaking for nine grandchildren should keep Mei Li busy for a long time to come. But this is America, not China. What if her grandchildren don't want their marriages arranged? What if they want to leave the ranch and strike out on their own?''

Cassandra's needle darted in and out as she stitched down a loose button. ''Mei Li understands that some of them are bound to go their own way. The girls, of course, will go with their husbands. And Thomas's son George wants to become an engineer. He's extremely bright, and your father has promised to help pay for his education. But Mei Li is hoping that at least some of them will stay here to raise their families. She loves having babies to hold.''

''And what about Jacob and Josh?'' Rachel asked, plunging into the quagmire. ''They were boys when I left. Now when I look at them, I see two young men.''

''Yes. Yes, they are men in some ways.'' The subtle tightening of her mother's jaw told Rachel she had touched a tender spot. ''In other ways, they're just boys, like two overgrown pups, running in circles and chasing their tails. It's as if they're unable to look beyond the next picnic or fishing trip to what the future holds. Nothing matters but the pleasure of the moment. I can't help thinking it's my fault. I loved them so much. I fear that I spoiled them when they were little.''

"Loving isn't spoiling." Rachel patted her mother's arm, aware of the shift in their relationship. She had left home as Cassandra's child. Now she had returned as a confidante as well as a daughter. The change was both a joy and a burden. "They're still young," she said, hiding what she knew. "Give them time. They'll grow up soon enough."

Cassandra had stopped sewing. She sat with her back rigid, her small, work-toughened hands clasped tightly on her knees. "It's more than that," she said. "I'm worried."

"Slade?" It was scarcely a question, and her mother's silence confirmed the answer. "How long has he been coming around?" Rachel asked.

Cassandra took up her sewing again. The needle worked furiously, jabbing in and out as she spoke. "He's the son of Lem's sister, and he came from Missouri to stay with the Carmodys about two months ago. Lem's never said so, but I get the impression Slade was in some kind of trouble there, and Lem offered to put him to work and give him a new start."

Rachel knew the Carmodys well. Lemuel Carmody, an affable, middle-aged widower, had been their neighbor on the east for as long as Rachel could remember. His son Bart had been one of Rachel's childhood playmates. "And how's Slade working out?" she asked. "Has Lem mentioned anything to you?"

"He doesn't have to. Slade spends more time over here than he does at Lem's place. Your brothers seem very much...taken with him." Her fingers quivered as she paused to tug at a tangled thread. "I've begun to notice changes in the boys since they started hanging around with him. They're becoming cocky, questioning almost everything we tell them. And the three of them disappear for hours on end—hunting, they say, or fishing. But it's not like the old days, when they used to come home laughing and happy, telling stories about their adventures. Now they come back silent, looking at each other as if they have secrets they don't want to tell us. Oh, Rachel—'' She shook her head. "I'm sorry. I wanted this to be a happy time for you, and here I am, pouring out my worries like a fussy old hen—''

Rachel's throat tightened as she squeezed her mother's arm. Her parents had always appeared so strong, so invulnerable in her eyes. Only now did she realize it was the way she'd chosen to see them. As a child, she had created an illusion of absolute safety for herself. But the time for illusions was over. Now it was her turn to be strong.

"Can you keep Slade from coming over here?" she asked. "Maybe if you talked with Lem—''

Cassandra shook her head. "Lem seems to think it's a good idea for his nephew to spend time with our boys. And there's no solid reason we can find to keep Slade away. We've never caught him doing anything wrong, and he's never contrary or impolite to us. He's just…'' The words ended in an explosive sigh of frustration.

"I know," Rachel said. "It's as if he walks the edge of any line you draw, touching it but not quite stepping over."

"Lem's a good neighbor. We've seen each other through some hard times. I hate to get crosswise with him over this fool boy. I just keep praying this time will pass, and Slade will go his own way before too much damage is done."

"Jacob and Josh will be fine," Rachel said, willing herself to believe her own words. "You and Dad have taught them right from wrong. Sooner or later, they'll see Slade for what he is." She took a quick breath, like a diver about to plunge off a high ledge. "Speaking of neighbors, I've never seen sheep this close to the ranch boundaries before. Who owns them?"

Cassandra thrust her wooden darning egg into the toe of a gray woolen sock. "Oh, another thorn in our side—an irritating man named Luke Vincente. He moved onto that section below the bluffs while you were away. Evidently, he's owned the land for years and refuses to sell it, even though both Lem and your father have made him fair offers."

"What's he like?" Rachel felt her pulse skip. She hated deceiving her mother, but she needed to understand how things stood between Luke and her parents.

"I've never met him—not many people in these parts have. He keeps to himself and doesn't seem to have a woman or any children about the place. Not exactly a neighborly sort—but maybe that's just as well. Lem had a detective friend do some checking on him. It seems Mr. Vincente spent time in prison for killing a man."

Rachel felt her heart lurch. Luke had hinted at a

dark past. But it stunned her to realize that she had melted in the arms of a killer and an ex-convict.

"What does Dad think about having a sheep man for a neighbor?" she forced herself to ask.

Cassandra worked a thin strand of wool through the eye of her darning needle. "You know your father. He's a fair man. I've heard him say that as long as Mr. Vincente keeps his sheep off Tolliver land, we've got no quarrel with him. But other people aren't as tolerant. Lem, for one, thinks the cattle ranchers should band together and run him out of the county."

She anchored the thread and began weaving a neat mat of stitches over the hole in the toe of the sock. When she glanced up at Rachel again, her delicate, almost childlike features were arranged in a smile.

"Enough of this worrisome talk on your first day back! I have some happier news. Bart came by the house with his father last week. He asked about you and wanted to know when you'd be home." Her eyes twinkled impishly. "You used to have quite a crush on him, as I recall."

"When I was thirteen!" Rachel forced herself to laugh. Bart Carmody, Lem's son, was two years her senior. They'd been friends as children, but thirteen and fifteen were a world apart. As young men do, he had left her behind.

"Bart had his eye on Lula Mae Evans," Rachel said. "She had blond hair and a bosom, and I didn't stand a chance. I always expected they'd get married one day."

"Lula Mae married Eddie Parker and moved to Nevada two years ago." Cassandra inspected her mending job, then snipped the thread with her little silver scissors. "And you're not thirteen anymore. You're prettier than Lula Mae ever was, and smarter to boot. I wouldn't blame Bart for being interested."

Rachel bit back a murmur of dismay. She was well aware that, at twenty-two, she was approaching the age of spinsterhood, and her mother was anxious to see her wed. She was also aware that Bart Carmody was considered the best catch in three counties. But right now she felt too drained to deal with the prospect of a new suitor, even one as handsome and eligible as Bart. Heavenly days, she had only just arrived home!

And she had come here directly from the arms of Luke Vincente.

"Why don't we go and visit Mei Li?" Rachel scrambled to her feet, seizing on the opportunity to change the subject. "Please—I would so love to see her! Can we go now?"

"Of course." Cassandra looked startled. "But you don't have any shoes on, Rachel. You can't expect to walk all the way to Mei Li's house on those poor feet."

"I'll be fine in my old slippers." Rachel started for the landing. "Wait for me, I won't be a minute!"

She forced herself to hurry as she mounted the stairs, willing the pain that shot from her tender feet to blur the memory of Luke's soul-blistering kiss. But the distraction did not work. The sensual heat of his touch lingered on her skin, burning deep, all the way to the warm, pulsing core of her body.

He had known exactly what he was doing, she lectured herself as she rummaged under the bed for her slippers. He had used her expertly, almost coldly. Even now he could be using her, knowing how the memory of that kiss would haunt her, making her ache with a desire that threatened to tear her loyalties away from her own family.

She would never go near him again, Rachel vowed. Luke Vincente was no better than a criminal. No, he *was* a criminal, she reminded herself. He had spent time in prison for killing a man.

How had it happened? she wondered as she worked her slippers onto her swollen feet. It couldn't have been cold-blooded murder, or Luke would have ended his life at the end of a rope. Manslaughter, perhaps? Never mind, whatever the circumstance, he had been judged guilty. That made him a criminal. And the hell of prison life had a way of twisting a man's nature, so that he was never again fit for decent society.

All the more reason to stay away from him, she thought. All the more reason to put Luke out of her mind and her heart.

Rachel bit back the pain as she eased her weight onto her feet and walked across the braided rug to the doorway. It would be all right, she told herself. She was home now, with the people she loved. Soon the pulse of her days would adjust to the familiar rhythm of life on the ranch. She would be busy and happy. There would be no need for her to remember the feel of Luke's arms around her or the way his kiss had spilled molten fire through her veins.

As for her brothers and what she had discovered, there could be only one answer. Family was family. Whatever they might have done, she would protect them. To keep them safe, she would lie, cheat, steal, fight, whatever was needed. And she would start by placing Luke Vincente squarely where he belonged— in the camp of the enemy.

Luke stood over the fresh mound of earth that covered the coffin of his friend. The two boys had gone their separate ways to finish the chores, Sebastian taking refuge in his god, and Ignacio taking refuge in his anger. But two of the four dogs remained to mourn their master, their sharp muzzles resting on their paws, their intelligent eyes deep, golden wells of sadness.

The service had been an awkward affair, with Luke struggling to speak words of consolation in Spanish that was barely adequate for working with sheep. Sebastian had fingered his rosary beads and muttered a prayer in what Luke guessed to be Latin. Ignacio had wept, cursing under his breath and glaring at the ground. When the words were finished, the three of them had shoveled the dirt into the grave and marked it with the simple cross that Sebastian had carved while his father lay dying.

All in all, it had been a miserable excuse for a funeral—a pathetic farewell to the gentlest and wisest man Luke had ever known.

Now he had a promise to keep.

Turning away from the grave, Luke stood for a moment gazing south along the mountains, in the direction Rachel had gone. It had only taken him a few minutes, at first light, to follow the prints of her narrow little boots across the muddy yard to where they disappeared amid the clumps of sage and rabbit brush. There had been no time to trail her farther, and no need. His little captive bird had fled home, and he would bet money she knew the way, even in the dark.

All the same, if it had not been for the burial, he would have gone after her. Rachel's water-damaged kidskin boots had been on the verge of falling apart, exposing her tender feet to rocks, stickers and worse. He could have offered her a ride, saving her a long, painful walk and giving them a chance to talk before he let her off a safe distance from the Tolliver ranch house.

But never mind, Luke thought irritably. It had been her choice to leave in the night. If the high and mighty Miss Tolliver had paid for her impulsiveness with cut, blistered feet, that was her problem.

But why had she gone? That was the question that pricked him like a burr. He had promised her the loan of a horse if she waited until morning. Had it been that explosive, startling kiss? Had she feared he would storm the locked bedroom and demand to take up where they'd left off?

Luke rejected that possibility out of hand. Rachel was no innocent. She had known exactly what she was doing when her honeyed lips had blocked his questions. She had kissed him with the sureness of an accomplished flirt. And he had returned the kiss with the intent of showing the little minx that he knew her game, and that this time she'd taken on more than even she could handle.

He had felt her stiffen with surprise. Then…Lord, what had happened? It was as if everything had spun out of control, and all he could think about was how much he wanted her. Her response had triggered a surge of molten heat that had flooded his loins, building to a pressure so exquisite that he'd feared he might burst if he held her too closely.

Had he pulled away or had she? Luke couldn't remember. But the sting of her slap still burned on his cheek. Even the slap, he recalled, had sent a jolt of wildfire streaking through his veins.

He would be crazy to go near her again, or even to remember how she'd melted like hot honey in his arms, Luke berated himself. If he was so all-fired woman-hungry, there was a house in Sheridan where he could put down his money, slake his lust and leave without regret. But he knew it wouldn't do him any good. Such experiences, the few he'd tried, only left him with a bitter, hollow ache in his gut.

And his business with Rachel Tolliver had nothing to do with finding a way between those lovely legs of hers. Rachel was his only key to finding Miguel's murderers. Last night he had pressed her for answers, and she had responded with evasive tactics that only a desperate woman would try. The more he thought about it, the more certain he became that she was protecting someone close to her. Someone she would rather die for than betray.

So how to get at the truth? Thrusting his hands into his pockets, Luke scowled at the cloudy horizon. Right now, short of kidnapping Rachel and holding her hostage, his only recourse was to wait. Sooner or later the raiders would make another move against his sheep, against his herders, against him. If he could stay a step ahead of them, he might at least be able to protect the sheep and Miguel's precious sons while he ferreted out the bastards who had beaten the old man.

But he couldn't be everywhere at once, Luke realized. He had to have some idea of what to expect, and that was where Rachel came in. If he could persuade her that there was no disloyalty in keeping her loved ones out of trouble—

But what was he thinking? Rachel would not even see him again, let alone listen to reason. She was as much his enemy as the four cowboys that had nearly run his herd over the cliff.

What he had sworn to do, he would do alone, Luke vowed. He would trust no one, depend on no one. And anyone who got in his way, including Rachel Tolliver, had damned well better be ready to pay the consequences.

Pressing his mouth into a thin, hard line, he turned away from the grave and walked back toward the sheds. He had a thousand sheep to shear, and one fire-haired devil of a woman to forget.

* * *

On the morning of her third day home, Rachel was able to work her feet into her beloved old boots. Walking downstairs in them sent tingles of pain up her legs, but never mind that. She would be able to ride with her brothers now, the three of them flying across the open range, laughing as they raced coyotes, jackrabbits and each other. It would be just like old times.

But nothing could be like old times—that reality slammed home as Rachel walked into the dining room and saw Slade lounging at the table with her brothers.

There was no one else at breakfast. Rachel remembered now that her parents had planned to leave early for Sheridan, Morgan to settle with the livery stable for the mule and wagon, Cassandra to pick up some needed supplies and enjoy the time with her husband. Even after more than two decades together, the two of them seemed to share a private world that no one, not even their children, could invade. Rachel had often wondered what it would be like to know such a deep, intimate connection to another person. She could not imagine how it would feel, let alone that it would ever happen to her.

"I told Bart you were home, Miz Rachel," Slade drawled in his lazy voice. "He perked up right smart at that news. Him and Uncle Lem plan to come by for a visit this afternoon."

The announcement caught Rachel off guard. "But my parents won't be here!" she protested. "They'll be making the trip for nothing."

Slade grinned. "Bart won't. It's you he wants to

see, not your folks. And Uncle Lem's just coming along so things will look proper.''

Masking her surprise, Rachel pulled out a chair, sat down at the foot of the table and made a show of spearing two hot flapjacks from a platter. From what Slade had just said, it almost sounded as if Bart Carmody meant to court her!

Three years ago, she would have given her soul to have Bart pay attention to her. His lack of interest, in fact, had tilted the balance in favor of her going away to school. Now, however, her first reaction to Slade's news was, *Why today?* Why did Bart have to show up when everything was such a confused mess? At a quieter time she would have welcomed him. She would have been flattered by his wanting her company, happy to renew their friendship and intrigued by what the future might hold. But *now?*

''Rachel, don't you think you have enough syrup?'' Josh's amused voice startled her out of her musings, and Rachel realized she had picked up the glass pitcher and poured nearly a pint of maple syrup onto her flapjacks. Her plate was a messy brown pool, with sticky little rivulets trickling over the edge and onto the white tablecloth.

Slade guffawed. ''I'd say your mind was someplace else, Miz Rachel. Like on my cousin, maybe.''

Rachel shot him a glare. ''Actually my mind was on going for a ride with my brothers this morning, and then maybe having a picnic lunch by the reservoir.'' She glanced at the twins. ''Are you up for that? I can ask Thomas to pack the basket.''

Jacob and Josh glanced uneasily at each other, then at Slade. Clearly they had made other plans, plans that did not include her. Maybe it was time she found out what those plans were.

"It's such a beautiful day," she persisted. "And I so wanted my first ride to be with the two of you, just like old times. Slade is welcome, of course, if he wants to come along with us."

Rachel forced a smile as she lied through her teeth. Slade's presence had already soured her morning. But she needed to know more about the young man and understand his influence over her brothers. How else could she fight against him?

Jacob cleared his throat. "Dad wants us to clear the lower fence and mend the broken places. Even with Slade helping, that will take us most of the morning. After that, Slade told his Uncle Lem that we'd ride out along the north range and check bait."

"Check bait." Rachel's distaste showed in her voice. She never had liked the idea of killing off coyotes by scattering strychnine-laced rabbit carcasses over their range. The coyotes who took the bait died in horrible agony, and the rabbits were also eaten by eagles, hawks, ravens and foxes, which suffered the same fate. Morgan Tolliver, no lover of coyotes himself, hated the practice and always used a rifle to kill predators that threatened his calves. Other ranchers, however, did not share the same view, and setting out poisoned bait was common, especially since the Cattlemen's Association had put a generous bounty on coyote tails. Many a young rancher's son had earned pocket money by revisiting a baited area, collecting the tails of dead animals and taking them to town for the reward.

"Checkin' bait's no sport for a lady, Miz Rachel," Slade drawled. "I daresay you wouldn't enjoy it much."

Ignoring him, Rachel glared at her brothers. "Dad won't be happy about your going," she said sternly.

"He won't know about it," Jacob said. "Not unless you tattle on us."

"Please, Rachel." Josh fixed her with what she'd always thought of as his puppy-dog expression. "It's Mom's birthday next week. We want to get her something nice."

"We saw a necklace and some earrings in town," Jacob chimed in. "They're real silver, with shiny blue stones, the same color as Mom's eyes. But the necklace and earrings together cost fifty-two dollars, and we don't have anywhere near enough money."

"Fifty-two dollars!" The story sounded fishy to Rachel, but she decided to play along. "At fifty cents each, that's more coyote tails than you'll find in a month!"

"Not if we get lucky," Jacob said.

"Get lucky? What are you talking about?" Rachel's eyes narrowed as she saw Josh give his brother a cautionary nudge. But it was Slade who answered her question.

"It's Uncle Lem who's offering to pay the bounty," he said with a lopsided grin. "Fifty cents for a coyote. Fifty dollars for one of those black-and-white sheepdogs."

Chapter Ten

Rachel strained forward in the saddle, her hands clutching the reins as the galloping bay leaped a wash and thundered through the scrub. The hot spring wind raked her hair, reddened her eyes and sucked the moisture from her skin. Her body, unaccustomed to the punishment of long rides, screamed for rest and shade. But a sense of urgency drove her on.

She should have been running *away* from Luke Vincente, not toward him, Rachel thought. He was the enemy, hated by her family and neighbors. Their last encounter had left her shamed and seething. Every shred of common sense she possessed told her to keep her distance from the man. But the thought of those graceful, intelligent dogs falling prey to a hideous death was more than she could stand. She had to warn Luke before something terrible happened.

What had possessed her brothers to become involved in such a scheme? Jacob and Josh had always loved animals. But they were young and impressionable, easy game for the older, more experienced Slade.

Rachel remembered an incident from her childhood—a gang of dogs that had run wild at night, attacking young calves, pulling them down wolf pack fashion and slashing them to death, not to feed on them but for the mere pleasure of killing. When the marauders were finally rounded up and shot, they were found to be ranch dogs and pets, friendly and docile at home but reverting to savagery when roused by their pack mates. It made sense that what was true of animals could also be true of people.

But she could not let herself believe that. Jacob and Josh were good boys. They'd been raised by good parents and taught right from wrong. It was the circumstances that had thrown everything into confusion—the idea that cruel acts were justified as long as they were committed against an enemy. It was the same idea that had triggered massacres, purges and pogroms from the beginning of history.

Slade was no fool. Neither was Lem Carmody. They had used that same logic to manipulate her innocent young brothers into joining their war.

The war against Luke Vincente.

Rachel's spirits quailed as she crested the last hill and saw the sprawl of buildings and sheep pens that marked Luke's ranch. Would he welcome her as a friend? Would he make angry demands, or would she be met with a wall of cold silence?

She hesitated on the hilltop, resting the horse and fighting her own fears. Luke's feelings toward her didn't matter, she told herself, urging the horse forward. She had come to warn him about the danger to his dogs, nothing more. She would deliver her message and go. After that, if she was smart, she would never set eyes on him again.

As Rachel neared the ranch, she could make out the gray-white clusters of sheep milling in the pens. She remembered now that Luke had brought in the herds for shearing. She could only hope the dogs would be there, too, safe from harm.

Even as the thought crossed her mind, she saw two of the dogs on the porch. A third, the big, shaggy mongrel, came racing around the house to bark at her as she rode into the yard. Alerted by the noise, Luke emerged from the shearing shed.

Rachel's heart contracted as she saw him. He was stripped to the waist, his sinewy bronze body gleaming with sweat. His eyes glared at her from behind a tangle of black hair that had tumbled over his forehead. His hands gripped a rifle, one finger resting on the trigger.

He lowered the gun as he recognized Rachel. But the wariness did not leave his coffee-colored eyes.

"Hello, Luke," she said, forcing herself to meet his stormy gaze. "You don't look very glad to see me."

"What are you doing here, Rachel?" His voice was flat and cold.

"I—" She cleared her dry throat. "I came to help you."

He muttered something under his breath. "Last

time you were here, I asked for your help. You answered me by running off in the night. Why should I believe things are any different now?''

His manner roused a spark of irritation in her. "All right," she snapped. "I didn't come to help you. I only came to warn you. I'll speak my piece and go."

He watched her in distrustful silence, waiting.

"Lem Carmody has put out a bounty on your dogs," she said. "He's setting out coyote bait where you run your sheep, and he's offering a fifty-dollar reward to anybody who brings in a dead sheepdog."

Luke's expression did not change. His eyes drilled into her, probing for the truth. It took all her strength of will to keep from turning the horse and riding away.

"Is that all you came for?" His question dripped innuendo.

Her cheeks blazed as the implication sank home. She felt the heat, the sudden tightening in her loins as his darkly insolent gaze swept over her. The awareness that he could arouse her like this, with the merest look, only heightened her fury.

"If you think I'd so much as come near you, you conceited, presumptuous, arrogant—" she sputtered, then broke off as she saw the smile tugging at the corners of his mouth. The insufferable man was toying with her. She had played right into his hands, and now he was laughing.

Rachel glared down at him, relief diluting her outrage. Some of Luke's anger, at least, had been for show. But that didn't mean she should stay and accept his insulting behavior. Mustering her dignity, she straightened in the saddle. "I've spoken my piece, and now I'll be going," she said. "The only reason I came here was to make sure your dogs were safe. You can take my warning for whatever you think it's worth."

Without waiting for his reply, she swung the horse around and nudged it to a trot.

"Rachel."

She had almost reached the gate when his voice stopped her. She reined in the horse and twisted in the saddle, looking back at him over her shoulder.

He was standing where she had left him, arms folded, sunlight glinting on his bare torso. "Thank you," he said. "I'm sorry if I was touchy. It's been a rough three days, and your leaving didn't make things any easier."

Rachel hesitated, torn by her own pride. If Luke was waiting for her to apologize in return, he could wait till doomsday. She owed him nothing. "I only came about the dogs," she said. "The rest is over and done with."

"Then you may have come for nothing." His voice and gaze held her captive. "I didn't know about the bounty, but I'm not surprised. The ranchers know we need the dogs to run sheep. But poisoned bait's always been a danger, so the dogs are trained not to touch carrion on the range. Traps and guns are even more of a worry because there's no protection against them. All we can do is try to keep the dogs in sight."

Rachel glanced toward the house, where two of the

sheepdogs lay on the porch, their pink tongues lolling in the heat. The third dog, the one that had barked at her, crouched a few paces from Luke's side, still eyeing her warily.

"Don't you have four dogs?" she asked.

"We do." He gave a low whistle, and waited with Rachel for the missing animal to come bounding around the corner of the house. When nothing happened, he whistled again. The other three dogs lifted their heads and pricked up their ears, but there was no sign of the fourth.

"Shep always stays close by, and he always comes to that whistle." Luke's expression had darkened. Hesitating only for an instant, he turned and strode toward the barn where the horses were kept.

"I'll help you look for him," Rachel said. "Two sets of eyes will be better than one."

When he did not reply, she chose to take his silence as consent. By the time he emerged, minutes later, mounted on the rangy buckskin, she had watered her horse and was waiting for him at the gate.

The surly dog that had barked at Rachel came at Luke's whistle and fell into step alongside his horse. At a terse command from Luke, it raced ahead, its sharp nose searching the ground.

"Do we just follow him?" Rachel asked.

"Dan's the best tracker of the four. If he can't find Shep—" Luke's words ended in a shrug. He was a man of few words, but Rachel felt his deep attachment to all of the dogs. They had been truer to him, she sensed, than most of the humans in his life.

As they rode, she found herself casting sidelong glances at his craggy profile. She had spent hours alone with this very private man, had known his arms and felt the raw hunger in his kiss. Yet he remained very much a stranger to her.

She burned to pry into his past, to ask him about his time in prison and the story behind the desperate act that had put him there. But then, she wasn't supposed to know about his conviction for killing a man. She had heard that story from her mother, who had heard it from Lem Carmody. To bring it up now would only put Luke on the defensive and heighten his distrust.

"Are you ready to tell me why you left?" His abrupt question jolted her, throwing her off balance.

"I think you know why," Rachel shot back the first retort that came into her head.

"All I can come up with is a couple of good guesses," he said, keeping his eye on the dog. "Either you didn't trust yourself to spend the night in the house alone with me, or you didn't want to answer any more questions."

"Maybe you were the one I didn't trust." Rachel was not fooling him, and she knew it. "I shouldn't have come here, Luke," she said. "There's a war on. You and I are on different sides, and whatever you might think, I don't owe you a thing. You have no right to demand anything from me, not even an explanation."

His hand flashed out and seized her wrist in a grip that was like an iron manacle. "A good man has died because of your so-called war. He died because he was working for me, and I owe it to his sons to find the murderers who beat him to death. If you know something, Rachel, if there's someone you're protecting—''

''No!'' She jerked so abruptly that her horse shied, but Luke did not let her go. ''I'll tell you the truth,'' she said. ''Out there on the range, when those cowboys chased your sheep, I thought I recognized someone. Who it was doesn't matter, because there's no evidence to connect any of them to your friend's murder. There are plenty of people who want you and your sheep gone, Luke. That doesn't make them killers.''

He stopped the horses, letting the dog go its way for the moment. ''How much do you know, Rachel? Damn it, you're my only lead, my only hope—''

''Then you have no hope at all,'' Rachel said. ''I don't know anything about what happened the night Miguel was beaten. I don't *want* to know.''

''But if you hear something, see something—for the sake of decency, Rachel—'' His fingers tightened around her wrist.

''No!'' She twisted away, but he maintained his firm grip. ''Don't you see? I can't help you. I can't take your side in this, Luke. When I leave here today, I don't intend to ever see you again. It has to be that way, or—''

The dog's frantic barking exploded from the direction of a sandy, scrub-filled wash that broke their path fifty yards ahead. Releasing her wrist, Luke spurred his horse in the direction of the sound. Rachel followed, even though her common sense told her that now would be the time to wheel her mount and ride for home. With trouble on his hands, Luke would not follow her. She could get away clean, and she would never have to face him again.

But she was already riding fast behind him. Dry juniper limbs lashed her face as the horse plunged down the side of the wash. Ahead of her, Luke had jerked his mount to a halt and flung himself out of the saddle. She could hear his curses mingled with the dog's plaintive, whining barks.

Tossing the bay's reins over a cedar limb, she leaped to the ground. Through the brush she could see the black outline of the dog, digging furiously at a fan of fresh earth at the side of the wash. Luke had dropped to his knees and was digging, too, clawing at the dirt with his bare hands.

"What happened?" Rachel flung herself down beside him.

"Some kind of cave-in," he muttered. "Don't know what caused it, but Shep's under here somewhere. I saw his tracks leading up to this spot."

"Do you think he's alive?"

Luke's only answer was a grim tightening of his mouth.

Rachel seized a flat slab of rock and used it to scrape at the loose earth. The big black-and-tan dog, no longer growling at her, sent up showers of dirt and rocks as they worked side by side. Bits of earth coated Rachel's hair, face and clothes. She was barely aware of them as she dug frantically to reach whatever lay beneath the caved-in bank.

Beside her, Luke labored in grim silence. She knew he was steeling himself for what he might find beneath the rubble, and she ached for him. The dogs were invaluable to the work of herding, and despite his gruff manner toward the diminutive black-and-white collies, Rachel could sense Luke's deep attachment to them. Finding one of them dead would be one more blow to a man whose soul was already bruised and bleeding.

What were the odds they would find the dog alive? Perilously slim, Rachel realized. They had been digging for a good ten minutes, but were barely halfway through the debris. And, aside from the fact that the loose earth was still damp, there was no way of knowing how many minutes the dog had been trapped before their arrival. Rachel scooped faster, harder. Perspiration trickled between her breasts as she battled the nameless dread that had settled over her spirit. Finding the collie's body, she knew, would break Luke's heart.

A yip from the big black dog shattered her musings. He was digging with renewed energy, his ears pricked forward, his dark muzzle coated with dirt. Little whining noises rose from his throat as he zeroed in on one spot and pawed like a demon.

"He can hear something—oh, Luke!" Rachel abandoned her scraping and plunged in beside the dog. Heedless of broken nails and raw fingers, she clawed at the earth, widening, deepening the hole.

"Careful." Luke caught her arm and jerked her back against him. "He could be trapped in what's left of the hole. We don't want to cave it in on him. Let Dan find him."

Quivering with fatigue, Rachel sank back onto her heels. Luke's hand gripped her arm, the warm pressure sending ripples of sensation through her body. But Luke seemed unaware that he was still touching her. All his attention was fixed on the dog as he held his breath, straining to listen.

"Can you hear anything?" she whispered.

He exhaled sharply. "All I can do is hope Dan knows what he's hearing."

"How do these things happen?"

"Washes like this one are riddled with dens. Fool dog chasing a fox or a badger, follows it into a hole and pushes a little too hard. I've seen hunting dogs lost that way. But sheepdogs?" He shook his head. "I've never known Shep to go chasing off like this. There had to be a reason—"

A rumble of earth interrupted him.

"The rest of the hole's caving in!" Rachel stared in horror, then flung herself forward and began to dig into the collapsing bank. If Shep was still alive he would be buried now, unable to breathe. They had seconds to find him.

Beside her, Luke was using his arms and hands to scoop away the gravelly soil. His bare chest heaved with effort as he clawed the dirt away, heedless of his bleeding hands. Dan was barking, racing back and forth. As the seconds passed, he pawed at the slide and then began to whine in frustration, or perhaps in grief. Luke was cursing vehemently.

"No!" Rachel calculated the now-buried spot where Dan had been digging. Bracing herself, she thrust her hands, then her arms, straight down into the loose earth. Dust filled her nostrils. Rocks scraped her skin, drawing blood, but she continued to grope deeper and deeper until her chest was pressed flat against the slide.

At first she felt nothing. Then her scraped, bleeding fingers touched the coarseness of long hair and the warmth of flesh beneath. "Here!" she shouted. "Luke, he's here!"

Luke plunged in beside her, ripping into the earth with his hands. He had not asked her whether the dog was alive. Even if he had, Rachel could not have told him. She strained deeper, trying to maintain some contact with the buried collie, to calm it, perhaps, if it was conscious, though that seemed less and less likely as the seconds crawled by.

Dan hung back, whining anxiously as if baffled by the other dog's disappearance. Luke clawed and heaved, using the strength of his whole body against the slide. By now he had cleared away what looked like a small mountain, but the dog remained trapped.

"Can you feel anything?" His voice was a rasp, his eyes like burning coals in his dirt-streaked face. "A heartbeat? Any sign of breathing?"

"I don't...know..." Rachel strained deeper and discovered that the soil was less resistant. She worked her hands lower, sliding them around the narrow body. "I have him! Help me!"

They worked furiously, Luke digging, Rachel tugging on the inert dog. Inch by inch she worked him upward through the loose dirt and gravel. His body was warm but he was making no effort to struggle. Luke's anxious eyes met hers. She shook her head.

Another moment and the little collie was free. Limp and dirty, he lay across Rachel's knees, eyes closed, tongue lolling. Dan shouldered his way between Rachel and Luke, sniffed his companion and whined. Tears welled in Rachel's eyes, one drop forming a muddy rivulet down the side of her nose. "Oh, Luke, I'm sorry," she whispered. "I'm so sorry."

"Give him to me." Luke held out his scraped, bleeding hands and worked them beneath the small, inert body. Laying the collie on the slide he probed along the motionless ribs. Rachel pressed her lips together, remembering Shep's shining golden eyes, his joyful gait and sharp little yips as he ran the sheep. Dan pressed against her side, seeking and giving comfort. She stroked the massive head, her throat tightening.

Luke's exploring hand stiffened, freezing on one spot. "He's alive. Here—get over here and hold him steady. Keep his head level."

While Rachel braced Shep between her knees, Luke began a rhythmic massaging of the dog's chest, squeezing and pumping the air in and out. Rachel listened to the soft rush of air, unconsciously matching its rhythm with her own breathing. Sweat pooled in the hollow of Luke's throat as the seconds crawled past. When would he give up? Rachel began to wonder. When would he abandon all hope that his dog would live?

Dan pressed against her side. Odd little coaxing sounds quivered in his throat. Could dogs pray? Against all reason, Rachel found herself believing it was possible.

Luke's hands stilled. A low sob escaped Rachel's throat. Then she saw the subtle rise and fall of ribs beneath skin. The little collie was breathing on his own.

Rachel's heart seemed to stop. Her eyes flickered from the dog to Luke's grime-streaked face. The naked emotion on his face touched a place so deep inside her that, until now, she had not even known it was there. Unbidden, her hand reached out and clasped his wrist. His throbbing pulse quivered upward through her fingers to become part of her own body. Her breath came in tiny, broken gasps.

Shep's dust-coated eyelids twitched. "Come on," Luke whispered, stroking the dog with his free hand. "Come on, boy, wake up."

Rachel's fingers tightened around Luke's wrist as Shep's golden eyes fluttered open. His pointed black nose twitched and jerked. Miraculously, he sneezed.

"Oh—" Rachel's hand crept downward into Luke's palm. She felt his fingers close around hers as the dog began to thrash and struggle. With Dan whining and nudging, the little collie scrambled to his feet, shut his eyes and shook with all his might. Showers of dirt flew in all directions.

Rachel had to close her eyes, but she could hear Luke's laughter, so rich and full, and so surprising, that her throat went tight at the sound of it. In the days, months and years to come, when she could not be with him, she knew that she would yearn to hear that laughter again. She would remember the sound of his voice and the strength of his big, callused hands, and she would ache to feel the way she always felt when she was with him—vibrantly alive, her heart pounding, her blood racing, her emotions blazing like a prairie wildfire.

Was this the way her mother felt about Morgan?

The dirt had stopped spattering her face. Rachel opened her eyes to find Luke watching her from the shadowed depths of his eyes, his thoughts as much a mystery as ever. He had let go of her hand. Rachel could not even remember when it had happened. But she felt the loss of it, that warm, electric contact of his flesh with hers.

The two dogs were standing side by side, Dan looming protectively over his smaller friend. Shep's muzzle was still caked with dirt. He was panting, mouth open, tongue lolling.

Self-conscious now, Rachel scrambled to her feet. "Shep looks as if he could use a drink. I've got a canteen on the horse."

Unlooping the canteen strap from the saddle, she pulled the stopper and walked back to the dog. Kneeling beside her, Luke shaped his hands into a tight bowl. Rachel poured the cool water into his mud-stained palms. The collie lapped noisily, a peaceful sound that mingled with the songs of meadowlarks on the clear morning air.

"You, too, boy. You're the hero of the day." Luke held out his cupped hands toward Dan. Again Rachel tipped the canteen and filled Luke's palms. His hands cradled the water, fingers pressing tightly together.

Rachel's eyes traced the lines of his profile. His expression was warm, almost tender as he watched the dog drink. Luke Vincente had killed a man, she reminded herself. He had been convicted of the crime and served time in prison.

What had happened to set this gentle, quiet man against the world? How deep were the wounds he carried beneath his granite-tough exterior? Rachel yearned to know his secrets, no matter how terrible they might be. She wanted to understand every part of him. But she knew better than to ask questions. If she so much as hinted at what she knew about him, Luke would close himself off like a door slamming in her face.

The dog finished drinking and turned away. As water fell through Luke's open fingers, he glanced up and caught her eyes on him.

Rachel's gaze dropped to her scraped, muddy hands. Color flamed in her cheeks. She felt the dizzying heat, the giddiness, as the bottom seemed to drop out of her stomach. What was wrong with her? She'd become as awkward and tongue-tied as a thirteen-year-old girl. Reason whispered that she should mutter some hasty excuse, sprint to her horse and gallop hell-bent for home. But her body had lost its will to move.

Slowly Luke rose to his feet. His hands reached out and cupped her face, the palms wet and cool against her hot cheeks. "If you're going to run, you'd better do it now, Rachel," he murmured thickly. "Because once I start kissing you, I might not be able to stop."

She gazed up at him, knowing she should pull away. But the memory of their last kiss burned sweet and hot, igniting ripples of sensation that pooled like quicksilver in the shimmering depths of her body. She wanted that kiss again, wanted to feel the wildness, the forbidden yearnings that only one thing could fulfill. Lord help her, she wanted *him*.

She strained upward as his lips closed on hers. His unshaven face was gritty with dust, and his mouth tasted of earth and coffee. Heaven. She quivered with need as his arms jerked her close—aching for him, shameless, wanton.

In her past flirtations with boys, Rachel had always played the tease. She had always been the one to hold back, measuring what she gave and making sure she never gave too much. But Luke was no boy. The urges his raw masculinity aroused in her were too powerful to resist. She was dizzy with wanting him.

Her mouth opened to his kiss, her tongue invading, exploring the moist, sensitive inner surface. He moaned and molded her hard against him. She gasped as his thumb brushed her swollen nipple, sending spasms of pleasure through her body. "Yes..." she whispered, and he touched her again, so lightly and exquisitely that she thought it would drive her mad. It was all she could do to keep from begging for more. She wanted his hands on her, his mouth on her, everywhere.

He groaned, low in his throat, as his free hand moved down to cradle her buttocks. "You shouldn't be here, girl. You shouldn't be letting me touch you, a man like me. You don't know who I am, where I've been...."

She stopped his words with another kiss. Words would only confuse things, and this was no time for confusion. Right now, to Rachel, the only thing that mattered was the way she felt in his arms.

Pulse racing, she caught his hand and laid it on her breast. Her heart drummed beneath his rough palm. The earth seemed to slip away from beneath her feet as he cupped her, stroking her through the thin fabric of her shirt. Her hands kneaded his shoulders, gripping and releasing in mute ecstasy.

"Tell me when you want me to stop," he whispered roughly. "I promise you, Rachel, I won't—"

He froze against her, distracted by an urgent yip from one of the dogs. Glancing down, Rachel saw that Dan and Shep were pawing furiously at an area near the deepest part of the cave-in, where Shep himself had been found.

Before Luke could let her go, she pulled away from him. Something was down there, she sensed. Something she didn't want to see.

Taking a step backward, she waited, her heart

pounding inexplicably. The morning sunlight was like bright golden butter. Lark songs, as pure as crystal, echoed across the prairie. But the darkness that had fallen over Rachel would not go away.

"What is it, you two ruffians?" Luke dropped to his knees beside the dogs. "What's under that dirt? A woodchuck, maybe, or even a badger?"

The dogs paid him scant attention. Both of them were intent on digging. Their muddy paws flew, scattering dirt in all directions.

Rachel, watching from behind, saw Luke go rigid for an instant. Then he began to dig, his hands rummaging in the earth to grasp something he had glimpsed below the surface.

When he looked back toward her, Rachel saw that the familiar wall of distrust had returned to his eyes. He knelt in the dust of the cave-in, his right hand clutching the frayed end of a rope.

Chapter Eleven

Luke's sinewy brown fingers gripped the rope, drawing it out inch by inch through the crumbling earth. For the first few seconds it came easily. Then it tightened as the pull met resistance from whatever was tied to the other end.

A chill went through Rachel as Luke began to dig in earnest. She watched him, sensing what he would find and fearing what it would mean. A moment ago she had been in his arms. Now she stood forgotten as he tunneled deeper, following the rope's taut path. His expression darkened, and she saw that he had come to a knot and discovered what was attached to it. Seconds later, he had it free.

The lamb was dead, its small body still warm and limp. Its condition told Rachel it had likely been alive until the final collapse of earth. Now it lay where Luke had placed it, its lifeless eyes encrusted with dirt. The rope had been knotted harness-fashion around its neck and shoulders, giving it no chance to work loose and escape.

Luke flung the rope down in disgust. The face he turned toward Rachel was a mask of icy rage.

"Bait," he muttered. "This was a trap. Damned clever trap at that—tunnel under the bank, shore up the roof of the hole, tie the lamb inside and set a trigger that a dog would touch off when it pushed past."

Rachel gazed at him in mute anguish, knowing where Luke's reason would lead him. She had opened the door herself, by coming here. Now there was little she could do or say.

His eyes drilled into her like lead-tipped bullets. "Who did this? You know, don't you?"

She shook her head, wondering how the man who had just held her in his arms and set her on fire with his kisses could look at her with such cold fury.

"You knew Lem Carmody had a bounty on the dogs," he said, rising to his feet. "But Carmody wouldn't pull a stunt like this in person. He's got too much to lose. What else do you know? Who would do this?"

Again Rachel shook her head. "Luke, I swear it on my life, I don't know."

"But you could find out." His hands cupped her jaw, their touch no longer gentle. "Whoever it was, they had the gall to come onto my property. The fact that this wasn't done on open range might give me some legal grounds—"

"Luke, no judge in the world is going to convict a man for killing a lamb and attempting to trap a dog, even if it was on private property."

"I know," he said impatiently. "But if I could get them into court, if I could see them, face them, it might give me a link to finding out who murdered Miguel."

Releasing her, he turned away and stared down at the lamb's smothered body. "The bastards would have to come at night to get so close. And they'd have to know we were shearing. They'd have to know when the dogs would be here—"

He spun back to face her. "You," he said in a cold whisper that was more menacing than a shout. "You knew. You could have told them. And you could have come here this morning to see if their plan worked."

"No!" Rachel stared at him, feeling as if he had just slapped her face. "I had nothing to do with this. I wouldn't, Luke. I couldn't—"

"Then tell me who did!" His hands caught her shoulders. "Was it one of your friends? Somebody in your family? Who are you protecting?"

Rachel shook her head. "I don't know who did this awful thing," she murmured. "I told you—"

His grip tightened on her shoulders. "You can't play this both ways, Rachel," he growled. "You can't come sashaying over here on some trumped-up excuse, wiggling your hips, making me want you so much my teeth ache. You can't playact like you want me, too, and then run home to report to your friends on what I'm up to. It won't work!"

"Stop it!" Rachel bit back tears of rage and hurt. "I wasn't playacting! When I kissed you, it was real! Otherwise it would never have happened!"

A muscle twitched in Luke's cheek, but he showed no other sign of emotion. "If it was real, then, choose your side, Rachel," he said in a flat voice. "I told you before, you can't have it both ways. If you care for me, help me find the answers I'm after and, so help me, girl, I'll do anything for you. But if you'd rather protect vandals, thieves and murderers, to hell with you! I won't have you or your kind sniffing around my property." He let go of her so abruptly that she stumbled backward. She caught her balance, facing him across a gulf that had widened to the proportions of the Grand Canyon. She could love this man, she realized, aching for him. She could happily spend her days working at his side, raising his children and building a future for generations to come. She could spend a lifetime of nights drifting off to sleep in his arms, warm and sleepy and sated with loving.

So help me, girl, I'll do anything for you. His words came back to haunt her now. All she had to do was reach out and take his hand, and everything she wanted could be hers.

But it was only a fantasy, Rachel reminded herself. Luke's terms demanded a terrible price. Her family was the center of her world. They had always been there for her, sharing their laughter, their strength, their love. To betray them even for the sake of justice—no, it was unthinkable. She would never be able to live with herself, or with Luke.

There was only one thing she could do. She would have to do it now, quickly, or she would be lost.

Steeling herself, she thrust out her chin and glared at him.

"How dare you?" She spat out the words, syllable by angry syllable. "You took me in your arms! You pretended to make love to me! And all the while you were scheming to get me to spy for you! Well, I won't do it! You and your sheep can go to hell, Luke Vincente! I never want to see you again!"

She spun away from him and stalked toward her horse. He stood like stone, making no move to follow her. Furious tears blinded her eyes as she fumbled for the stirrup and swung into the saddle. He would not call out to her, she knew. Luke was a proud man, and she had wounded him deeply. Almost as deeply as he had wounded her.

The dogs watched her with their wise golden eyes as she wheeled the bay and dug her boot heels hard into its flanks. Iron-shod hooves spattered gravel as they shot up the side of the wash. On level ground, Rachel gave the horse its head. It knew the way and would carry her home.

The hot wind raked her hair and dried her tears to thin, salty streaks. She would not look back, she vowed. Not even once. She had made her choice, and she was through with Luke Vincente forever.

Luke watched as Rachel's mounted figure crested the top of the ridge. He should move out of her sight, he thought. The last thing he wanted was for Rachel to turn and see him standing there like a fool.

But it made no difference that his legs felt as if

they were rooted to the earth. He knew that Rachel would not look back. She was too angry, and with good reason.

Luke swore under his breath as she vanished behind the ridge like the setting sun. What in hell's name had ever led him to believe he had a way with women? Years ago, it might have been so. But no more.

If he'd had his wits about him, he would never have laid a hand on her. He would have remained calm and persuasive, appealing to her compassion and her sense of fairness. Instead he had grabbed her like a caveman, all but ravished her on the spot, and come damned near to proposing marriage.

He had generally prided himself on keeping a cool head with women. But there was something about Rachel that threw him out of control. All she had to do was look at him with those sea-colored eyes, and he found himself doing things that he was bound to curse when he came to his senses.

But cursing now was only a waste of time and words. Rachel was gone. He had asked her to choose sides, and she had chosen loyalty over justice—and over him. He'd been a fool to think she would choose any other way. She was a cattleman's daughter. And he would lay money that one day she would be a cattleman's wife.

Thrusting her out of his thoughts, he turned back to the cave-in. The two dogs crouched a few feet away, watching with curious eyes as Luke pawed through the dirt to find the rude framework that had supported the tunnel and the stick that had functioned as the trigger, bringing the bank down when the collie pushed it aside. To set such a trap would require more skill than most men possessed—the skill of an Indian, maybe, or someone who had spent time with Indians.

Luke did not know his neighbors well. It was no secret, however, that Morgan Tolliver was the son of a Shoshone woman and had been raised by his mother's people.

Why would anyone, let alone Morgan, go to so much trouble to trap a dog? Luke pondered the question as he scooped out a grave for the dead lamb. To earn Lem Carmody's bounty, the culprit would have to return to the cave-in and dig out the carcass. For a wealthy rancher, the risk of getting caught would hardly be worth the fifty-dollar reward.

But there were people out there who would go to any lengths to run a sheep man off the range—killing sheep, burning sheep wagons and even beating an elderly herder to death. This latest episode with the dog was just one more attempt to break him, Luke concluded. This time it hadn't worked, but they were sure to try again. He had to find a way to stop them. But first he needed to know who they were.

Was Morgan Tolliver behind what had happened? Luke had never clashed openly with his nearest neighbor, but the Tollivers were cattle ranchers and that made them enemies. The fact that Morgan had made offers on his land only lengthened the shadow of suspicion. Luke had received other offers, including one from Lem Carmody, but it was Morgan's agent who'd staked the best price and raised it when Luke refused to sell.

It was no secret that Morgan Tolliver wanted Luke's ranch. But how far would he go to get it?

And how far would Rachel go to help him?

Rising to his feet, Luke turned away from the small heap of rocks he had made to cover the lamb's carcass. The dogs trotted behind as he wound his way down the wash to where his horse was tied.

His thoughts had come full circle, returning to Rachel as they had so many times over the past three days. Her kiss had haunted his dreams at night and tormented his reason while he labored in the sweltering heat of the shearing shed. He had cursed her, wanted her, ached for her.

Today she had been like molten flame in his arms, her passion so hot that even the memory of it seared him down to his vitals. Luke was experienced enough to know when a woman was faking, and he could have sworn that Rachel's explosive response to his kiss was real. But then, he'd been fooled before.

Lord, how he'd been fooled!

When the prison doors had clanged shut behind him, Luke had vowed never to trust a woman again. Rachel, with her wide aquamarine eyes, her halo of titian curls and her fiery spirit had tempted him to forget that vow. But she was the last person on earth he could afford to trust right now. The woman had every reason to betray him, and if he could lay bets on it, he would wager she had already done so.

But deception was a game two could play as well

as one. Rachel had said she never wanted to see him again. But Luke knew better than to believe her. One way or another, he calculated, the little schemer would be back. When she came, he would be ready for her. And he would not be satisfied until he had learned every last one of her dirty secrets.

The buckskin was waiting by the dead juniper, where he had tied it. Luke had one foot in the stirrup and was about to swing into the saddle when he noticed the bootprints in the red sand that lined the bottom of the wash. He recognized one set as the thick-soled brogans he wore for shearing and another, elegantly small with narrow heels, as Rachel's riding boots. But scattered among them was a third set of prints—man-sized, pointed cowboy boots that did not belong to anyone on the sheep ranch.

Disengaging himself from the saddle, Luke dropped to one knee to study them. The tracks, which led up the floor of the wash toward the cave-in, were dry and lightly weathered, as if they had been made sometime in the night. In their haste to reach the trapped dog, he and Rachel had trampled on the earlier trail, obliterating most of the prints. The dogs had added to the damage. Only a few impressions had been left untouched.

Luke leaned close to examine the prints. Judging from their size and the distance between them, the man who'd made them would be about his own height, and fit enough to walk with long strides. It took a few minutes of searching before Luke found one perfect impression. It had been made in the shadow of a large chamisa, where the ground was still damp from the rains of a few days earlier. The track faced inward, toward the center of the bush, as if the man making it had turned aside for a piss before continuing down the wash. The muddy earth had dried, holding precisely the contours of the boot sole.

Luke knew exactly what he was looking for. When he found it, the hair on the back of his neck bristled like a wolf's.

The boots that made the prints had been half-soled in the recent past. The sole of the left boot had come loose beneath the arch and curled forward enough for the edge of the leather to leave a line where it touched the ground.

Luke's mouth tightened as he brushed a fingertip along the telltale line. He had seen the same bootprint before, on the ground of the mountain clearing where Miguel was beaten to death.

Rachel rode like a fury across the flat, pushing the bay hard, as if fighting some invisible force that would draw her back to Luke like iron to a magnet.

Luke had done his devilish best to break her. His kiss had turned her to simmering jelly inside, setting her senses ablaze. She had wanted him more than she'd ever dreamed she could want a man, wanted his mouth crushing hers, his hands cupping her breasts. She had wanted to feel the heat of his flesh welded to her own, easing the empty ache that had been there from the first moment she saw him.

But Luke had wanted only one thing from her—

her help in unmasking his enemies. To get that help, he had manipulated her shamelessly, demanding that she choose and holding himself out as the prize. The arrogance of the man! As if she would betray her people in exchange for a lifetime of cooking mutton stew and trying to scrub the sheep smell out of his dirty clothes!

If Luke had really cared for her, he would have fallen at her feet and begged for her love. Instead he had come dangerously close to making a beggar of her.

A flock of crows passed overhead, their raucous calls echoing across the sky. *Fool! Fool! Shame! Shame!* Their cries seemed to be mocking her. Never again, Rachel vowed, thrusting out her chin. She had her pride and her values, and the determination to get whatever she wanted. There was no excuse for letting a man, *any* man, reduce her to a quivering lump of physical need.

Choose, Luke had told her. Well, she had chosen. She was through with him and his kind. From this day forward, her head would rule her heart. She would be wise, calculating, even cold. And no man would ever, *ever* dare to hurt her again.

In the distance now, she could see the sprawl of buildings and corrals that formed the heart of the Tolliver Ranch. Behind it the rugged peaks of the Big Horn Mountains towered like protective giants. Two golden eagles rode the updrafts, spiraling in lazy circles against the blue sky. Rachel shaded her eyes, watching the pair until they vanished into the blinding glare of the sun. Something in her ached in envy of their fierce bonding, male to female, so natural, so perfect. If only human mating could be so simple.

But it wasn't, for a fact. With rare exceptions, like her parents, men and women fought, manipulated and struggled against each other. Rachel had seen it many times. Now she had experienced it for herself, and she felt utterly drained. The emotions she had experienced with Luke this morning—the rage, the hurt, the vulnerability—had caused her more pain than she ever wanted to feel again.

Eager for a bucket of oats and a rubdown, the bay broke into a trot. Rachel leaned forward in the saddle and kneed the horse to a gallop. They flew across the prairie, the wind whipping her hair and stinging her eyes. Every stroke of the bay's powerful legs carried her farther away from Luke Vincente's insolent gaze and blistering kisses. She would be safe now, she told herself. She was almost home.

As she galloped the horse through the gate, Rachel remembered that she was spattered with dirt from the top of her head to the toes of her boots. She bit back a groan of dismay. If anyone in her family was watching her arrival, there would be questions. The answers to those questions would force her to lie. Her only hope of escape lay in making it to the barn, and from there to her room, without being spotted.

Scanning the house and yard anxiously, she reined the horse to a walk and swung its head toward the barn. She was safe, she concluded, relaxing a little. It was far too early for her parents to be back from

Sheridan, and there was no sign that her brothers had returned from their outing with Slade. Johnny Chang and his boys were on the mountain with the cattle, and if any other members of the Chang family had glimpsed her from the house, they would be discreet enough not to mention her appearance.

Dismounting outside the barn, she led the horse into the shadows. The aromas of fresh hay and manure surrounded her as she slipped off the bay's bridle and poured some oats into a bucket. Her face felt hot in the coolness of the barn, her skin as taut and dry as parchment.

While the big bay munched oats, Rachel unbuckled the cinch, hefted the saddle and carried it to the rack on the north wall of the barn. Pulling a clean rag from the gunny sack that hung next to the stalls, she slid the blanket off the horse's back and began rubbing down its warm, damp coat.

Little by little the motion of the rag, gliding over the gelding's silken contours began to soothe Rachel's ragged nerves. Her explosive encounter with Luke had shaken her to the core. But Luke Vincente's dark presence was enough to unsettle any woman, she reminded herself with a bitter little smile. Time would dim her memory and heal her heart. But for now...

She began to tremble as the memory swept over her. Luke's arms around her, his hands on her breasts, his hard body pressing hers as his kisses roused her to a frenzy of exquisite need. Would she ever feel it with anyone else—that aching burst of joy, like the soaring of eagles toward the sun?

Her mind's eye filled with the sight of him crouched over the unconscious sheepdog, his hands tender, his eyes welling with hope and despair as he urged it back to life. She would have died for him at that moment. And later, when the little collie had scrambled to its feet and shaken its coat, showering dirt in all directions, and she had heard Luke laugh for the first time…

Rachel sagged forward, pressing her face into the solid warmth of the bay's shoulder. Heaven help her, how was she going to live without him? How was she going to face waking up every morning of her life knowing that she would not see his face or hear his voice or feel the roughness of his morning whiskers on her skin?

She closed her eyes, blotting bitter tears against the gelding's satiny coat as she fought the temptation to saddle the horse once more, ride hell-bent for Luke's ranch and fling herself into his arms. That would be the worst thing she could do, she admonished herself. Seeing Luke again would only fan the flames of trouble and tragedy. She could not, would not let it happen. Not ever.

A long shadow fell across the straw-covered floor of the barn. Rachel sensed rather than saw it. Reining in her emotions, she forced herself to turn around.

For an instant she was blinded by the glaring rectangle of sunlight that shone through the barn door. As her vision began to adjust, a tall, lean silhouette emerged through the brightness, moving toward her.

"Luke?" The whispered name escaped her lips before she could think. For the space of a heartbeat, her pulse leaped. Then the figure moved into the shadow of the barn. Rachel bit back a groan as she recognized him.

"Where the devil have you been, Rachel?" Bart Carmody's white-toothed grin flashed in the darkness. "I've been waiting half the morning to see you!"

Chapter Twelve

Clasping her by the shoulders, Bart grinned down at her. Under different circumstances, Rachel might have been glad to see her old neighbor and childhood friend. But right now all she could think of was making a swift getaway to her bedroom.

"How...nice to see you, Bart." She forced each sticky word from her mouth. "Where's your father? I'd like to say hello to him, as well."

"Dad's lumbago was acting up this morning, so I decided to ride over alone and deliver the invitation."

"Invitation?"

"We're having a barbecue and dance at our place on Saturday night. Your whole family's invited. I know it's short notice, but we only decided on it when we heard you were back. It's a welcome home party!"

Rachel stared up at him, perplexed and more than a bit unsettled. It struck her as odd that neighbors who had paid her scant attention when she was growing up would go to the trouble of throwing a party to celebrate her return. To question such a generous act, however, would be churlish. Good neighbors were the lifeblood of this lonely country, where blizzards, drought, fires and sickness were never far out of anyone's thoughts. If she planned to spend the rest of her life here, she would be wise to build bridges, not tear them down.

Bart's smile broadened as he studied her. "Look at you!" he exclaimed, thrusting her out to arm's length for a better inspection. "All grown up and prettier than ever, but still a tomboy, I see, and still getting into trouble. Right now you look as if you've been rolling in a buffalo wallow."

He laughed at his own joke, his blue eyes twinkling with a charm that had been breaking hearts since he was in grammar school. Rachel's vulnerable young heart had been among them. But if Bart had seen her at all, it was as a scrawny, freckle-faced kid with perpetual scabs on her elbows. From the time he was old enough to sneak out at night, Bart had preferred the company of the more experienced and buxom town girls. He had never looked at Rachel...the way he seemed to be looking at her now.

"Feisty little Rachel," he scolded gently as he brushed the dirt from the tip of her nose. "You always did have a talent for getting bumped and scraped and splattered. What happened to you this time?"

"Nothing. Just a...silly accident." Her voice sounded high and shaky in the hollow space of the barn. Bart seemed too charming, too attentive. He was beginning to make her nervous.

"Accident!" He laughed. "Seeing you like this reminds me of the time you and your brothers tried to dig your way to China!"

"You'll find that I clean up nicely these days," Rachel said with a strained laugh. "But it's been a few years since we played together, hasn't it? What have you been doing all this time, Bart?"

"Not much." His hands had begun to massage her shoulders, kneading the tautly aching muscles. "Just helping Dad run the ranch and counting the days until you came home."

In the silence that followed this declaration, the bay chose to raise its tail and drop a steaming clump of manure onto the straw, scant inches from Bart's immaculately polished calfskin boots. For a rancher's son, Bart had an inordinate distaste for anything dusty, dirty or smelly. Nostrils twitching, he released Rachel's shoulders and edged carefully to one side.

Rachel forced herself to laugh. "I was just wondering what to say to your remark, but I think the horse just said it for me."

He looked puzzled. Rachel took advantage of his momentary shock to turn away and resume the task of rubbing down the gelding's coat.

"And what's that's supposed to mean?" he demanded.

"You say you've been waiting for me to come home. How on earth can you expect me to believe that, Bart? You barely gave me a second glance when we were growing up. You were too busy chasing after girls like Lula Mae.''

"I was a fool." He moved to the opposite side of the horse, where he could face her as she worked. "But I've come to my senses, Rachel. Deep down, I've known all along that it would be you and me some day. We have the same memories, the same values. We're very, very right for each other."

His hand slid across the horse's back to capture hers, the fingers curving under to lightly massage her palm. Rachel stiffened at his touch. "I think this whole thing is moving a little too fast for me," she said in a small, cold voice.

The motion of his fingers stopped, but he kept her hand imprisoned in his. "Then I'll slow it down, if you say so. I'll do whatever it takes to win you. But understand this, sweetheart. I'm a determined man. When I go after something I want, I don't give up until it's mine. And I want you."

He ducked under the horse's neck, caught her waist, and swung her off her feet. Rachel had no time to catch her breath before his mouth ground onto hers, hot and damp and demanding. Years ago she had fantasized about kissing Bart and how romantic it would be. But now that it was happening, she was too stunned to respond. She froze in his arms.

When his tongue invaded her mouth she began to resist. Her hands worked upward to push against his chest, but his arms held her fast. The voice of common sense shrilled that Bart was offering her everything she'd always wanted, and that she would be a fool not to accept him. But as he was kissing her, Rachel felt nothing except a slow-rising panic. It was too soon. She had only just come home.

She had only just come from Luke.

Her struggles had thrown him off balance. Staggering backward, he suddenly went rigid. What had begun as a kiss ended in a muttered curse. Carried by her own momentum, Rachel spun out of his grasp, stumbled and fell into a pile of loose straw.

For an instant she sputtered upward, ready to fight like a wildcat should he leap on her and try to wrestle her down. Then, as she swept her vision clear of hair and straw, she realized what had happened.

Bart had backed into the clump of fresh horse manure. It oozed over the soles of his polished boots and clung to the hem of his spotless trousers. The earthy stench rose like a miasma around him.

Bart's handsome face, its chiseled mouth and chin smeared with dirt from their ill-fated kiss, was a study in shocked revulsion. Unable to help herself, Rachel began to giggle, then to chuckle, then to belly laugh in a most unladylike fashion. Her hands clutched her aching ribs as she bent double, rocking back and forth in the straw. Tears of laughter left rivulets of mud down her dusty cheeks. Was she laughing at Bart or crying for Luke? Either way, she realized, the knot of tension in her chest was slowly loosening.

Bart glared down at her as he scuffed the sides of his boots in the straw. "That wasn't funny, Rachel," he snapped. "And I won't have you laughing at me. It's…disrespectful."

"Disrespectful, is it?!" She wiped her eyes with the back of her hand. "Why, just look at you, Bart! If you had a mirror and could see your face, you'd be laughing, too!" It was all right now, she thought. Surprise had allowed him a brief advantage, but she was back in charge now, as she liked to be.

Bart continued to scowl at her. "That may be, but it's not your place to laugh at me, Rachel. As my future wife—"

"Your future *wife?*" On the offensive now, Rachel scrambled out of the straw to confront him. Her eyes blazed with fury through her tears. "What makes you think you can just come storming over here and claim me like an unbranded heifer, Bart Carmody? Any man who wants to marry me can damn well earn my favor first! He can bring me flowers and chocolates and take me dancing in the moonlight! He can pay me pretty compliments and curry favor with my parents! And when the time comes, he can fall on his knees and *beg* me to be his! And even then, I might say no!"

She glared up at Bart, her mind churning in the silence. Would Luke have brought her flowers and chocolates? Would he have taken her dancing in the moonlight and whispered pretty words in her ear? Perhaps long ago, before life had twisted his soul like rawhide in the sun, he might have done such things. But surely not now. Not the Luke she knew.

Would he have begged her to be his? Rachel's heart contracted as she realized how close she had come to begging *him.* But a match with a man like

Luke would be an invitation to disaster. She had no choice except to forget him and move on.

Little by little the muscles of Bart's face relaxed into a smile. He shook his head. "Little Rachel. You certainly haven't lost any of your spit and vinegar. You and I are going to have an interesting life together."

Rachel stifled a sigh. It was as if Bart had chosen to ignore everything she'd just told him. He still assumed that all he needed to do was open his arms and she would fall into them, along with her twenty-percent share of the Tolliver ranch.

She was not so naive as to think he loved her. The ranch had to be the reason Bart was courting her so ardently. He was thinking of his future, and what a tie to the Tolliver family would mean. There might be other girls more to his liking, but none with the kind of dowry Rachel could bring to a marriage.

The thought of his motives hurt and annoyed her. But there were two sides to every coin. Bart was Lem Carmody's only son, and the Carmody ranch was a fair piece of land. A union between Bart and Rachel would be smiled on by both their families. She would be foolish to toss his proposal aside like so much chaff.

Rachel's head had begun to ache. Bart was saying something to her about the barbecue, and how he would make it a point to dance with her in the moonlight, but the air in the barn had suddenly become stifling, her brain too befogged to concentrate on his words.

"Would a glass of cold lemonade on the porch be too much to ask?" His face wore a determined smile. "I'll finish with your horse while you run to the kitchen and get some for me."

"Yes...thank you." Rachel spun away from him, grateful for any excuse to leave the barn. Thomas Chang made fresh lemonade most summer days and kept it in the spring house. Nothing tasted better after a long, hot ride. And she could hardly expect Bart to turn around and go home without some refreshment and polite conversation. She would be safe enough, she knew. Thomas would be close by, his presence a safeguard against any improprieties. All the same, she was not looking forward to the next hour.

She had just cleared the shadow of the barn when a cacophony of war whoops and clattering hoofbeats reached her ears. Shading her eyes, Rachel saw Slade and her brothers racing full out through the ranch gate. Jacob was in the lead, leaning over the neck of his lathered horse. Slade followed, waving a severed coyote tail like a war trophy, with Josh riding just off his flank. A long cloud of dust trailed behind them.

The flood of relief that washed over Rachel was laced with worry. What sort of mischief had the three been up to this morning? Had they invaded Luke's property, perhaps visited the site of the rigged cave-in?

Rachel strode out into the yard, waving her hands above her head. The three young riders whooped in return and slowed their horses to a ragged trot. All of them wore broad grins across their dusty faces.

With a sigh, Rachel turned toward the house. She would order lemonade all around. Then she would deal with whatever troubles had blown in with the boys' arrival.

A ripe golden moon hung low in the sky above the Carmody ranch house. The savory aromas of beans, biscuits and barbecued beef floated on the night air, mingling with the sound of voices and the lively whine of a solitary fiddle. Children played hide-and-seek among the wagons and high-wheeled buggies, squealing with laughter as they darted in and out of the moonlit shadows. Where men stood talking, their cigarette tips made glowing points of red in the darkness. Smoke spiraled upward, ghostly against their weathered faces as they passed around discreet flasks of whiskey.

Every cattle rancher within a forty-mile radius was here with his family. Luke had not been invited, but he was here, too, lingering in the deep shadows beyond the lamplight, watching and listening.

That morning, by pure chance, Luke had met the elderly fiddler, who'd hailed him to ask directions to the Carmody place. The two had shared a pleasant drink, and the old man had mentioned that he was on his way to fiddle for what he'd called a grand whoop-de-do that evening. There'd be dancing till the moon went down, he'd declared, and half the county was going to be there.

Half the county, including the men who'd murdered Miguel.

The thought had been too much for Luke to resist. The boot track he'd found was the only lead he had, and it wasn't enough. He needed faces. He needed names. Heaven help him, he needed solid proof. If he didn't find it soon, Ignacio's fragile patience would explode, and the boy would be gone.

Taking care to keep his face out of the light, Luke strolled the fringes of the crowd. There were plenty of cowboys dressed as he was, in denims, boots and clean plaid shirts. Aside from his height and the broadness of his shoulders, he did not stand out in any way. Even so, as he strained his ears for any meaningful snatches of conversation, the loudest sound Luke could hear was the pounding of his own heart. He was strung so tightly that if anyone had so much as touched him, his nerves would have snapped like frayed bowstrings.

As he drifted in and out of the shadows, he struggled to focus his attention on the murmuring clusters of men, and not on the glowing circle of light where couples whirled and danced to the lively strains of the fiddle. If he looked in that direction, he knew he would see Rachel dancing with Lem Carmody's son. The sight of her in another man's arms would turn him into a jealous, hotheaded fool. Worse, it might make him careless, and he could not afford to be careless tonight.

Even so, he could not resist a glance as she and her tall blond partner rounded the circle of dancers. Rachel was wearing a daffodil-yellow gown of a fabric so light it seemed to float around her. The heart-shaped neckline, puffed sleeves and ruffled hem accentuated the curves of her trim little body. The dark-green sash at her waist matched the ribbon in her hair, which hung down her back, gleaming like amber silk in the lamplight. Her eyes sparkled. Her mouth smiled as she responded to something her partner was saying.

Luke's throat contracted at the sight of her. But his reasons for being here tonight had nothing to do with Rachel. The two of them had ignited a few very hot sparks, and that was all. The sooner he could forget about her, the better.

A gangly teenaged girl, a stranger, glanced in his direction. Nervous about being recognized, Luke turned away and faded into the shadow of a covered buggy. That was when he almost stumbled over the circle of youths shooting dice in the moonlight.

"Hell, man, I'll bet you two coyote tails against that box of rifle bullets your pa gave you." The speaker was the young whelp called Slade who'd come to live with the Carmodys a few months back. Luke had met him in town and disliked him on sight. For all his bantam size, the little pill had walked with a swagger that took up the entire sidewalk and made a show of being mean to anything and anyone too weak to fight back. Luke would have wagered his best saddle that Slade had been one of the riders chasing his sheep and was likely involved in other mischief as well. But there was not a shred of proof against him.

Keeping to the shadows, Luke ambled past the

boys, who were on their knees in the dust, intent on their dice game. A quick glance at Slade's boots confirmed that they were too small and narrow to have made the prints Luke was trying to match. In fact, none of the boys in the circle, including Morgan Tolliver's twin sons—Rachel's brothers—had large enough feet to have left the tracks that were burned into Luke's memory. That fact alone did not prove their innocence. It only reminded Luke that he needed to learn more, much more.

Making a mental note to check the area around the cave-in for smaller tracks, Luke turned away. He was about to move on when he heard another of the boys, a stranger, ask in a nasal twang, "Store-bought bullets is worth more'n a couple coyote tails, Slade. What about that dog hide you said you was gonna get? The one you said Lem was gonna give you fifty dollars for? Why not put that up?"

"He can't put up what he hasn't got." The speaker was one of the Tolliver twins. "What happened, Slade? You never did tell us."

Slade cursed. "Rode by there the other night and saw the place was all dug up. Knew I wouldn't find the damn-fool dog, so I skedaddled fast. But I'll get me one yet. So if I promise, can I use it to bet for your bullets?"

"Can't bet what you ain't got," the boy said. Slade cursed again, and the boy laughed. "Now if you could promise me a roll in the hay with Beth Ann Harper…"

The youths burst into raucous laughter. As the conversation swung to the inevitable subject of girls, Luke thrust his hands into his pockets and drifted off in another direction.

So Slade had been involved in setting the dog trap. Who, then, had made the larger tracks Luke had found? Could it have been Lem Carmody's son?

Against his will, Luke's gaze wandered toward the dance floor, seeking Rachel. His gut ached at the thought of her with another man, and he found himself yearning to stride into the swirl of dancers, seize her by the waist and claim her in the eyes of every cattle-raising mother's son there.

But Rachel wasn't his to claim, Luke reminded himself. He hadn't come here to make trouble for her. In fact he could no longer see her among the dancers. Both she and her tall blond partner had disappeared.

Luke scanned the crowd, apprehension gnawing at his insides. He was dangerously close to making a fool of himself, something he could ill afford to do. Let jealousy get the upper hand, and anything he might gain by being here tonight would be thrown to the winds.

Wrenching his thoughts away from her, Luke moved on through the edge of the darkness. In the shadow of a big cottonwood tree, he passed a man and woman passionately locked in each other's arms. His pulse lurched. He had taken a step toward them, one fist raised, before he realized the woman was a plump brunette with a long braid hanging down her back.

Turning away, Luke shook off the tense fury that

had seized him. He had no claim on Rachel. Yet here he was, bristling like a bull elk in rut because he thought he had seen her in another man's arms. What he needed right now was an ice-cold dunk in the sheep pond.

Suddenly, a dozen yards ahead, he caught sight of two figures through the crowd. All distracting thoughts fled as he realized he was looking at the pair of men who worried him most—Lem Carmody and Morgan Tolliver.

Getting close to them was not difficult. They were standing on the outer edge of the crowd with the darkness behind them. Morgan was watching his pretty wife polka around the floor in the arms of a gangly young cowboy. Head tilted back, face laughing, Cassandra Tolliver looked like an older, softer version of her daughter. For the space of a breath Luke studied her, comparing in his mind. Rachel was taller, her features sharper, her body more angular, her hair more gold than red, and instead of curling like her mother's it fell in soft, sun-streaked waves around her face....

Rachel again. He shoved her out of his thoughts and focused his attention on the two men. Lem Carmody, short and stocky with a bull neck and a thick gray moustache, took a long puff on his cheroot. Smoke curled upward as he spoke.

"My boy and your girl make a right fine couple, don't they, Morgan? Speakin' for myself, I wouldn't mind havin' a few grandkids around to liven up my old age."

Morgan let a moment of stillness pass before he answered. In that stillness, Luke felt his stomach clench.

"If it's what Rachel wants, that's fine," Morgan said at last. "But we're hoping Bart won't rush her. She's only just come home. We'd like the chance to enjoy her as part of the family for a while."

Lem snorted. "Sometimes I think you're too patient. Maybe it's the Injun blood in you. Me, I don't like to wait. When something needs pushin', I like to jump in and push."

Again Morgan was silent. His eyes were on his wife, but there was no sign of jealousy in his expression. His mouth wore a faint smile, as if he were simply enjoying her beauty and waiting for the moment when she would come laughing back to him. That was how things should be between a man and a woman, Luke thought. No gut-wrenching uncertainty, no jealous rages, just simple trust and love. It was all too rare.

Lem Carmody cleared his throat and spat in the dust. "Don't know about you, but I'm ready to do a little pushin' right soon. That sheep man, Vincente, is gettin' too big for his britches, runnin' those woolly maggots of his all over the range, spoilin' the land for our cattle. A bunch of us want to band together and pay him a visit, burn him out and send him back to wherever the hell he came from. Can we count on you and your boys to help us?"

Morgan exhaled sharply. "I don't like sheep any more than you do. But as long as Vincente's running them on open range, and not on anyone else's land, he's not breaking any laws.''

"Then maybe we ought to make our own laws!'' Lem snarled. "If we all stick together, that's law enough for me.''

"What you're suggesting could land the lot of you in jail,''' Morgan said quietly.

"Not if we don't get caught!'' Lem argued vehemently. "And even if we do, no jury is going to convict us if every rancher in the county is in on it. Hell, the whole system would go broke without us. There'd be no jobs, no taxes paid, no business at the stores…'' Lem cleared his throat and spat again. "That's why we need everybody to do it together. It's why we need you.''

Listening in the shadows, Luke felt the strain in every raw nerve of his body. Beads of sweat congealed on his forehead. The Tollivers owned more land and cattle than any other family in the county. If Morgan agreed to join Lem, the other ranchers would fall in behind them. Blood would be spilled, and in the end, no matter how it happened, Luke would lose everything.

His thoughts flashed to the two boys, Miguel's sons. Even if they insisted on staying, he would not put them in danger. But, Lord, how could he keep them safe? Where could he send them?

Luke's breath rasped in his dry, gritty throat as he waited for Morgan to answer. The distant sounds of the fiddle buzzed in his ears, in an odd counterpoint to the hammering of his pulse.

"So what'll it be?" Lem demanded. "Are you and your boys with us?"

Morgan's gaze lingered on his wife, where she flitted among the dancers like a bright little hummingbird. When he looked back at Lem, his face was as impassive as a Shoshone warrior's.

"My answer is no, Lem," he said. "I won't risk my sons to that kind of trouble, and I won't put my wife and daughter through the worry of it. As long as the sheep man keeps his animals off my land and does no harm to me and mine, I won't have any quarrel with him."

Luke felt his knees go weak with relief. Drops of perspiration trickled down his face, wetting his cheeks like tears.

The polka ended on a single crashing note. Dancers broke apart, laughing and sweating. Lem Carmody scowled up at Morgan, looking as if he wanted to argue. But there would be no more time to talk. Cassandra Tolliver had left her young partner. She was making her way back to her husband, her blue eyes sparkling, her arms reaching out in anticipation.

It was time for him to get out of here, Luke thought. He had seen his enemies. He had heard their threats. To stay longer would only tempt fate.

Still, Luke found himself hesitating. He had come here for one reason—to find solid evidence against the men who had murdered Miguel. For all he'd learned tonight, he had failed to get what he really needed.

But how could he push his luck any further? his

cautious side argued. What did he expect to do, follow the men around and examine their tracks? This was, after all, a party. The owner of the boots with the curled insole would likely be wearing something more presentable tonight. Searching for the print here would be as fruitless as it was risky.

His eyes made one last brief scan of the crowd, but Rachel was nowhere in sight. And that was for the best, Luke told himself, turning away. If what he'd heard was true, she would soon be marrying Bart Carmody. The sooner he burned her image out of his heart, the better.

The sounds of music and laughter faded as he walked past the outbuildings toward the corral fence, where his horse was tethered alongside a half-dozen others. He had not found the proof he needed. But at least he knew who to watch. Everything he had learned pointed toward the Carmodys. With luck, if he shadowed them long enough, he might learn who was behind Miguel's murder.

A glimmer of movement in the shadow of the granary caught his attention. Instinctively Luke froze, ready to defend himself. Then the sounds of heavy breathing reached his ears. More lovers. They seemed to be everywhere tonight. Maybe it was the full moon.

Willing his taut nerves to relax, Luke moved quietly past them. He had gone only a few steps when he realized he was hearing the sounds of a struggle.

"Why, you little hellcat!" a man snarled. "Scratch me, will you? I'll show you once and for all!"

"No!" a woman's voice rasped with desperate fury. "Let me go! I won't let you—"

The rest of the words were muffled, but Luke had heard enough to recognize that voice. It was Rachel's.

Chapter Thirteen

The warning voice in Luke's head shouted that he should ignore the struggle and keep walking. Rachel had clearly gotten herself into this mess; she could damned well get herself out of it. He had his own skin to think of.

But he was already plunging toward the sound of her voice, driven by a possessive rage so hot and so primal that, for one blinding instant, he could have killed Bart Carmody with his bare hands.

The impact of his charge struck Bart's shoulder, knocking him off balance. With a startled gasp, Rachel spun out of Bart's arms. The bloody streaks her nails had left down the side of his face flashed in the moonlight as Bart turned. A split second later, Luke's fist crashed into his jaw. Stunned, Bart reeled like a drunkard and stumbled sideways against the wall of the granary.

"Get out of here, Rachel!" Luke growled. But Rachel did not move. Her hair was disheveled, her pretty yellow gown torn off one shoulder. She stared with

wide, frightened eyes as Bart recovered and came a
Luke, head lowered like a bull's.

The impact drove Luke backward. He was stil
staggering when Bart came at him again, fists flying
Bart was a powerful man. Younger than Luke by a
decade, he had the advantage of lightning-quick re
flexes. But Luke had honed his fighting skills in the
hellpit of the Louisiana State Penitentiary. He knew
tricks that could cripple a man, or even kill him
Driven by fury, it took all his strength of will not to
use them now. The last thing he wanted was to end
up behind bars again.

He met Bart's charge from a crouching angle tha
brought him up below the younger man's arms, al
lowing him to drive into Bart's chest and belly with
the power of his fists. Grunting with pain and surpris
Bart staggered backward. Luke's eyes flickered to
ward the shadows, where Rachel seemed to be scram
bling for something she could use as a weapon. Foo
woman.

"Get out of here, blast it!" he hissed at her
"Run!"

He cursed when she showed no sign of leaving, bu
there was no time to reason with her. Bart's nex
charge hit him like a freight train, knocking him fla
and dashing all hope that, once Rachel was safe, he
could get loose and make a dash for his horse.

Seizing the advantage, Bart leaped on him, punch
ing, kicking and gouging. Luke brought his knees up
to counter the blows. His thoughts flashed briefly to
the small pistol stuck in his boot. He fought the temp

tation to reach for it. Draw a weapon, and he might as well be a dead man.

"Fight! Fight!" The shout went up, setting off a stampede of onlookers. Luke heard the sound of running feet and glimpsed a forest of legs closing into a ring around them.

"Jehosephat, it's Bart and the sheep man!" a man's voice shouted. "Go to it, Bart! Kill the bastard!"

"Five dollars on the sheep man!" another voice called out. "Heard tell he killed a fellow down south with his bare hands!"

"Ten dollars on Bart! Come on, Bart!" People were hooting and cheering, as if they were at a rodeo. They wanted blood, Luke thought. His blood.

"Please, somebody stop them!" Luke heard Rachel's desperate cry through a blaze of pain as Bart's fist slammed into his nose. He glimpsed her yellow skirt flashing around them, glimpsed her hands brandishing a grain scoop. What in hell's name did the woman think she was doing?

The grain scoop swung through the air and slammed into the side of Bart's head. It was only a glancing blow, but it caught Bart off guard for an instant—long enough for Luke to roll like a cat and spring to his feet. Still dazed, Bart lurched upward, but Luke had the advantage now. A single, well-aimed blow from his fist crashed into Bart's jaw. Bart's eyes rolled back in his head as he collapsed in the dust like a poleaxed steer. It was over.

But it was far from over, Luke realized. The watchers, recovering from their surprise, were closing in around him, muttering and cursing. Too late, Luke realized they had every reason to believe *he* was the one who'd attacked Rachel, and that Bart had come flying to her defense.

"Tar and feathers!" a voice shrilled. "Come on, let's get 'im!"

Behind him, Luke caught a glimpse of Rachel, looking pale and frightened. Scores of eyes had seen her hit Bart with the grain scoop. When the mob remembered that she'd struck out against one of their own to save the sheep man, she would be a pariah.

Glancing around for an opening, Luke calculated that he might still be able to escape. But the mob wanted a victim. If he left her here, they could turn on her, and not even Morgan Tolliver would be able to stop them.

There was only one thing he could do, and Luke did it.

Moving like quicksilver, he slipped the pistol from his boot. His free arm flashed out to capture Rachel's waist and jerk her in front of him, holding her like a shield, with the muzzle of the small gun pressed against the soft, white flesh of her neck.

"Stay where you are, all of you," he said in a flat, cold voice. "I don't want to hurt this little lady, but if even one of you moves a muscle, so help me..." He left the rest of the threat to the crowd's imagination.

A hush fell over the watchers. In the sudden silence, Luke could feel their stunned disbelief as they edged out of harm's way. The fear that hung in the air was as real as the haze of tobacco smoke and smell of horses on the warm night wind.

Rachel's body was taut and still against him, her breathing a shallow flutter. Where his arm crossed her breast, he could feel the pounding of her heart against his wrist. He could only hope that she understood what he was trying to do, and why.

"Don't do this, Vincente." Morgan Tolliver had pushed his way through the crowd. He faced Luke across the ring of open ground, one arm clasping his wife, who looked as if she wanted to plunge headlong to her daughter's rescue.

"She's never done a thing to hurt you." Morgan's black Shoshone eyes caught glints of moonlight. "Let her go now, and I'll see that no charges are brought against you. But harm one hair on her head and, so help me, I'll track you down and kill you with my own hands."

Studying Rachel's father across the distance, Luke sensed that here was a man who lived by his word. He ached to tell Morgan that he would rather cut off his arm than hurt his precious daughter. But he had to maintain the fiction. If he let Rachel go, there was no guarantee that Morgan could stop the crowd from rushing him and tearing him apart. And the longer he could appear to threaten her, the more apt they were to believe she'd meant to strike him, not Bart.

Luke's grip tightened around her waist. "I don't take much stock in a cattleman's promise," he said. "This little lady is my best insurance policy, and I mean to take her along when I ride out of here. We'll take an extra horse, and once I'm satisfied nobody's come after me, I'll send her back.'' He began edging toward the corral. Rachel moved with him, her feet stumbling over the toes of his boots. As he steadied her, it suddenly came to him that he could not leave yet. He had something to say to these people, and this might be his only chance to say it.

"Please.'' Cassandra Tolliver strained against her husband's arm. "We love her so much. Please don't hurt her.''

Luke felt the quiver of emotion that passed through Rachel's body. Looking across the moonlit circle, into her mother's tearful eyes, he knew that this was one person he could not lie to. "Believe me, ma'am,'' he said gently, "hurting your daughter is the last thing I want to do.

"But I came here for a reason,'' he continued, raising his voice so that even those at the back of the crowd could hear him. "A band of masked men attacked one of my herders, a fine old gentleman who would never harm any of you. They set fire to the sheep wagon where he'd taken refuge, and, when he stumbled outside, they beat him with their fists and kicked him with their boots. They did it again and again and again. Miguel was a tough old man. He lived long enough to tell me what happened.''

A hush had fallen over the listeners. Some of them stared at the ground, refusing to meet his gaze. From somewhere near the house, a child began to wail.

"A few days ago I buried my friend. He left two

young sons. They're part of the reason I'm here.'' Luke scanned the crowd, his eyes lingering on one man, then another, on Lem Carmody and then on Bart, who lay twitching on the ground, just beginning to awaken. "The men who beat Miguel are cowards and murderers," Luke said. "If they're here tonight, I want them to know that the death of Miguel Agustín Ibarra y Sandoval will be avenged. One way or another there'll be justice for him and for his sons. One way or another, his killers will pay."

For the space of a breath there was no sound except the whisper of the night breeze through the branches of the cottonwoods. Then the crowd began to mutter, and Luke knew it was time to leave.

"Nobody move!" he warned as he backed Rachel toward the horses. "Don't make me hurt her!"

Getting her into the saddle was awkward and dangerous. Luke feared that the onlookers would choose that vulnerable moment to rush them, but the menace in his eyes and Rachel's evident fear kept everyone at a distance. Swinging up behind her, he seized the bridle of the horse that was tied nearest his own. Nerve-grinding seconds later, they were galloping through the gate of the Carmody ranch, onto the open plain, with the spare horse trailing alongside them.

Rachel did not speak. She clung to the front of the saddle, her body tense, her hair fluttering back into Luke's face. Was she frightened? Angry? Would she be cold and distant when they finally stopped, or would she fly at him like a wildcat? The longer they rode, the less certain Luke became that he had done the right thing by forcing her to come with him. He could almost feel her mind churning, building up to an explosion of anger that would surely come when they stopped.

Two miles beyond the gate a low bluff rose out of the plain, its rocky crest overlooking the way they had come. Here they could stop, rest the horses and make sure no one was following them.

Luke swung the horses off the road and circled behind, to the sloping side of the bluff, where a narrow, hidden game trail wound its way to the top. Only as the horses slowed to pick their way up the twisting path did Rachel begin to speak.

"You've set yourself up for more trouble, you know." She sounded shaken, but calm. "After tonight, they'll never leave you in peace."

"That's what I'm counting on," Luke replied, grimly. "If I can't find the buzzards who killed Miguel, I'll just have to let them find me."

"But they'll kill you!" The worry in her voice almost undid him. He had expected her to be outraged, even hysterical. But Rachel's first concern was for him.

"They'll have to catch up with me first," he said. "When they do, I'll be ready for them."

"Ready how?" she pressed him. "I've been to your ranch, Luke. It's not exactly an armed fortress— just you, the boys, the dogs and those fool sheep. And after tonight, it won't just be Miguel's killers hunting you down. It will be every cattleman in the county."

"Including your father and brothers?"

The question silenced her. Luke could hear her shallow breathing in the darkness. He could feel the tension where her legs rested lightly against his own, cupping his knees as the horse wound its way upward. The full moon rode the crest of the sky, veiled now and again by scudding clouds that made pools of shadow on the rocky landscape.

When Rachel did not answer his question, Luke forced himself to speak. "I overheard your father talking with Lem Carmody. He said that as long as I kept the sheep off his land and didn't interfere with him or his family, we had no quarrel."

"But now all that's changed!" she cried. "You've made an enemy of a man who was willing to leave you in peace!"

"I know." Luke shifted in the saddle, balancing her weight as the horse rounded the last bend in the path. "But after so many people saw you swing that grain scoop at Bart Carmody, I couldn't leave you there, Rachel. I couldn't stand the thought of what they might do to you—now and in the future."

"You should've left that to me!" she snapped. "For that matter, you should have let me deal with Bart. I can take care of myself!"

"Is that what you were thinking when you let Mr. Carmody lead you off behind that granary in the first place? That you could take care of yourself?"

They had reached the level ground at the top of the bluff. Luke reined their mount to a halt, feeling dark and ugly. What had he been thinking? That he was saving her? That he had had some kind of claim on her? He'd heard the talk between Lem Carmody and Morgan Tolliver. According to Lem, at least, Rachel and Bart were as good as engaged.

If that was true, Luke lashed himself, he had just interfered in a private spat, knocked out a woman's fiancé and kidnapped her at gunpoint.

Swinging a leg over the horse's rump, he dropped to the ground. A quick scan of the moonlit plain below confirmed that no one had followed them. But Luke knew his troubles were far from over.

Still in the saddle, Rachel gazed down at him. Moonlight shone down from above her, casting her eyes in shadow and giving her eyelids a heavy, sensual look.

"That's not fair, what you just said." Her voice was so low he had to strain to hear her. "I've known Bart all my life. We grew up together. Tonight we were joking around, just playing, and suddenly he was grabbing me, tearing at my gown. I was scared. I started to fight him. That was when you came by."

"You should have run when I told you to," he muttered. "If you had, we wouldn't be in this mess now."

"I couldn't. I was afraid he was going to hurt you. Oh, Luke!" Her lips began to quiver. She seemed to be fighting tears, but she did not cry.

Reaching up, he clasped her waist to help her down from the horse. Her hands gripped his shoulders for balance, and it seemed the most natural thing in the world that she should fall into his arms. But that did not happen.

The instant her feet touched the ground she pushed away from him. She stumbled toward the spare horse they'd brought, as if she meant to leave. Then, suddenly, she spun back to face him, the wind fanning her hair around her face like a moonlit flame.

"Don't you realize what you've done to me?" She hurled the words at him. "I came home because I wanted to build a life here on the ranch with my family. I wanted to pass my days in simple contentment, to have a family of my own when the time came, knowing that everything I needed was close at hand. But you—you've made that impossible, Luke Vincente! You've ruined everything!"

Luke gazed at her, drinking in her beauty and wishing passionately that the two of them had never met. His circumstances had been difficult enough before she arrived. Now everything he'd worked so hard to build was at risk.

"All my life, I've managed to get whatever I wanted," she said. "A new dress, a trip to town, a new pony, art school—nothing was out of my reach. Until I met you."

Luke felt his chest jerk as if he'd been lassoed by an invisible noose. He cleared his throat, but no words emerged. He could only stand there gazing at her like staked bait while she tore at his heart.

"Don't you know why I was with Bart tonight? It was because I knew I could never have *you,* and it hurt. All the way through me, it hurt. I wanted that hurt to stop, Luke. I wanted to forget that I'd ever met you. And Bart was there, saying the pretty words

I'd longed to hear for half my life. Everyone was so happy, seeing the two of us together. I wanted to keep them happy. I willed myself to make it work...but I couldn't do it. As soon as he put his arms around me, you were there, between us, and I couldn't...I can't. And I don't know what to do!''

Defiant and vulnerable, she faced him in the moonlight. Luke gazed back at her, knowing she had just said the worst thing she could possibly say to him. If she had cursed him, shrieking her hatred to the sky, it would have made things easy compared to the torture she was inflicting on him now.

He tore his eyes away from her and glared at the ground, fighting for self-control. "Get on that horse, Rachel," he said. "Climb into that saddle now, and ride hell-for-leather back to your family. They'll be worried sick about you."

She made a little sound of protest and took a tentative step toward him, but he shook his head, stopping her. "There's no law that says you have to marry a jackass like Bart Carmody," he said, aching to hold her. "There are good men out there, and sooner or later the right one will come along and give you all the things you deserve. But that's in the future. Right now, you've got to go home and forget every word you just said to me. It's the only way, girl. The only way you'll be safe."

"Safe!" She flung the word back at him like an epithet. "I've been safe all my life, Luke! There are better things than safe!" Once again she took a step toward him, and Luke felt his will begin to crack. He bit back a groan of need.

"Stop it!" he growled in a fury of desperation. "Do you think you can have your little adventure with me, then just wipe the dirt off your boots and go on as if it had never happened? It doesn't work that way. Damn it, Rachel, *life* doesn't work that way. The dirt stays on you—for good!"

Her head went up like a wild mare's. "I know you killed a man, and that you went to prison for manslaughter," she said in a low, taut voice. "You're the gentlest man I've ever known, Luke. If you took a life, you must have been sorely driven to it. But that's behind you now. You've paid your debt, and it no longer matters. Not to me!"

"Then sit down and listen." Luke's voice had dropped to a growl. She stared at him with large, bewildered eyes. "Do it!" he barked. "You're going to hear the whole ugly story, and when I get to the end of it, you're going to leap onto that horse, ride down that hill at a mad gallop and count yourself lucky to be rid of me!"

Rachel glanced around her, then walked to a flat-topped rock and sat down, gazing at him with expectant eyes, as if she had already pardoned him for what he was about to tell her.

She would change her mind when she heard the story, he thought.

She had left room for him on the rock, but Luke did not trust himself to sit beside her. Thrusting his fists into his pockets, he stared up into the vast, dark bowl of the sky, where the stars shone like glittering handfuls of sand. If he went to her now and took her in his arms, there would be no more talk. But that would only put off the inevitable hurt. He would tell her now, before he sent her home to the family who loved her. That way, he knew, she would not come back.

"I'm waiting," she said softly. "Tell me."

Turning around, he forced himself to meet her luminous eyes. "It started with a woman," he said, watching her flinch with the impact of each word. "Her name was Cynthia."

Rachel would have chosen to hear Luke's story with his arms around her, strong and reassuring. Instead she willed herself to remain seated while he stood before her like a schoolboy, moving in and out of moonlight so that his face was alternately hidden and revealed. His expression was a granite mask, his voice so flat as to be almost a drone. But the twitching of a muscle in his cheek and the subtle clenching of his left hand gave mute evidence that he was in torment.

"I met her at a party in Baton Rouge." His words came awkwardly at first, then moved into a flow that was almost hypnotic. "A mutual friend introduced us. She was a true Southern belle, with long black hair, eyes the color of spring violets and a way of laughing that drew men to her like moths to a lantern."

Rachel's gaze fell as he paused to gather his

thoughts. She had never had any trouble attracting men, but she knew that her carrot-colored hair, freckled nose and tomboy manners were no match for the dazzling beauty that haunted Luke's memory.

"She lived in a huge fortress of a house with a widowed father who was as rich as Midas, and when she chose me from a score of beaux, I couldn't believe my luck—me, a wild ruffian from the bayou, with no money, no education and no more family pedigree than a mongrel dog. I was too giddy to wonder why. Through one long, delicious summer, we rode together, danced together, picnicked together—I felt like I'd stumbled into the Garden of Eden." He paused, his breath jerking out in a long, bitter sigh. "But what would any Eden be without its serpent?"

"Her father?"

Rachel had spoken on impulse. He flashed her a startled glance, as if he had sunk so deeply into memory that he'd forgotten her presence. "He was dead set against me, of course," he said, ignoring Rachel's question. "What father wouldn't be? After he forbade Cynthia to see me, we started meeting in secret—that was a new game, with its own excitement because we had to spend our time alone. I was as hot-blooded as any young fool, and it wasn't long before I started demanding more than kisses from her."

He paused and looked directly at Rachel, as if he were studying her reaction, measuring the depth to which he'd hurt her. She forced her back to stay ramrod-straight, her face to remain impassive as she met his eyes. They glittered in the moonlight, like the cold eyes of a wolf, challenging her to stay and hear the rest of the story.

"Go on," she said, knowing he intended to spare her nothing.

He answered with a sharp intake of breath, then began speaking again. "The first time I tried to touch her—touch her intimately—she cried out and shrank away from me. At first I didn't know what to make of it—she'd been telling me that she loved me, that she wanted me.

"Finally, after hours of talking and crying, the story came out. Her father, she said, had been getting drunk and forcing himself on her for years, threatening her with ruin if she tried to leave."

Rachel stared at him, shocked speechless, not only by the unthinkable crime, but by the fact that Luke could speak of it with such dispassionate frankness, especially to her.

"I was hard put to believe her at first," he said. "Her father was one of the most respected men in the state, active in politics, known for his generosity to good causes. But then she showed me the bruises, on her legs, her arms, her breasts..." He shook his head. "I had no choice except to believe her then."

A bank of clouds had drifted across the moon. Luke stood in darkness now, his face unreadable, his black hair fluttering in the night wind. From somewhere off in the darkness, a coyote yipped its melancholy song to the sky. Rachel felt as if her heart had crawled into her throat to form a hard knot that kept her from speaking. If she'd been capable of words, she would have begged him to stop this heart-wrenching tale that was as painful for him as it was for her. But like a man bent on self-destruction, Luke sighed and continued.

"I begged her to elope with me. But she was afraid her father would hunt us down, destroy me, and treat her worse than ever. Only when she felt completely safe from him, she insisted, would she be capable of the kind of love she wanted to give me."

"Things came to a head the morning I decided to confront her father. He'd banned me from the house weeks before, but, fool that I was, I pushed the old butler aside and stormed up the stairs into his study. He was seated at his desk, a big, red-faced bull of a man, still in his dressing gown. At the sight of him, and the thought of what he'd done to his daughter, I went wild with loathing. If I'd had a weapon on me, I'd have been sorely tempted to use it.

"I told him what I knew and threatened to go to his political enemies if he didn't let Cynthia go. The man seemed…thunderstruck. He denied everything I'd said, called me a liar and some other names I won't repeat, and said he'd see his daughter in her grave before he saw her married to me."

He paused, his eyes searching Rachel's face in the darkness. She remained on the rock where she was seated. To move closer, she sensed, would only feed the demons that tore at every part of him. He needed to tell this story, and she needed to listen.

A flicker of moonlight cast his eyes into black pits of shadow as he took a long breath and continued.

"I told him he had no choice. I was taking his daughter with me now, and I would see him ruined before the day was out. With that I turned on my heel and strode out of the room.

"The second floor of the house had an open landing with an iron balustrade that overlooked the marble foyer below. He caught up with me there and laid into me with his ivory-handled walking stick. I knocked it away from him and we started to grapple. I was younger and quicker, but he had the advantage of weight and bulk. When he started pushing me toward the balustrade, it struck me that he meant to shove me over the rail. That, and the thought of what the man had done to his daughter, gave me the strength to keep fighting...."

His jaw tightened as the words trailed off. Rachel made a futile attempt to clear the tightness from her throat. If Luke heard the little strangled noise she made, he gave no sign of it. He was lost in the memory of the woman he had adored—the woman he had killed for.

Rachel blinked back the tears she was too proud to let him see. How could she have been so naive as to think Luke might return her feelings? His heart was buried in the past, with the raven-haired beauty who would hold it forever.

All that remained now, Rachel told herself, was to endure to the end of this bitter tale. Then she would mount the spare horse, jab her heels into its flanks, and gallop down the trail without a backward glance.

As if drawn by the thought, her gaze flickered back

the way she and Luke had come, across the rolling plain that spread beyond the foot of the bluff. Clouds drifted across the face of the moon, casting shadows that moved, making the stark landscape seem to undulate and flow.

It was only by chance that her eye caught a flicker of movement along the road that cut across the hills like a long, pale scratch mark. At first glance, Rachel dismissed it as a shadow—the thin, dark shape that followed the road, breaking into dots, then coming together to form a single line, like a company of galloping riders.

Only when they paused, and she saw the flicker of torches being lit, did she realize what was happening.

Her father and the other ranchers had not waited for Luke to let her go. They were coming after her, moving closer by the second.

Chapter Fourteen

Rachel felt Luke move up behind her. His chest brushed her shoulder as he studied the column of riders that moved along the moonlit road. Even in this anxious moment, his closeness made her ache.

"They're coming fast," he muttered. "It won't be long before they pass the place where we turned off the road."

"And if they pick up our trail?"

He shot Rachel a dark glance, his silence allowing her to draw her own conclusion. If the riders followed the path they'd taken, it might still be possible for him to pick his way down the steep, rocky face of the bluff or to hide in the honeycomb of buttresses and hollows until they had taken her away. But that was not Luke's concern, she realized with a lurch of her heart. A mile beyond the bluff, a rutted wagon trail branched off the road, cutting south through clumps of sage and stands of juniper. It was the trail that led to Luke's ranch.

A nightmare vision flashed through Rachel's

mind—haystacks and buildings in flames, the screams of dying animals, and two terrified youths, battling to hold off a band of ruthless marauders. Would her father and brothers be among them? A shudder passed through her body. She fought to control her horror, to think, to act.

Her hand seized Luke's wrist, fingertips digging into hard bone and tendon. "I've got to stop them! You need to let me go, Luke!"

"Let you go?" A muscle twitched at the corner of his grim mouth. "You were never my prisoner, Rachel. You don't need my permission to leave."

"I know that." Her grip tightened on his wrist. If she was to reach the main road ahead of the riders there was no time to lose. But it tore at her to go with so much unsaid between them. With an all-out range war about to erupt, it was possible—even likely—that they would never meet again.

"I'll do my best to turn them back," she said, "or at least try to stall them for a few minutes."

His head jerked in a brusque nod. "I know a shortcut back to my ranch. With luck, I can get there ahead of them."

Rachel nodded, fighting back a flood of unspoken questions. What would he do when he reached the ranch? Would he scatter the sheep? Would he send his young herders and the dogs off with them and stay to face his enemies alone? Would he live through this terrible night?

Turning toward her, he caught her chin and cupped

it with his free hand, tilting her face into full view. His hooded eyes lay in shadow.

"I'm sorry, Rachel." His voice was like crushed granite, sharp-edged and gritty. "Under different circumstances, I might have gone to your father and asked his permission…" The words trailed off as if he'd thought the better of what he was about to say. "This isn't your fight. I should never have involved you in it. Go on, now, back to your family. Live your life and be happy. I can take care of my own problems."

Rachel gazed up at his stoic features, knowing he was wrong. Whether Luke liked it or not, this was her fight as well as his. If she'd had the sense to put Bart in his place before he forced her behind the granary, Luke would have gotten away clean and no one would have been the wiser. Now everything he held dear was in danger, and she had only herself to blame.

As for his taking care of his own problems, that was a lie as well. Luke could not stand alone against an armed mob. He needed her—needed her badly.

The truncated story he'd told her flashed through her mind—the raven-haired belle from Baton Rouge, her father's unspeakable crime and Luke's tragic love. It was, as he had said, an ugly story, but it was easy enough to surmise the ending. Luke had killed a profoundly evil man in self-defense and paid with his freedom. How could anyone hold that against him?

How could she?

His eyes devoured her face, as if hungry to find some sign of understanding. "Go, Rachel," he whispered. ''Our time's run out. If I don't make it through the night—''

Her kiss stopped his words—a wild, sensual, clinging kiss that held all of her heart. The earth seemed to pulse beneath them as he moaned and caught her close. His strong, sweet mouth took her, roused her, dizzied her with need. She could die kissing him like this, Rachel thought. The feel of his arms, the smoky taste of his mouth as his tongue set her body on fire…it was heaven, weighted with the hell of knowing she would have to let him go.

''I love you, Luke,'' she whispered against his searching lips. ''I don't care what you may have done—it's past and gone. And whatever happens tonight, or tomorrow, it won't change anything for me. I'll never stop loving you.''

''Don't, Rachel,'' he groaned, but even then his hands were moving over her body, skimming her breasts, cupping her hips to pull her in against his straining shaft. ''Lord…don't, girl. I want you so much I can hardly stand it. But there isn't time, and I'd only hurt you. You've got to get out of here, before it's too late.''

Rachel clung to him, burning with need, but knowing that every second she spent in his arms made his situation more dangerous. Luke was right. Their time had run out. She had to let him go.

Facing back a sob, she tore herself away from him. Luke's hands dropped to his side, making no move to hold her or to thrust her away. His eyes were dark hollows in his tired face.

"Go," he murmured. *"Vaya con diós, amor de mi vida."*

Only much later would she realize that he had said, *Go with God, love of my life.*

Blinded by tears, she plunged toward the spare horse Luke had brought along. The animal snorted and danced skittishly, but she managed to seize the reins and scramble into the saddle. Seconds later she was flying toward the long sloping side of the bluff, the night breeze buffeting her skirts and raking her hair. She knew that if she were to look back, she would see him standing in the moonlight, watching her. She did not look back. If she did, Rachel knew she would not be able to go on.

She took the zigzag trail with reckless haste, trusting to the instincts of the horse. If she failed to reach the road ahead of the mounted searchers, and if they missed the trail that led onto the bluff, she would be riding behind them, galloping frantically to catch up. If they left the road for the trail, and she met them while she was coming down the bluff, they would know that Luke was somewhere above her, and they would go after him.

Her best hope lay in meeting the searchers on the road at a point where they could not see which way she'd come. Only then would she have a chance of turning them back, or at least stalling them long enough for Luke to get away.

The breeze had quickened to a gusty wind. Ragged streamers of cloud swept across the sky, hiding the moon and darkening the path. When she dared to look down, Rachel could see the road below. It wove through the scrub like a discarded ribbon, bare and desolate, with no sign of the riders. Were they still approaching, or had they passed the cutoff and gone ahead? Rachel clung to the horse's neck, her lips moving in silent prayer as they plunged downward through the darkness.

The lurch of the horse as they hit level ground flung her backward in the saddle. She fought her way upright, jerking the reins to stop the animal's momentum. They had reached the road at last.

A frantic glance in both directions confirmed that no one else was in sight. But were the riders ahead of her or behind her?

Stroking the horse's neck to calm it, she strained her eyes and ears. It was too dark to look for tracks, but the air held no unsettled dust from the dry road. Did that mean the riders hadn't yet come this far, or that their passing had given the dust time to settle back to earth? Lives could depend on the answer to that question.

Rachel hesitated, weighing the odds. Then, praying that she'd guessed right, she wheeled the horse to the left and dug her heels into its flanks. The animal exploded into a gallop, bearing her back the way she and Luke had come, in the direction of the Carmody ranch.

Behind her, in the west, inky clouds were spilling over the horizon. Sheet lightning danced in the distance, followed seconds later by a growl of thunder. But Rachel paid no heed to the weather. All her attention was fixed on the pale stretch of road that wound its way into the darkness.

Where were they?

Suddenly, far ahead, she saw the flicker of torches held high. Giddy with relief, she urged the horse to a sprint. As they drew nearer, dark shapes materialized out of the night. The shapes became a half-dozen mounted men, each of them taking on his own form and features. The flickering light fell on the long, hawkish face of the lead rider. A little sob caught in Rachel's throat as she recognized her father.

Catching sight of his daughter, Morgan spurred the tall buckskin toward her. They met in a swirl of dust and plunging, snorting horses. He held up his torch as if to inspect her, his black eyes worried, probing.

"I'm all right!" Rachel exclaimed before he had a chance to ask. "You have nothing to worry about."

"Where's Vincente?" Morgan's voice was flinty with suppressed anger.

"Gone. He sent me back to you. Luke would never have harmed me. You have to believe that!"

Morgan gripped her arm. "Your mother's beside herself. We need to get back to her."

Swinging his mount, he seized the bridle of her horse and led it back toward the milling riders. In the dancing light, Rachel could make out the faces of Lem Carmody, Slade, and three neighboring ranchers who were longtime friends of her family. Her brothers were not with them. Neither was Bart.

"Rachel says she's fine," Morgan announced. "We've got what we came for. Let's go home!"

"The hell you say!" Lem Carmody bellowed from the darkness. "Vincente beat up my son and kidnapped your daughter, Morgan! In my book that's reason enough to burn the bastard's place to the ground and slaughter those damned filthy sheep— now, tonight, while we're all together!"

"No!" Rachel's voice rose in frantic protest. "Luke Vincente didn't kidnap me! He rescued me!"

"Sure he did!" Lem snorted and spat in the dust. "Come on, we're wasting time!"

"No!" Rachel swung her mount in front of him, blocking his way. "Listen to me, Mr. Carmody. Listen, all of you. Bart was behaving like a caveman! He'd torn my dress, and I was trying to fend him off when Luke came along! What you all saw was Luke fighting Bart to protect me, not the other way around!"

Lem Carmody started to grumble, but he was interrupted by one of the other ranchers.

"If Vincente was rescuin' you, why was he holdin' you at gunpoint? Answer that one, missy."

Rachel's hands whitened on the saddle horn. She knew she would be judged for what she was about to say, but she squared her chin and answered with the truth.

"Things were getting ugly. Luke was worried about what might happen if he left me. Pretending to take me hostage was the only way to get us both safely out of there. The gun was part of the act. I went with him of my own free will."

Behind her, Rachel heard the sharp intake of her

father's breath. All her life, Morgan had given her unconditional support and trust. Now she had betrayed that trust by falling in love with an enemy.

"I'm taking Rachel back to her mother," he said in the cold, flat voice he used when he was furious. "The rest of you can do what you damned well please, but I won't be going along."

"Come on, boys!" Lem Carmody pushed Rachel's horse aside and nudged his stocky piebald forward. "Just 'cause Morgan's got a weak stomach doesn't mean we can't do the job ourselves."

Slade followed him, avoiding Rachel's eyes as he slunk past, but the other three men hung back. "You said you was with us, Morgan," one of them quavered.

Morgan scowled, looking as proud and fierce as his Shoshone ancestors. "I came to find my daughter. As long as she's safe, and the sheep man didn't hurt her, I have no quarrel with him."

"You're sayin' you believe her?" Lem's voice oozed contempt. "Hellfire, the bastard's probably had her more ways than—"

"That's enough, Lem!" Morgan's low voice belied his fury, but Rachel knew the signs, and the knot in her stomach tightened. "I've never had reason to doubt my daughter's word. Until I have proof that her story isn't true, I'll choose to believe her." His blazing eyes flickered toward Rachel. "We've wasted enough time. Let's go."

Turning his back on the five men, Morgan swung his horse toward the Carmody ranch where his wife and sons waited for news. Rachel hesitated, her heart clenching like a fist as the drama continued behind him.

Lem swore at Morgan's back as the wind whipped around him. Then he turned his anger on the three ranchers who clustered together, heads bowed against the coming storm.

"Well, what'll it be, you lily-livered cowards?" Lem roared. "Which of you is man enough to come with me and take care of that stinking sheep ranch once and for all?"

The three exchanged glances, no doubt thinking of their worried families back at the ranch. As one, they turned and followed Morgan up the road.

Rachel did the same. She had upset her father enough for one night. She would be foolish to try his patience further.

"Cowards!" Lem howled at the three. "There's not a one of you fit to—"

The deafening boom of lightning, cracking across the sky like a giant whip, drowned out the rest of his words. Like a sudden, violent burst of tears, the rain began to fall, pelting down in torrents from the boiling black clouds. Lem swore loudly, then motioned to Slade. The two of them fell in at the rear of the procession, their torches doused by the rain.

Light-headed with relief, Rachel lifted her face to the storm, loving the water that streamed off her skin and soaked her hair and clothes. There would be no range war tonight, no shooting, no torching, no kill-

ing. The rain had brought the gift of a peaceful re-
prieve.

For a moment, Rachel allowed herself to think of
Luke, riding home in the storm, the rain soaking his
clothes and streaming off his hair. Luke. Safe and
free. For now.

But morning would bring the same dangers, the
same gut-wrenching worries. In his effort to find Miguel's killers, Luke had flung down the gauntlet. Men
like Lem Carmody would not rest until they had broken him for good.

As for herself—if she truly loved Luke, she would
stay away from him. Their being together would only
fan the flames of hatred and turn even her stubbornly
neutral father against him. If Morgan turned against
the sheep man, every rancher in the county would
follow his lead. Morgan commanded that kind of respect. That was why Lem had tried so hard to win
him over.

The tension reminded Rachel of a keg of black
powder, ready to explode at the touch of a match. She
and Luke could not be the ones to provide that match.
If full-scale violence broke out people would die—
and some of them, she knew, would be people she
loved.

The rain had turned leaden, trickling down Rachel's back and between her breasts, chilling her to
the bone. She huddled against the cold, shrinking into
herself as she imagined the days of her life without
Luke. She imagined those days passing into months,
the months into years. She imagined finding someone

else and trying to love him as she had loved Luke, knowing it would never be the same.

For Luke's sake and for her own, she would have to forget him. But every day that followed would be like the cold, dreary rain that drizzled from the sky. And the first days would be the worst of all.

Forcing Luke's image to the back of her mind, she nudged the horse to a trot and pressed forward to catch up with her father. It was time for the forgetting to begin.

Rachel awoke to the blinding glare of morning sunlight through her bedroom window. For a moment she lay still, her eyes closed against the harsh yellow brightness as she forced her mind to remember that this was the day she had resolved to stop thinking about Luke.

The trouble was, the very intention of forgetting brought a flood of remembered sensations—the aching contraction of her loins when he touched her breast, the taste of his mouth on hers, the way his hair curled and clung to her fingers when she reached up to pull him close. It was as if Luke was burned into every part of her, and her senses refused to let him go.

From the direction of the corral, the sound of hammering reached Rachel's ears. Yawning, she rubbed her eyes and forced herself to sit up. She had spent most of the night tossing in her bed or staring up at the dark ceiling, her emotions churning. Only as the sky had begun to gray had she finally slipped into an exhausted slumber.

She was grateful that her family had let her sleep this morning; but the extra hours in bed had only put off the inevitable. Much as she'd dreaded the moment, it was time to get up and face them all.

Her gown and petticoat lay sodden on the floor, where she had stripped them off in the dead of night. Once the frothy yellow voile had been one of her favorites, but no amount of washing would remove the mud stains from the skirt, and no seamstress's skill could mend the rip where Bart had torn it off her shoulder. It was good for nothing but the rag box now.

Rachel felt like a candidate for the rag box herself as she staggered to the washstand and splashed her face with cool water. A glance in the mirror revealed bloodshot eyes, matted hair and chapped lips. Her head ached dully, and her body was damp and clammy beneath the thin muslin nightgown.

She frowned sternly at her reflection in the mirror. No, by heaven, she wasn't going to be sick! The last thing she wanted was to spend the day lying in bed and feeling sorry for herself. That would be a surefire recipe for misery. Today she needed the distraction of hard work, like mending the pasture fence, oiling harness or mucking out the stable.

Setting her jaw, Rachel jerked on her denims and boots and shrugged into a clean cotton work shirt. A dozen hard brush strokes slicked back her hair to the point where she could tie it with a bandana at the nape of her neck. An accidental glimpse of herself in the wardrobe mirror confirmed that she looked tired, sad and uncaring. Never mind. It didn't matter. No one who gave a fig about her appearance was going to see her today.

She was walking toward the door when everything caved in on her like an avalanche—the danger, the loneliness, the gut-grinding fear that would not leave her until she knew he was safe—or dead.

Oh, Luke. It came like physical pain, so real and intense that she doubled over, clutching the door frame with white-knuckled fingers.

Luke…my love…my dearest, only love.

Chapter Fifteen

Like a knitter picking up stitches from an unraveling shawl, Rachel groped for the ragged edges of her self-control. Gripping the door frame, she forced herself to take long, deep breaths, filling her lungs with the sunlit morning air and the aromas of bacon, biscuits and eggs from the kitchen below. She would be all right, she told herself. She would make herself be all right.

She would go downstairs, eat, smile and make pleasant conversation, she resolved. She would behave as if everything was fine—as if last night's encounter with Luke had meant nothing, and she had no concern for what became of him.

Coldhearted? Yes. But it was her only hope of protecting Luke and her family from the hatred that threatened to destroy them all.

Squaring her shoulders, Rachel strode across the landing. She had just reached the top of the stairs when a gunshot, muted by distance, rang out from the ridge above the ranch.

For an instant her heart clenched with dread. Then, as two more shots followed in quick succession, she recognized the familiar signal—one that had always brought a surge of joy whenever she heard it.

Breakfast forgotten, she flew down the stairs and out onto the porch. She was scanning the ridge, one hand shading her eyes against the glare, when her mother hurried out onto the porch.

"Can you see anything?" she asked, a little out of breath. "Your eyes are better than mine."

Rachel squinted into the yellow sunlight, searching the high trail that emerged from the aspens to wind downward along the ridge to the foothills. At first she could see nothing. Then her eyes caught a flicker of movement that slowly became two riders moving single file, trailing a pack mule behind them.

"There—just above the rocks! See them?"

Cassandra stretched on tiptoe, straining upward as if the extra inches would give her a better view of the trail. "I see something! Is it—?"

"Yes!" Rachel had begun to wave frantically. "Look, they've seen us! They're waving back! It's Ryan and Molly!"

While her mother bustled off to the kitchen to arrange for more breakfast, Rachel dashed out into the yard to join her father, who had just come out of the barn. "There!" Rachel pointed to the moving spot along the distant thread of trail. Morgan nodded, his careworn face relaxing into a smile. Ryan's presence would be a blessing to them all, especially today.

Rachel had adored Morgan's younger half brother

from the time she was old enough to toddle behind his long-legged stride. In the twenty years since his marriage and his move to a mountain ranch on the Canadian border, her family had seen far too little of him. Ryan's visits were always joyous occasions, especially when he brought along his wife Molly and their two adopted Cheyenne children. Mary Bright Wing and John Dark Eagle would be grown by now, Rachel realized, counting the years. They would be pursuing their own lives, leaving Ryan and his beautiful Molly to make this visit alone.

Cassandra had returned from the kitchen by the time the two riders cantered their mounts in through the gate. As they reined in the horses, Rachel broke away from her parents and bounded across the yard like a ten-year-old. At the sight of her, Ryan whooped like an Indian and flung himself out of the saddle. Her welcoming embrace almost knocked him off his feet.

Laughing, he pried her away from him, holding her at arm's length for inspection. "Rachel! Lord, girl, what happened to my little fishing partner? It's a grown woman that's come back from that fancy eastern school!"

She grinned up at him, grateful beyond words that he had come. Ryan had aged in the three years since she had last seen him. The creases had deepened at the corners of his twinkling blue eyes, and his dark blond hair was lightly silvered at the temples. A leg broken in a hunting accident had left him with a slight limp. Otherwise he appeared as lean and athletic and handsome as ever.

Glancing past his shoulder, Rachel saw Ryan's wife laughing down at them from the back of her horse. She, too, had been touched by the years. But even with her suntanned face etched by laugh lines and her waist-length golden braids streaked with platinum, Molly Ivins Tolliver was still the most stunning woman Rachel had ever seen. Raised by the Cheyenne, she had spent her life outdoors, and she moved with the grace of a powerful golden cat. Perhaps if time allowed, Rachel thought, she would ask Molly to pose for some sketches, or even a portrait. She would make a spectacular model.

But something about Molly suddenly struck Rachel as strange. The Molly she remembered would have been out of the saddle in a flash, striding across the yard to embrace Cassandra and Morgan. Instead she sat patiently on the horse, as Ryan disentangled himself from Rachel and walked back to help her dismount. She placed her hands on his shoulders, and he swung her to the ground so gently that she might have been made of porcelain.

Only as the morning breeze blew Molly's loose flannel shirt against her body did Rachel see the reason for his care. Molly, at the age of forty-four, was well along with her first child.

"Oh!" Cassandra's hands went to her mouth. "Oh, my dearest Molly!" Darting across the yard, she flung her arms around her tall sister-in-law. "What a surprise! Why on earth didn't you let us know?"

"But we did!" Molly exclaimed. "Ryan wrote two months ago to say we'd be coming! You mean to tell me—?" Her words ended in a sigh of resignation. Lost mail was a fact of life in the remote country where they lived.

"I've talked Molly into having the baby here," Ryan said. "Given her age, and this being her first time…"

There was no need for him to say more. The worry was there, in his eyes and in his voice. For this precious birth, he wanted his Molly where she would have the support of other women, and where a doctor could be summoned if anything went wrong.

"But how wonderful!" Cassandra's radiant smile swept away the uncertain shadow that had fallen over them all. "You'll be staying for a while, and it will be so much fun, having a sweet little baby to hold. Wait till I tell Mei Li! She'll be thrilled!"

Linking her arm with Molly's she guided her toward the house, chatting excitedly all the way. Rachel fell into step with Ryan and her father, but her eyes were on the two women. What would it be like, she wondered, to be a part of that secret society of women who had made love with their men and carried babies inside their bodies? The things that came so naturally to them were couched in discreet terms when *she* was present. Now Rachel found herself aching to be part of that intimacy, a sharer of those dark, wonderful woman-secrets.

Would it ever happen to her? Would she ever pass the initiation and join the club? Having grown up on a ranch, she was not unfamiliar with the facts of life. But seeing the herd bull mount a fertile cow was one thing. Lying in Luke's arms with his body thrusting deep and hot into hers would be quite another, almost beyond imagining...

Rachel gulped back a groan as she realized where her thoughts had taken her. Every path her mind wandered seemed to lead back to Luke. His face was there when she closed her eyes; his voice whispered to her on the prairie wind. Every part of her held some memory of him, with a yearning so raw that she wanted to curse. She had been happy before she knew him. Why couldn't she be happy again now that they were apart?

"Where are your boys, Morgan?" Ryan's question broke into her reverie.

"Riding fence with the neighbor boy on the north pasture. I promised they could take a lunch and go fishing if they finished before noon."

"They're with Slade?" Rachel's heart sank. "After what happened last night?"

Morgan shot her a cautionary glance. "Lem came by this morning, before you were up, to make peace," he said. "Slade came with him. When the boy offered to help Jacob and Josh with the fence, I couldn't very well turn him down without offending Lem and starting last night's trouble all over again. It's past and done with, Rachel. I won't war with my neighbors."

"What's all this?" Ryan's brows shot upward. "Is something wrong between you and Lem?"

''I said it's past and done with,'' Morgan growled. ''No reason you even need to know about it.''

Ryan's eyes flashed to meet Rachel's. Both of them knew that the more something was bothering Morgan, the less inclined he was to talk about it. Clearly, last night was still bothering him a great deal.

Sooner or later, Rachel knew, the truth would emerge. Ryan would insist on knowing everything. But how much should she tell him?

In her growing-up years, Ryan had always been her confessor, the one who heard her little sins and granted her absolution with a smile and a hug. If she did not guard her words now, he would pry the whole story out of her, including her relationship with Luke. She needed a few minutes alone to think about what she would say.

''You two go on inside and visit,'' she offered. ''I'll turn out your horses and mule and fetch one of Thomas's boys to carry your things upstairs.''

When Ryan hesitated, she forced herself to grin at him. ''Go on! I haven't become so fancified that I can't get a little mule sweat on my hands!''

Ryan laughed as he limped across the yard to rejoin Morgan, but Rachel had not missed the knowing flicker in his keen blue eyes. He would be back. It was only a question of how soon.

She had unsaddled Molly's horse and was starting on Ryan's when he walked into the barn. His long shadow fell across the straw as he limped over to the mule and began unlashing the bulky pack.

''I managed to convince Morgan you'd need my

help with the mule,'' he said in his straightforward way, ''but you know why I'm here. You look as if somebody's just died. Your old man's as testy as a buffalo bull with the mange, and your mother's so fluttery I can barely get near her. I don't think I'm just imagining that we came at a bad time. I'm only hoping it isn't my fault.''

This last was said with a wink, intended to put Rachel at ease. But she felt more like crying than laughing. She stared down at Ryan's boots, afraid that if she looked up into his face she might burst into tears.

When she did not speak, he cupped her chin and lifted it, forcing her to look up at him. ''What is it, girl? We've always been able to trust each other. Even if there's nothing I can do to help, I need to understand what's going on.''

When he released her she turned back to the horse and began fumbling with the bridle. At first no words would come, but Ryan gave her time. As they unloaded the animals and rubbed them down, the story emerged—slowly at first, as each word was forced from her mouth, then suddenly surging like a flash flood down a dry gully.

She told him almost everything—how she'd come to be with Luke the day of the rain, how the masked riders had nearly driven the sheep to their deaths, and how she'd recognized one of them as her brother. She told him about the murder of Luke's elderly herdsman, and about the threats against Luke's dogs, his sheep and his ranch. And finally, she told him what had happened last night at the party.

Ryan listened quietly, his fingers untangling the burrs from the mane of Molly's horse. His expressive blue eyes reflected, in turn, surprise, dismay, shock and compassion.

"And no one else knows you saw one of the twins with those masked riders? You haven't told your father?"

Rachel shook her head.

"And you haven't confronted Jacob and Josh? You haven't demanded to know if either of them was there when the old man was beaten?"

Again she shook her head, her lips forming a thin barrier to the words she could not speak. Anyone who was present at Miguel's beating would be an accessory to murder, or worse. The safest and most honest way she could protect her beloved brothers was simply not to know.

But the weight of uncertainty was crushing the life out of her.

Ryan put his hands on her shoulders. "Poor little girl," he said, and at his simple words of kindness, Rachel felt herself crumbling around the edges. She began to shake uncontrollably, her breath coming in tightly constricted sobs.

"I don't know what to do," she whispered. "What's right...what's wrong... When I try to see clearly, it's nothing but a blur. Why does life have to be such a mixed-up mess, Ryan? Why can't things be simple, the way they used to be?"

He made a move as if to gather her close, then checked himself. Years ago, a comforting embrace would have been a natural gesture. But Rachel was a woman now, and it was no longer the proper thing to do.

"Things are never as simple as they seem when we're young," he said gently. "It takes growing up to understand that."

"Then I'm not at all sure I like being grown up."

He studied her for the space of a long silent breath. "Tell me about this sheep man of yours," he said.

Rachel felt her heart lurch. She had avoided any mention of what had happened between her and Luke, but Ryan had missed nothing—his choice of words had made that clear.

But how could she begin to describe a man like Luke, who loved and hated with equal passion—Luke whose fierce gentleness had awakened needs she had not even known she possessed.

"He's...a very proud man," she began awkwardly. "All he wants is to hold on to what's his. But people like Lem won't leave him in peace. If things don't change, sooner or later he'll have to start fighting back." She inhaled sharply. "You'll find this out sooner or later. He served time in prison for killing a man—an evil man, in self-defense. He's bitter, but he's not a criminal."

"And how do you know all this?"

She dropped her gaze to hide the color that flooded in her cheeks. That simple gesture, she realized, would be enough to confirm Ryan's suspicions. He was experienced enough to recognize a woman in love.

"Little Rachel." He shook his head as he caught the mule's halter to lead it out to the corral. "What are you going to do?"

"I'm going to stay away from him," she said. "There's too much at stake here, too many people who could get hurt."

"Have you told your parents?"

"My mother's no fool. I'm sure she's guessed. But my father acts as if he doesn't want to know. You won't tell him, will you?"

"You know me better than that." He matched her shorter strides as they led the horses and mule to the corral gate, turned them in with the other animals, and headed back toward the house. "The last thing I want is to make more trouble for you."

"And I for you," Rachel said. "Stay out of this, Ryan. Molly needs you, and this isn't your fight."

"Wrong. It's our family's fight, so that makes it mine. But it would help to know exactly who it is we're fighting, wouldn't it?" His eyes twinkled with sardonic humor.

Rachel did not return his smile. "Please, Ryan. If anything were to happen to you, especially now, with a baby on the way, I'd never forgive myself."

They had reached the house and were mounting the porch steps. The aromas of bacon, eggs and fresh coffee floated out through the screen door. A mourning dove called from the roof of the chicken coop, its cry sweet and peaceful on the clear morning air.

"Please!" Rachel caught his arm as they reached the porch. "Promise me you won't get involved in this!"

He grinned and patted her hand. "I promised you I'd keep still. That will have to do. Now, smile for me, sweetheart. Let's make them think we've been talking about what you learned at that fancy eastern art school of yours."

Arm in arm they entered the dining room, where Morgan, Cassandra and Molly were seated at the table. Rachel's parents, who had eaten earlier, were sipping coffee while Molly wolfed down a small mountain of Thomas Chang's scrambled eggs. She looked up, grinning, as Ryan and Rachel pulled out their chairs. "Forgive me for not waiting. I—*we*—were starved."

"Excuses! You've talked about nothing but Thomas's cooking for the past three days." Ryan grinned back at her, brushing his knuckles lightly along her cheek before he seated himself. The love in his eyes seemed to light the whole room. What she wouldn't give, Rachel thought, to have a man look at her that way, especially—

No, she could not let herself keep thinking about Luke, not now, not ever.

Molly's haunting violet eyes sparkled back at her husband. She looked radiant but was clearly exhausted from the long, arduous ride over mountain trails. The child she carried was a sweet miracle after so many barren years, but Rachel could understand

Ryan's concern, and she murmured a private prayer that all would go well for them.

"Molly's been telling us about John and Mary," Cassandra said. "Mary has two years of medical school left. Then she wants to go back to the reservation and help her people."

"Is she happy, Molly?" Rachel helped herself to three strips of bacon. Mary Bright Wing, Ryan and Molly's adopted Cheyenne daughter, had always been a serious child, hungry for knowledge and quick to learn, but who would have guessed she would choose such a difficult path?

"It's what she's always wanted," Molly said. "But it's been a struggle for her, both as a Cheyenne and as a woman. My worst fear is that her own people won't accept her now that she's been trained in *ve hoe* medicine. After all she's been through, that would be a terrible blow."

"Mary's a strong girl," Ryan said. "She'll find her way."

"What about John?" Rachel asked, thinking fondly of the younger boy, who had been her junior companion in mischief and misadventure through their growing-up years. Ryan had always claimed that trouble multiplied by a factor of ten when John Dark Eagle and Rachel were together.

"He's minding the ranch for us," Ryan said. "John's very content in the mountains. He's never wanted any other life."

"Especially since he met Little Swan," Molly added, laughing. "She lives in the canyon with her parents, who guard her like the treasure she is. Such a pretty thing, and so sweet. The two of them are counting the days until they're old enough to marry. Judging from the way they look at each other, I imagine we'll have grandchildren running all over the place before long.''

''And Mary?'' Cassandra asked. ''She was always such a beautiful girl, with those big, dark eyes. Does she have a young man?''

Molly sighed. ''Not that she mentions in her letters. She's probably too busy with her studies for much of a social life.'' She downed another forkful of scrambled eggs, savoring Thomas Chang's secret mélange of wild herbs and seasonings, then reached for her coffee cup. As Molly sipped thoughtfully, Rachel braced herself for what she knew was coming next.

''You were always surrounded by boys, Rachel,'' Molly said. ''Is there anyone special? Not that I'm trying to rush you, but I know your mother would love some grandchildren underfoot, and as for this little mischief—'' She patted her swollen belly. ''He, or she, is going to need some playmates when we come to visit, and your brothers are far too young and scatterbrained to provide them anytime soon.''

Rachel had been dreading the question, but Molly's approach had been so innocent and well meant that she could not help smiling. ''I confess I hadn't thought that far ahead,'' she demurred. ''But right now, the answer is no, there's no one—''

Her words were cut short by a sound that galvanized them all. They froze at the table, hearing the ominous cadence of approaching hoofbeats—a lone horseman—thundering through the gate and up to the house, the scream of the horse as the bit jerked tight, pulling it to a sudden halt.

Morgan and Ryan scrambled to their feet, but before they could rush outside, Slade burst into the dining room, wild-eyed and out of breath.

"What is it, Slade?" Morgan had gone white around the mouth. Cassandra's hand was ice-cold where it gripped Rachel's arm.

"It's that damned sheep man!" Slade gasped, sagging against a corner of the table. "You should've let us go after him last night. The bastard just shot Josh."

Morgan's face turned ashen. Cassandra groped blindly for her husband's hand and clasped it as if she'd fallen into a whirlpool and could not swim. Rachel felt strangely paralyzed, unable to breathe, speak, think or feel. *Not Josh! Please, God, not sweet, funny, gentle Josh!*

It was Ryan who recovered enough to take charge. "Where's Jacob?" he demanded.

"He stayed with Josh," Slade said. "They're down along the north fence, past that outcrop of red rocks— that's where the sheep man was hiding when he shot Josh. I saw the bastard ride away after he done it."

Rachel stifled a cry. *You're wrong!* she wanted to scream at Slade. *It couldn't have been Luke! He would never do such a thing!* But she held her tongue. With Josh's life hanging in the balance, this was no time to argue blame.

"How badly is he hurt?" The question had to be asked, and Ryan chose to be the one to ask it.

"Bullet went in his chest and out his back," Slade said. "He was still breathin' when I left to come here, but, Lord, I never seen so much blood!"

Cassandra looked as if she were about to faint. Molly moved to her side and slipped a supporting arm around her shoulders.

"We'll need you to take us to the boys," Ryan told Slade. "Morgan, you can go with him. We'll need the wagon—I'll hitch up the team and bring Cassandra and Rachel with me."

"No!" Cassandra had found her voice. "He's my boy, and I need to get there as fast as I can. I'll ride with Morgan and Slade. Saddle the horses while I get my medical kit."

"I'll see to things here," Molly volunteered softly. "He'll need a clean bed and plenty of hot water, and I brought along some of the good herbs I use for poultices…" Her words trailed off as the same thought struck her that had struck them all. By the time they got Josh back to the house he might not need anything except a clean suit of clothes and a pine box.

They moved like automatons, each of them gripped by a dread too awful to voice. Cassandra flew upstairs for her bag of medical supplies while Morgan and Slade sprinted for the corral. By the time she came back downstairs they had saddled two of the fastest horses. Seconds later the three of them were racing for the north fence that separated the Tolliver ranch from Luke's property.

While Ryan hauled the wagon into the yard and brought out the harness for the draft horses, Rachel and Molly raided the bedrooms for quilts, blankets and pillows to soften the wagon bed. Rachel was back outside in time to help buckle the husky bays into their traces. They did not speak of what had happened. It was as if a single word might tip the balance of fate in the wrong direction and shatter all hope of denial.

Molly stood on the porch, watching with tragic eyes as the wagon lumbered toward the gate. She would alert Johnny Chang, who would inform his parents and send one of his sons galloping to Sheridan for the doctor, or even go himself. No one dared voice what they all feared—the possibility that the doctor might not be needed.

Ryan drove the bays hard over the rutted washboard road, slapping the reins like whips onto their broad, coppery backs. Rachel spread the quilts and blankets as best she could manage in the jouncing, slamming wagon bed. Then she clambered up onto the bench to sit beside him.

Ryan did not look at her. He was hunched over the reins, his lips pressed together in a grim line. Rachel clung to the seat, feeling the weight of his silence—a weight that grew heavier by the minute, until she could no longer bear it.

"Luke wouldn't do this, Ryan," she said. "He's

not that kind of person—and my father's never raised a hand against him.''

''But at least one of your brothers did. You told me that yourself, Rachel.''

''But I didn't tell Luke!'' Rachel shot off the bench as the wagon hit a rut and scrambled to regain her place. ''He suspected I was shielding someone, but he never found out who that person might be. *I* don't even know which one of the twins I saw!''

''Then maybe something happened this morning,'' Ryan said in a leaden voice. ''Maybe the boys were messing around, doing something he didn't like, and he—''

''No!'' Rachel grabbed the side of the wagon as it lurched around the last bend. ''He wouldn't! No matter what was happening, Luke wouldn't shoot an innocent boy, especially one of my own brothers. He—''

''There they are.'' Ryan's head jerked to the left.

Following his gaze, Rachel saw the horses clustered along the distant barbed wire fence. Figures were huddled around something in the long grass. She recognized her mother, her father, and Slade, who was still sitting his horse. As the wagon rumbled closer, she caught sight of Jacob, kneeling on the ground, his hands balled over his eyes, his shoulders heaving spasmodically.

''Hurry,'' she begged Ryan. But Ryan needed no urging. The horses had left the wagon road now, and were pounding their way across the open grassland. The wheels bumped and flew, flinging Rachel off the seat. She clung to the side of the wagon until it had stopped. Then she dropped to the ground and raced across the remaining distance.

Was her brother alive or dead? Seconds from now, she would know.

Chapter Sixteen

As Rachel stumbled through the grass, she could see Josh lying on his back with his eyes closed. His shirt had been torn away, and his chest was packed and bound with strips of muslin. His face was as white and still as alabaster, and his body lay in a veritable lake of crimson. Rachel's heart lurched as she realized she was looking at her brother's blood.

Her throat moved. "Is he—"

"He's alive." Cassandra's face and arms were smeared with red. Her voice was a strained whisper. "But he's lost so much blood…" She swallowed hard. "Bring a blanket, Rachel. We'll need it for a stretcher to get him into the wagon."

Ryan backed the wagon in close. Rachel seized the topmost blanket and helped her mother work it beneath Josh's body. By the time they finished, her own hands and sleeves were streaked with blood.

"Help us, Slade. You, too, Jacob." Morgan's face was a stoic mask as he directed the moving of his son to the wagon bed. Ryan, Slade and Rachel took one side of the blanket, Morgan, Jacob and Cassandra the other, supporting the fragile body as best they could. Josh seemed as insubstantial as a bird as they carried him to the wagon. He moaned as they shifted him onto the planks, the sound as startling as a scream in the morning silence.

Cassandra scrambled in beside him. "I'll ride here," she said, touching Josh's white face as if memorizing the colorless features. "Rachel, you take my horse."

Morgan swung onto the wagon seat without a word and took the reins. He would be the one to take his boy home. This time the ride would be slow, with the urgency to get Josh home warring with the need to avoid bumping his fragile, wounded body.

Slade had remounted. "Reckon I'll go home," he said. "Uncle Lem will want to know about this. But don't you worry. Whatever happens, we're gonna find that sheep man and see that he pays!" Flinging this last remark at Rachel, he spurred his horse. Iron shoes spat gravel as he wheeled away.

Rachel mounted her mother's gray mare, her limbs leaden and her stomach churning with the sickness of dread. Was this tragedy her fault? Could she have prevented it if she'd behaved differently last night?

Muttering something about helping Molly get things ready, Ryan galloped off on Morgan's tall buckskin. That left Rachel to ride behind the wagon with Jacob, trailing Josh's pinto alongside their horses.

Jacob rode with his shoulders hunched and his

black hair hanging down in his eyes. His bare arms and torso were smeared with blood. Rachel surmised that he had used his shirt in an effort to stanch his brother's wound. His face, what Rachel could see of it, was blotchy and swollen from weeping. From the moment of their conception, Jacob and Josh had been inseparable, like two halves of the same person. Rachel could only imagine what her brother must be going through now.

Reaching out, she laid a comforting hand on his back. At her touch, a shudder passed through his body. A strangled sob broke in his throat.

"What happened, Jacob?" she asked.

He exhaled brokenly, his shoulders quivering beneath her hand. "Lord, Rachel, I don't know. Josh was helping me mend a hole in the fence. I heard a shot, and the next thing I knew, he was lying there on the ground with blood…all that blood…" Jacob's body heaved with anguish. "I don't know! I've gone through it a hundred times in my mind, asking myself how I could have saved him. And I don't know—it all comes down to that!"

"You say Josh was helping you mend the fence. Where was Slade?"

"Slade had left the wire cutters a half mile back where we'd fixed the last bad spot. He rode back to get them. After Josh was shot, he came tearing up on his horse, said he'd seen the sheep man behind the rocks, with a rifle, said he'd seen him ride off."

"And you believed him?" Rachel demanded.

Jacob groaned. "What was to believe? Josh was

shot. I thought he might be dead. The worst part was, if the sheep man had shot anybody, it should've been me!''

''What?'' Rachel stared at him. Scalded by her gaze, Jacob hung his head.

''I—Slade and I—we've played some tricks on the sheep man. No harm, mind you. Just chasing the sheep, teasing the dogs, things like that. Josh, he wouldn't go along—said he wouldn't cause trouble for somebody who was only trying to make a living.'' Jacob's voice broke. ''Don't you see? If that sheep man was set on shooting somebody, it should've been me, not Josh... Lord, Rachel, it should be me lying in that wagon right now! I only wish to heaven it was!''

Rachel stared at the rear of the wagon, where it rolled ahead of them in the brutal sunlight. She gazed at her father's rigid, solitary back where he guided the team as carefully as if they were walking on eggshells. Then she glanced back at her brother. There was one question that remained to be asked. If she did not ask it now, she knew she might never get another chance.

''Jacob,'' she said, speaking gently, ''the night that sheep wagon was burned, and the old man was beaten, do you know about it?''

He nodded wretchedly. A fresh tear trickled down his salt-encrusted cheek.

''Were you there? Did you see it?''

The breath that rushed into his lungs was like the sound of something tearing apart. ''No,'' he whispered. "Slade wanted us to sneak out that night, and I was all for it, but Josh wouldn't let me. He said he had a feeling something bad was going to happen, and that if I tried to go, he was going to wake Pa and tell him. I was so mad I wouldn't speak to him all the next day."

Rachel felt the lift of relief, in spite of all that had happened. Her brothers had not been involved in Miguel's death. They were innocent.

But they had not escaped punishment.

"Who else was with Slade that night?" she asked, her heart drumming a high-pitched tattoo in her ears.

Jacob shrugged. "We never knew for sure, but I'd guess it was Bart and some of the ranch hands. Slade did tell us they burned the sheep wagon and gave the herder a good scare. He called us chicken for not showing up. We didn't know until we heard it from the sheep man last night that the old man had died." He sucked in his breath, the sound like the rasp of a claw in his tight chest. "And now Josh... Oh, Lord, he didn't do anything. Why'd he have to go and get shot? I was the bad one! It should've been me!"

He began to rock back and forth in the saddle, his arms holding his sides. Rachel edged her horse against his and slipped her arm around his bony young shoulders. They rode that way, leaning on each other, until they passed between the gateposts of the Tolliver ranch.

The hours that followed would always remain a blur in Rachel's memory. She would recall the crimson-stained sheets and wrappings, the endless treks to fetch hot water, and the pungent aroma of Molly's poultices. She would remember her mother's stoic face and the sight of Josh's sweaty black hair clinging to his waxen skin. She would remember her father, reeling between rage and grief, alternately hovering over his son and staring out the window in helpless fury.

The bullet had passed at an angle through the right side of Josh's chest, a hand's breadth below the collarbone, and gone cleanly out the back just below the shoulder blade. Miraculously, it appeared to have missed his heart and lungs, but he had lost a staggering amount of blood.

He lay still now, his eyes closed, his breath barely strong enough to stir the bit of feather that Mei Li had placed beneath his nostrils. Chang's tiny, silver-haired wife had tottered in on her bound feet, bringing a pot of ginseng tea which Cassandra had carefully spooned between her son's bloodless lips. For all their ministrations, Josh had not opened his eyes or shown any other sign of gaining strength. But at least he was still alive.

Johnny Chang had ridden off like a madman that morning to fetch the doctor from Sheridan. Now the sun was getting low in the sky, and there was no sign of him or the doctor's high-topped buggy. Ryan had ushered the exhausted Molly to bed, but the rest of the family continued to keep watch, hovering around Josh's bed or standing on the porch, staring into the twilight and straining their ears for the sound of approaching hoofbeats that could signal the doctor's arrival.

Darkness had fallen and the moon was rising when Jacob burst into the house. "Somebody's coming!" His bloodshot eyes burned with hope. "I can hear their horses! Maybe it's Johnny and the doctor!"

But it was neither the doctor nor Johnny Chang who clattered in the yard a few minutes later. It was Lem Carmody, with Slade trailing him like an obedient whippet. Rachel was relieved to see that Bart had not come with them.

Morgan and Rachel had come out onto the porch, leaving Jacob to sit with his mother. They waited as Lem climbed awkwardly out of the saddle and lumbered up the front steps with Slade at his heels.

"Slade brought me the news," he said, laying a thick hand on Morgan's shoulder. "I'm right sorry about your boy, Morgan. I rode over here to see if there was anything I could do."

Morgan gazed past him into the darkness, his mouth a bitter line. "Are you a saint who can save my son with your prayers, or a doctor who can save him with your medicine?"

"No," Lem said. "But I can round up enough of the boys to go after that murderin' sheep man and get rid of him once and for all. Are you with us now, Morgan, after what he done to your boy?"

Morgan's eyes flashed in the darkness. Rachel's heart seemed to stop beating as she waited for her father's reply.

"You're asking me now, Lem, when all I can think

about is Josh, lying in that bed?'' Morgan asked indignantly. "If the sheep man did what Slade claims, I'll see him turned over to the law and I'll gladly watch him hang. But I have another son to think of, and I won't see Jacob grow up thinking that mob violence is the way to see justice done.''

Startled by Morgan's vehemence, Lem took a step backward, then cleared his throat and spat over the porch rail. "Do you know what I think?'' he growled. "I think you're yellow. You're sitting pretty here, with your land and your money and your fine family, and you don't have the guts to risk any trouble, not even to avenge your son's death!''

The silence that followed this outburst was so absolute and so terrible that Rachel felt her knees go weak beneath her. Morgan had always been slow to anger, but Lem had clearly pushed him over the brink.

Holding her breath, she waited for the explosion. When it came, Morgan's words were as soft as the step of a stalking panther and cold enough to freeze the sun to a crackling ball of ice.

"I'll thank you to remember that my son is still alive, Lem,'' he said. "And I'll also thank you to take that sniveling little weasel you call your nephew and get off my property before I get a shotgun and run you off.''

Lem's pudgy face had paled to the color of bread dough. He took another step backward. Then his eyes flickered toward Slade, and he nodded. The younger man tossed his cigarette to the ground, peeled his lean body away from the rail and followed his uncle off the porch.

Lem made a beeline for the horses, but Slade paused, turning back at the foot of the porch steps. His acid gaze fixed on Rachel where she stood in the shadow of the doorway.

"This is all your fault!" he hissed at her. "You ought to be ashamed of yourself, you sheep man's whore!"

Rachel stood frozen in place as he stalked away, feeling as if someone had just drenched her in blood. She knew her father had heard Slade's parting shot, and that there would be a reckoning. Quivering, she braced herself for what was bound to come next.

Morgan gazed after the vanishing riders for what seemed like an eternity before he turned toward her. His face was impassive in the moonlight, revealing nothing. "Is it true?" he asked in a tightly controlled voice.

Rachel's gaze dropped to her own clenched hands. She forced herself to lift her head and meet his anthracite eyes. "No," she whispered, knowing the time for lies was over. "Not the way Slade put it. I've done nothing to shame our family. But I've spent enough time with Luke Vincente to know that I love him…and to know that he couldn't have done this terrible thing to Josh. He would never do anything to hurt me or my family. I'd stake my life on that!"

He studied her sadly, and the flicker of heartbreak in his eyes told her how much she had hurt him. "Rachel, I won't condemn you for anything you might have done," he said. "But a woman in love is no judge of a man's character or his motives. Know that I meant every word I said to Lem. I mean to get to the bottom of what happened this morning, and if guilt points to Vincente, I'll see the man behind bars or dangling from the end of—"

"Morgan!" Cassandra's cry echoed down the stairs from Josh's bedroom. "Come here! Hurry!"

Morgan and Rachel raced inside, to be met by an elated Jacob. "It's Josh!" His tearstained face was shining with relief. "His eyes are open! He's awake!"

By the time the doctor arrived twenty minutes later, Josh had closed his eyes and drifted back into sleep. He was not strong enough to speak, but his face showed a hint of color now, and his breathing had become more regular. The doctor's careful inspection confirmed that Josh had passed the crisis. Barring unforeseen complications, he would live.

"The boy's had good treatment," the old man observed as he wiped his instruments and laid them in his black leather bag. "I've heard city doctors say that heathen medicine—Indian, Chinese, or what have you—is nothing but superstitious hogwash, but I've seen enough cures in this country to know better. You and your friends did right by this lad."

Jacob was sobbing openly. Rachel wrapped her arms around him, holding him in a long, hard hug that needed no words. As she hurried downstairs to give Chang the good news and ask him to prepare a quick supper for the doctor, she discovered that her knees had gone watery beneath her. Only now did she realize how terrified she had been.

She left the elderly cook grinning as he stoked the fire in the stove and set a kettle of soup on an open burner. Josh had been a favorite of his from the time the boys were big enough to toddle into the kitchen and tug at his apron.

Crossing the parlor, Rachel felt a wave of dizziness. She'd intended to go back upstairs to her family, but the warm, steamy air in Josh's room had been rank with the odors of disinfectant, herbal potions, blood and sweat. A breath of air would do her good, she told herself as she walked back toward the kitchen and slipped out the screen door, onto the back porch.

The cool night breeze rushed over her as she sank down on the stoop. Closing her eyes, Rachel gulped it into her lungs, filling her senses with the sweetness of prairie grass and damp earth. Everything would be all right, she told herself. Her dear, lighthearted Josh was not going to die at the age of eighteen with his adult life unlived. Jacob would not be torn apart by the loss of his twin—a loss that could have thrown him into a spiral of despair and self-destruction. Her parents would not spend their day in quiet mourning, weighed down by the knowledge that they would never know their son as the man he would have been, never see his work, never laugh with his wife or cradle his children in their arms. There would be no sad grave on the hillside where each member of the family would go alone to weep.

But some things had not changed, Rachel reminded herself. A crime had been committed against her family, and there would be no rest for any of them until justice had been served.

Tomorrow, as soon as he felt that Josh was well enough to be left, Morgan would be on the trail of the shooter who had nearly killed his son. And the first place that trail would lead him would be to Luke Vincente's ranch.

And then what?

Rachel clutched her arms around her rib cage, shivering with sudden dread. The wisdom in her father's words—that a woman in love is the worst judge of a man's character—had not been lost on her. How well had she come to know Luke in the short time they'd spent together? Could love have blinded her to who and what he really was?

She stared up at the waning moon, her mind playing out what the next day might bring. If Luke was guilty of shooting Josh, he would be expecting Morgan to come with enough men to take him. He would be armed and ready, and if they cornered him he would not go down without a fight. Any way that fight went, Rachel knew that people she loved could die.

If Luke was innocent, he would be unprepared. Unaware of what had happened, he could expose himself to danger. Tempers would flare as his protests went unheard or disbelieved. In the end, he could be shot dead on the spot or dragged off to spend the rest of his life behind bars.

Only one person was in a position to keep more blood from being spilled—Rachel herself. She would have to go to Luke now, and talk with him before it was too late. If he was innocent she would warn him, and she would remain to stand with him, shielding him from her family's anger until the truth could be heard.

If he was guilty… A chill passed through Rachel's body as she thought of the loaded revolver her father kept on a hook in the back of his wardrobe. She would take the gun with her; and if she discovered that Luke Vincente had shot her beloved brother, by all that was holy, she would bring him to justice herself!

Swiftly and silently she stole up to her room, where she scribbled a note and left it on her pillow. Then, slipping back downstairs, she took the gun from her parents' bedroom, crept out the back door and sprinted for the barn.

Luke stood alone on the front porch, peering through the darkness. Every small sound—the cry of a bird, the crackle of dry grass—galvanized his raw nerves. His eyes burned with exhaustion. His finger trembled on the trigger of the rifle he balanced against the crook of his arm.

Knowing there was bound to be trouble, he had sent them all off into the hills—the sheep, the dogs and the two young herders that Miguel's death had placed in his care. Sebastian had entreated Luke to come away with them. Ignacio had pleaded with equal fervor to be allowed to stay and fight at his side. But Luke had ordered them both away for their own safety. Now he stood alone, not knowing where the danger would come from, but certain that it would come.

Last night he had tipped the fragile balance that held all his enemies in check. Now he could do nothing but wait and see who would be first to ride against him.

Would it be Lem Carmody, using his son's humiliation as an excuse to get rid of Luke once and for all?

Would it be Morgan Tolliver, driven to action by the fact that Luke had dared lay hands on his daughter?

Would it be Miguel's murderers?

It was this last hope that had kept him here, against a fool's odds. He had flung down the gauntlet at the party, knowing it might be his only chance to draw the killers out of hiding. If they rose to the bait and came for him, he planned to stay out of sight, to watch and listen for any sign that would give away their identities. Once he knew who they were, he could take his evidence to the law. If the law refused to act, then it would fall to him to avenge his friend's death any way he could.

It was a dangerous game he was playing—a foolhardy game, some would say. But he could think of no other way to accomplish his promise without bringing harm to Miguel's tender young sons. As for his own safety…a wry smile twitched at the corner of Luke's mouth. It would not be the first time he had gambled all he had, and lost.

As the moon drifted behind a wispy veil of clouds, his thoughts drifted to Rachel and what their life together might have been like if things had been different. He imagined waking up to the warmth of her body in his bed, the amber glow of dawn on her face as he roused her with kisses. He imagined loving her, filling her with his seed, holding their children in his arms and watching them grow up. It was a beautiful dream, he told himself, but it was all of Rachel he would ever have. The path where life had led him was too rough and dangerous for her to follow.

The death scream of a rabbit, taken by some night predator, yanked his thoughts back to the present. Too edgy to stay on the porch, he slipped down the steps and checked the buildings that surrounded the open yard. His horse stood saddled and bridled beneath the eave of the nearest shed. Chickens dozed in their coop. The two milk cows stood together in the fenced pasture—safer there for the night than in the barn. Everything was quiet. Maybe too quiet.

His pulse exploded as his ears caught the sound of hoofbeats, still distant but moving rapidly closer. Straining his ears, he moved into the inky pool of shadow at the side of the house. There was only one rider, his senses told him. One rider, galloping fast, making no effort to hide or sneak. Still, a man couldn't be too cautious. Luke sank deeper into the shadows and waited, the rifle cocked, his finger on the trigger.

His throat jerked as the rider wheeled into the yard, and he recognized Rachel. Dressed in a mud-stained shirt and denims, with her hair blowing wild in the moonlight, she had never looked more beautiful to him. But she could not have chosen a more dangerous time to come.

Still wary, he lingered in the shadows, watching as she flung herself out of the saddle and raced toward the house.

"Luke!" She mounted the porch steps, calling his name in a breathy whisper. "Where are you? I need to talk to you!"

Luke had left the house dark and the front door locked, but she seemed to sense he was nearby. She rattled the doorknob and pressed her face against the window, her efforts ending in a little sob of despair.

"Luke, please…"

"You shouldn't have come here, Rachel." He stepped around the corner of the house, startling her, so that she gasped as she turned to face him.

"I had to come," she said, her voice turning steely. "There's something I have to know." She stepped into the moonlight. Only then did Luke see the glint of a revolver in her hand. Shocked into silence, he stared at her.

"My brother was shot this morning, while he was mending the fence along your property," she said, and Luke suddenly realized that it was blood, not dirt, that streaked her clothes. "He's alive, but barely. Somebody said they saw you do it."

So it had come to this. Luke groaned, aching for what she'd been through. "Somebody lied," he said.

"How do I know that?" she demanded.

"Because you know me. You know I wouldn't hurt you or anyone you loved." He took a step toward her. His gaze holding hers. "Put the gun away and get out of here, Rachel. After what happened last night, I'm expecting some dangerous company. This is no place for you to be."

"Right now the only dangerous company you need to worry about is Rachel Tolliver." Her knuckles gleamed white where they gripped the gun. "My father won't be going anywhere until he knows Josh is out of danger. And Lem Carmody slunk off with his tail between his legs when my father refused to ride with him. It's just you and me, Luke, and I want the truth."

"The truth?" He took another step toward her. She inched backward, the pistol still leveled at his chest. "Lord, Rachel, I wouldn't hurt your brother. I didn't even know he'd been shot until you told me."

"How do I know I can trust you?" Her eyes glimmered with unshed tears. "You killed a man once—an evil man, in self-defense to be sure, but all the same—"

"I killed an evil man in self-defense?" Luke felt the burst of bitter, angry laughter—laughter that startled him as much as it did her. "Rachel, my sweet, you never heard the rest of the story, did you? Never mind, you're going to hear it now. And once you do, maybe you'll understand why I have nothing to hide from you.''

The gun barrel wavered, then steadied. ''I believe we left off where Cynthia's father attacked you with his cane,'' she said. ''You were struggling with him, on the landing, and he'd pushed you back against the balustrade.''

''That's right,'' he said, wondering how many times she'd gone over the story in her mind. Doubtless, she'd pieced together what she knew to create a satisfactory ending. Well, by damn, the real ending was a lot less satisfactory, and she was going to hear it now.

''Out of the corner of my eye, I saw Cynthia come out of her room,'' he said. ''She was dressed in her robe, and I expected her to fling herself between us and try to stop the fight, but she only stood and watched, staring at us with those beautiful, cold blue eyes of hers.'' Luke shuddered as the next memory came. ''Her father had gone red in the face. His eyes were bulging. All at once he made a choking sound and clutched at his chest. One hand fumbled in the pocket of his dressing gown and came up empty.''

''He was having a heart attack!'' Rachel exclaimed, her eyes huge in her pale face.

''His weight was still holding me. I shouted at Cynthia to get help, or find his medicine if he had any, but she just stood there, staring at us as he reeled away and toppled over the rail to the marble floor, eighteen feet below.''

"He died of a heart attack!" The gun had dropped to Rachel's side. "Luke, you were innocent!"

Luke shook his head. "He died from the fall, Rachel. His neck was broken. While he was still lying there, Cynthia sent for the police and calmly told them that there'd been a fight, and in the course of the struggle, I'd pushed her father over the balustrade. I went to prison for manslaughter and counted myself lucky the charge hadn't been murder. Cynthia went to Paris, with her father's money and the Tennessee gambler she'd loved all along. As far as I know, she's living there still."

"But she set you up! She used you, Luke!" Rachel made a move to go to him, but the bitterness in his eyes held her in check. "How can you go on thinking of her? How can you let such an evil woman haunt you?"

"It's not Cynthia that haunts me."

She stared at him. "What, then?"

"At the trial, the prosecution brought out the good deeds the dead man had done—the charities his money had supported, his honesty, his kindness..."

"But all those years he'd been forcing himself on his daughter! He deserved to—" Rachel's jaw dropped as the truth struck home. "Oh, Luke!"

"When my lawyer brought up this matter, the prosecution countered with medical evidence of a riding accident the victim had suffered when his daughter was two years old. The accident had left him impotent, with no hope of recovery."

Luke gazed into Rachel's stricken face, knowing

she held his naked soul in her hands. He was asking her for his life—not because he feared she would shoot him but because he knew that if she walked away, his life would be over.

"There was no excuse for what happened except pure, blind stupidity," he said. "My temper and bad judgment caused the death of a good man. That's what haunts my nightmares and wakes me up in a cold sweat. That's what I can't forget or forgive. And if you think I would ever again take an innocent life, Rachel, you can point that gun at my heart and pull the trigger."

She gazed up at him, her lips soft and open. He could feel the struggle in her, the pull of old loyalties, the terrible weight of consequences.

"Once I asked you to choose," he said. "I'm asking you again, for the last time. If you decide to stay, I'm not in a position to promise you anything except that I'll love you forever, and that I'll work my fingers bloody to provide for you and our family. The timing couldn't be worse, I know. But maybe together you and I can put an end to this crazy war that's become living hell for us all.

"If you go, it will be to a better life, safe and familiar, with all the good things you deserve." He raked his hair back from his forehead, his knees threatening to give way beneath him, he wanted her so badly.

"I know it's not much of a choice," he said. "But I'm asking you to make it, Rachel. Here and now. Choose."

Chapter Seventeen

Rachel gazed up into Luke's face and saw the vulnerability there. She saw the raw need and the warm, protecting love. He was looking at her the way her father looked at her mother, the way Ryan looked at Molly—the way she had never dared hope that a man would look at *her*.

In the face of terrible danger, he had just offered her his soul. Did she have the courage to accept his gift and offer her own in return?

The choice she was about to make lent new meaning to the word *forever*.

Choose, he had said, and she knew Luke's pride would not allow him to ask her again. Until now, she had thought only in terms of choosing between Luke and her family. But suddenly Rachel realized that she could—and must—choose both. Turning her back on Luke, or on the parents and brothers she adored, would throw up a wall that would never come down. Only by choosing them all, with love, would she have any hope of bringing them together.

Luke had not asked her to choose between him and her people. He had simply asked her to choose him or not—a choice that was as easy as it was joyful.

The revolver dropped to the earth as she opened her arms to him. He caught her close in a long, tender kiss that swept away all traces of doubt. The kiss lingered, growing deeper and more passionate as his tongue found hers, thrusting into the damp warmth of her mouth in a sensual pantomime of what they both wanted so desperately.

Pools of liquid desire seethed and shimmered in the depths of Rachel's body. She arched against him, offering her throat, her breasts, her hips, every part of her, to his touch. Through the tight fabric of her denims, she felt the exquisite pressure of his hardness. She opened her legs, wanting more, wanting all of him.

He drew back slightly. "Rachel...sweet heaven, girl, what are you trying to do?" he murmured. "You'll burn both of us alive!"

Rachel drew him back against her, sensing the darkness and the danger around them. Love was no guarantee of safety. She could lose him, she realized, her throat tightening with sudden fear. It could happen anytime—tomorrow, even tonight.

"Love me, Luke," she cried softly. "I want to be yours tonight, now, so that if anything happens to either of us—"

"Don't." He kissed her gently. "Don't invite trouble with your words, my love. We'll find a way to stop this craziness. Together we can do anything."

"Love me," she whispered insistently, and felt his resolve begin to crumble. His next kiss was swift and hard.

"Go inside," he said, slipping the key into her hand. "I'll get your horse out of sight."

She brushed his cheek with her palm. "Hurry!" she urged him.

Luke allowed himself the pleasure of watching her flit up the steps and disappear into the house. Then he picked up her gun where she'd dropped it and led her horse toward the shed, where his own mount was tied. He felt the dark weight of uneasiness as he looped the reins around a post. Rachel had said that her father would not be coming before morning, and had intimated that Lem Carmody was too much of a coward to act alone. But what if she was wrong? Or worse, what if she was acting with them? What if she'd come here to betray him, to throw him off guard while his enemies closed in.

Why trust her? the voice of reason argued. Why trust any woman who professed to love him? He'd been taken in once and ended up behind bars. Only a fool would let himself be taken in again.

He made a careful circuit of the house and yard, his rifle in one hand and Rachel's pistol in the other. With every step, his suspicion deepened.

Should he send her packing here and now? The war inside him raged as he mounted the front porch. The very thought that she might be playing him false was enough to jerk the knot in his innards as tight as a hangman's noose, especially when he wanted her so much, not only now but forever.

Something stirred in the shadows next to the front door. Luke's pulse lurched before he recognized the big mongrel dog that he'd sent off with his herders. He sighed as the shaggy creature padded toward him, head repentantly lowered, tail wagging.

Luke patted the massive head. "Dan, you old rascal," he scolded affectionately. "I should have known you wouldn't stay with the others. All right, stay and earn your keep. If anybody comes close, you make enough racket to rouse the devil from hell. Then maybe I'll forgive you." He gave the battle-scarred ears a final scratch, grateful that the dog had shown up. Having Rachel here would be less of a worry with the protective animal on guard.

Dan settled back onto the porch as Luke opened the door and walked lightly into the house. The kitchen was dark except for a moonlit square on the wall opposite the window. There was no sign of Rachel. It crossed his mind that she might have gotten cold feet and decided to sneak out the back. And that was just as well, Luke reminded himself as he moved cautiously into the back hallway. It would save him the trouble of sending her away.

The bedroom door was closed. He took a deep breath, then turned the knob and slowly swung the door open.

Rachel was in his bed. She was sitting up, the moonlight falling like gold dust on her tousled hair and naked shoulders. The bedsheet, draped loosely beneath her arms, covered her breasts, but it was very evident that she had nothing on beneath it.

She gave a shy little laugh as Luke walked into the room. When she spoke, her voice quivered nervously. "Well, don't just stand there staring, Luke. I meant every word I said to you out there. Now come here and…kiss me."

The words, spoken with a little stammer, would have been a brazen tease coming from some women Luke had known. In Rachel's tremulous voice, they went straight to his heart. Lord, how could he not trust this woman? How could he not cherish and love her?

He walked toward the bed, but even as he reached out to touch her hair, the old doubts gnawed at him. She was a rich man's pampered daughter; he was an ex-convict, a misfit, fighting to keep what little he had in the world. The weight of who he was would drag her down for the rest of her life.

"Dearest Rachel," he murmured, smoothing back her tangled curls. "I love you more than I've ever loved anything in my life, but sometimes love isn't enough. I'm no good for you, girl. I'm in no position to keep you safe or give you the good things you deserve—"

"Hush," she said, rubbing her head against his hand. "I love you, too, Luke. That's the only thing that really matters. If we love each other, we can work out the rest as we go along."

Her hand reached out, caught his belt buckle and gently but firmly drew him toward her. Luke's breath caught in his throat as she worked at the buckle with unsteady fingers until its parts separated. By the time she started on his trouser buttons he was all but bursting. The color rose in her cheeks as her fingers brushed his hardness through the taut fabric, but she did not stop.

Luke groaned. "Rachel, if you don't—"

"Hush," she whispered, her sea-colored eyes brimming with love. "I want to do this. I want to see you, to touch you—oh!"

As the last button fell away, he caught her and pulled her up against him. Still gripping the sheet around her, he kissed her face, her lips, her soft, pale throat. Her hand fumbled with his shirt buttons and found the bare chest beneath, with its crisp mat of hair. She smoothed it with her fingers, touching his nipples, finding the dark path that led down the midline of his torso to the shallow indentation of his navel, then lower still to—

She hesitated, suddenly trembling. Aching for her touch, he caught her hand and raised it to his lips. "Don't be afraid, Rachel," he murmured, "there's no part of me that will hurt you."

Gently he guided her hand downward, and this time there was no hesitation. A shudder passed through Luke's body as her fingers closed around him.

"Oh," she whispered, her voice husky with wonder.

"What is it?" he teased.

"You're…so big and hard and fierce, and yet so soft, like steel wrapped in velvet…beautiful…" She began to stroke him, her fingers exploring his shape and texture until Luke feared he would explode in her hand.

"Lie down, love," he whispered, lowering her to the pillows. "If we're going to do this, we're going to do it properly."

Rachel watched as he stripped off his shirt, dropped his boots and trousers and stood leaning over her in moonlight that threw every nick and scar on his muscular body into stark relief. Those marks spoke more eloquently than words of the life he had lived. Luke Vincente was a man who fought, worked and loved with his whole heart and soul. Now she was his, and this loving would be the start of their life together.

He began with her lips, his kisses gentle and teasing. His sensual, nibbling mouth ignited hot rivulets that flowed downward to form shimmering coils of need in the depths of her body. Her hands caught his hair, pulling his head down to her breasts. His mouth found her nipples, his tongue licking, caressing each one until she wanted to scream with pleasure. When he began to suck her, she felt the sudden tightening, the sweet, ancient rhythm of her body responding to his. She cradled his head against her breasts, her hips rocking against him, her thighs slick with her own wetness. Wanting more, she moaned and arched upward against his hard belly. "Take me…" she whispered. "Please…"

"Wait," he murmured, his hand moving down to the source of the wetness, fingers parting her flesh, stroking her, arousing the most exquisite sensations Rachel had ever known. She began to move against his hand, desperately, urgently, feeling herself explode against his fingers.

"Oh!" she gasped like a drowning swimmer, lost in a whirlpool of sensation. "Oh, Luke…"

He shifted upward between her legs. She heard the rasp of his breath, felt a slight, tearing pain that swiftly passed as he filled her. This, then, was the mystery, the wonderful secret. It was so simple, and yet so much more than she had ever imagined. He was part of her; she was part of him, and she felt nothing but a sweet, overpowering love.

Instinctively, she raised her hips and felt him glide deeper. Her whole body began to sing as she moved with him, meeting his strokes with her own thrust. He moaned, and suddenly it was as if they were soaring together, spiraling up and up to a bursting release that left her weeping with the pure joy of it.

He buried his face in her hair, clasping her tenderly as they drifted back to earth.

They lay together on the bed, fully clothed now as they waited in the late-night darkness. Rachel could feel the tension in Luke's body as she nestled against him. He was wide awake, alert to every changing shadow, to every small night sound that reached his ears—the scurry of a wood rat, the breathy shifting of the horses beneath the shed, the drone of cricket songs in the woodpile outside the bedroom window.

He had tried to talk her into leaving, but Rachel had argued that, whatever the danger, her place was with him. When her father found her note and came

looking for her, as he surely would, it was urgent that
she be here. She needed to convince Morgan that
Luke was innocent of shooting Josh before tempers
flared and another tragedy occurred.

As for the rest... Rachel sighed and slid a loving
arm across Luke's chest. She could only hope that
Ryan would come along as well, and that his support
would help Morgan accept Luke into their family.

Luke brushed a trail of kisses along Rachel's hair-
line. "It'll be getting light in a couple of hours," he
murmured. "I'll breathe easier once this business
with your father is over."

Her arms tightened around him. "Promise me
you'll stay inside the house until I get him settled
down," she said. "He's been through a bad time.
Seeing you right away will only make things worse."

Luke exhaled slowly. "All right. But I wish we
could have done this the right way, love, with me
coming to court you and going to him to ask for your
hand."

"I know," Rachel whispered in the darkness. "But
he's a fair man. He'll come around. If only—"

"Ssh!" Luke had gone rigid against her. "Listen!"

Rachel held her breath, straining her ears in the
darkness until she heard what Luke was hearing—the
sound of horses, mingled with the low, breathy growl
of the dog.

"Someone's coming." Luke was on his feet at
once, reaching for his rifle.

"No!" Rachel caught his sleeve. "We can't have
you stepping out on that porch with a gun. Stay inside

while I talk with my father—that's what you promised me.''

He strode into the dark kitchen and peered cautiously out the front window.

"Do you see them yet?" she asked anxiously.

Luke shook his head. "I don't like this, Rachel. Three o'clock in the morning is no time for your family to come calling."

"Someone went looking for me and found my note, that's all," Rachel said. "Get me a lantern. I'll be fine."

Luke took a lantern from above the stove, struck a match and touched it to the wick. Soft golden light flooded the kitchen. "Be careful," he said. "I'll be watching. Wave the lantern if there's trouble—"

"There won't be any trouble." She kissed him lightly. "But you'd better keep Dan inside. I don't want him raising too much of a fuss."

She took the lantern and waited until Luke had called the dog into the house before she stepped outside. As she closed the door and turned to face the darkness the worries she'd held back for Luke's sake swept over her.

She hadn't expected anyone to find the note on her bed until morning. Why would her father be looking for her at this hour? Could Josh have taken a turn for the worse?

Holding the lantern high, she plunged down the steps and raced toward the gate. Merciful heaven, what if her brother had died? What if it had happened while she was here, thinking of nothing but her own pleasure?

Clouds had spilled across the sky, hiding the moon and plunging the landscape into blackness. Rachel's lantern provided no more than a tiny circle of light as she paused to listen for the horses. The night was eerily silent.

Her heart began to pound. Where were they? She had heard them. So had Luke. What was happening here?

As if in answer to her question, a big, rough hand was suddenly clapped over her mouth. Strong arms jerked her backward, off her feet. As she kicked and clawed, the lantern fell to the damp ground, flared briefly and flickered out, plunging everything into darkness.

''Help me hang on to this hellcat!'' a familiar voice growled. Rachel's heart dropped as she recognized Bart Carmody.

Hands grabbed her wrists and elbows, holding her fast. As Rachel's eyes became accustomed to the darkness, she found herself staring at three bandana-masked faces.

Under different circumstances she might have laughed at their pathetic disguises. It was easy to recognize Lem Carmody's bull neck and bulging belly, as well as Slade's narrow eyes and ferret-thin face and body. Bart would be the one behind her, his fingers digging into her ribs where he gripped her body. The fourth man was one of the hands at the Carmody ranch, a surly, unkempt Irishman whose name Rachel could not recall, but whose shaggy black eyebrows she would have known anywhere.

She swallowed the scream in her throat. The last thing she wanted was to bring Luke charging outside to her rescue—that would be exactly what the Carmodys were counting on. But it made no difference whether she screamed or not, Rachel realized. Luke would have seen the lantern drop and go out. For better or worse, he would know there was trouble.

"Rachel!" At the sound of his voice, her heart sank. She could see him now beneath the overhanging eave of the porch. He had come out with the rifle, closing the door behind him. "Rachel!" he called again. "Are you all right? What's happening out there?"

Rachel fought against Bart's smothering hand as she tried to call out a warning. But it was no use. Bart gripped her tightly, all but cutting off her breath. She writhed helplessly as Slade drew his pistol and took a step forward.

"We got your whore, sheep man!" he crowed. "Less'n you want to hear the little lady scream, throw that gun off the porch and come out where we can see you, with your hands up."

Luke did not move. "Let her go!" he shouted. "When I know she's safe, I'll do anything you say."

In reply, Bart removed his hand from Rachel's mouth and gave her arm an abrupt twist behind her back. The pain in her shoulder was so excruciating that a sharp little cry escaped her lips. "No, don't—"

she called out. "Luke, don't listen to them! My father will kill them if they hurt me!"

But Luke had already flung the rifle to the ground. Rachel heard the gun thud against the earth. She saw him moving down the steps with his hands in the air. "What do you want with me, Carmody?" he demanded. "Let Rachel go, and you can have it. Your fight is with me, not with her."

Lem lumbered forward, pushing Slade aside. With a snort of impatience he jerked the useless mask off his face. "I didn't come to fight you, Vincente," he growled. "I came to bargain. I have a bill of sale for your land right here." He drew a folded paper and a fountain pen out of his vest. "Sign it, and your little bird goes free."

"No, Luke! It's a trick!" Rachel struggled in Bart's arms, scratching and clawing. "Don't—"

Her vision exploded as Bart slapped her, snapping her head to one side so that she felt the blow all the way down her spine. Luke made a lunge for Bart, but the big Irishman stepped between them and jabbed the muzzle of his shotgun into Luke's belly. "Don't you move, man, or I blow your guts out," he said.

The moon had emerged among the thinning clouds, casting a ghostly light over them all. Bart's arms gripped Rachel like a vise. From where his blow had split her lip, she felt the blood trickling down her chin, dripping onto her shirt.

"You could've had me, Rachel," Bart muttered in her ear. "You could have been my wife and had everything you ever wanted in this world. Instead you chose *this*...a sheep man, a killer and an ex-convict. Look at him! Take a good long look."

Rachel's gaze met Luke's through the moonlit darkness. In his eyes she read worry, anger, and a love so deep and strong that it filled her soul. Lem did not intend to let either of them live—Luke knew that and so did she. They both knew too much. The only advantage they had left was the fact that they had nothing to lose.

"Let her go, Carmody," Luke said. "When I know she's safe I'll sign anything you put in front of me. Otherwise you're not getting anything. I'll let you kill me before I sign away my land."

Lem scowled. "Sign, and she's as good as home," he lied. "Give us any more trouble, and we'll tie you up and let you watch the show while we all have our fun with her. How'd you like that, sheep man? I'll wager you've had your turn with her already. How was she, eh?"

A vein throbbed in Luke's temple. He strained against the shotgun that held him in check, and Rachel knew he was dangerously close to making a lunge for Lem's throat.

Grasping for some diversion, she fixed her eyes on Slade. "It was you who shot my brother, wasn't it, Slade?" she demanded. "It couldn't have been very hard. All you had to do was go back for the wire cutters you'd left behind, circle around the rocks and take aim. What a lying, cowardly, low-bellied snake you are!"

Slade flashed her a lopsided grin, as if she'd just paid him a high compliment.

"I even know why you did it," she continued, driven by desperation. "Your family wanted my father to join them in attacking Luke. When he refused, you had to give him a reason to change his mind. And that old sheepherder, Miguel. Your family was responsible for beating him to death, too. Am I right? Give me that much satisfaction before I die, Slade."

"Shut that woman up!" Lem snarled at Bart, and Rachel felt Bart's sweaty hand clamp over her mouth again. Lem turned back toward Luke. "So what'll it be, sheep man? Sign the paper or watch the show?"

"I'll sign." Luke's voice was like winter ice. "But first I'd like to know why you're so all-fired anxious to own what amounts to nine hundred acres of sheep pasture. Are you planning to go into the wool and mutton business, Carmody?"

Lem's mouth tightened, but Slade, who was standing behind him, hooted with laughter. "Hellfire, he's gonna die anyway! Let's tell him and watch him squirm! Your land's got oil under it, sheep man! Beautiful black gold! We found it this spring, bubblin' up around that bad water hole! Looks like enough there to make us all filthy rich!"

"Shut up, you little fool," Lem snarled. "Let's get this over with!"

Luke's expression had not even flickered. "Give me the pen and the paper," he said. "Congratulations, Carmody, you're going to be a rich man if you can live with yourself."

Lem stepped forward with the legal document and the pen, but the big, slow Irishman was standing in his way. There was a moment of awkward shifting, and in that moment Luke moved.

Knocking Lem and the Irishman aside, Luke made a headlong drive for Bart. "Run, Rachel!" he yelled as the two smashed together. "Get to your horse! Get out of here!"

Bart reeled backward as his flailing arms let Rachel go. Then recovering, he came at Luke. Rachel burst out of the melee of flying fists and bodies, her eyes frantically assessing the scene. The Irishman had fallen badly. He was struggling to stand, whimpering as he clutched his shoulder. Lem was fumbling for his pistol. Slade was dancing back and forth, trying to get a shot at Luke without hitting Bart instead.

Luke had told her to run. But even if she made it to the horses without being shot, she could not, would not leave him behind.

The thought flashed through her mind that she could get both of their horses and come charging back for him. But the odds that she would be too late were fearfully high. She was still weighing them when she caught sight of the rifle Luke had dropped. It lay in the dirt, a dozen paces from the front steps. If she could get to it—

With no more time to think, Rachel dived for the rifle. Her hands groped for the stock; her finger found the trigger. With agility that would have done credit to a cat, she rolled and came up onto her feet with the barrel leveled at Lem Carmody's heart.

"Tell your boys to back off, Lem, if they want you to live," she said, her voice flat and cold. "I'll shoot you. Don't think I won't."

"Rachel, sweetheart!" Lem smiled affably. "You can't shoot us all, you know. You'll be gunned down before you can get off a second shot."

"Fine," Rachel snapped. "But I won't go down without taking you along with me, Lem!"

Luke and Bart had stopped grappling. The Irishman had fallen back against the woodpile, still clutching his shoulder. Slade simply stared at her dumbfounded. For the interval of a heartbeat, everyone seemed to freeze. Then Rachel glimpsed something in Bart's hazel eyes—something she recognized as pure, naked greed.

As Bart's hand moved to his holstered pistol, Rachel's mistake slammed home. Her threat to Lem's life would not stop Bart from shooting Luke. With his father out of the way, Bart would inherit the ranch and all that went with it. Nothing would suit him better than to have Rachel pull the trigger.

She was aiming at the wrong man.

"No!" She jerked the rifle toward Bart and fired. The shot went wild, but in the confusion, Luke managed to deliver a solid punch to Bart's jaw, knocking him onto his back.

"Come on!" Luke grabbed the rifle in one hand and Rachel's arm in the other. Together they started for the shed, where their horses were waiting.

They had gone only a few steps when Slade's pistol rang out behind them.

Rachel felt Luke's body jerk. He spun sideways, blood streaming from the wound in his shoulder. The rifle dropped from his hand as he pushed Rachel away from him. "Go on," he gasped. "You can make it, love! Run!"

"No!" Rachel shoved herself beneath his good arm. The horses were out of reach, but if she could get him inside the house, they could barricade the door long enough for her to bind his wound and find another gun.

Slade and the Carmodys were closing in around them. Only the fact that Luke had not signed the paper was keeping them from killing him outright, Rachel realized. If she could get him inside, they might have a chance. But how could she get him up the steps before time ran out?

From the inside of the door came the sound of frantic snarling and scratching. Only then did Rachel remember they had left the dog in the house.

Leaving Luke on the steps, she made a lunge for the door and flung it open. The big mongrel came barreling across the porch and shot into the yard. Snapping and snarling, it leaped on Slade and locked its fangs into his upper arm. Rachel heard him shriek before she dragged Luke over the threshold, slammed the door shut and shoved the bolt home.

Luke was bleeding badly. Ripping off her own shirt, she pressed it hard against the wound, praying it would stanch the blood. Cradling him in her arms, she crouched beside him in the darkness. She dared not leave him, even long enough to look for a gun. There was nothing to do now but wait.

Luke's eyelids fluttered open. His fingers groped for Rachel's hand, found it and squeezed hard. "I love you," he whispered. "Whatever happens, remember that."

Rachel kissed his damp hair, his forehead, his eyelids. "No whatevers," she murmured. "We're going to get through this, my love. We're going to be together always and live to see our grandchildren grow up. Now rest, my dearest. Save your strength…"

Outside, the night had grown strangely quiet. Suddenly she heard the clamor of galloping horses and shouting voices. Moments later, frantic footsteps echoed across the porch. Fists pounded on the door.

"Rachel!" a voice shouted. "Rachel, are you in there? Are you all right?"

The voice was Morgan Tolliver's.

Epilogue

July 2, 1901

"Turn around, Rachel! Let me look at you!" Molly laughed with delight as she rested against the pillows, nursing her newborn son. The tiny golden-haired boy, who had entered the world just two nights ago, was beautiful and healthy and perfect. But his birth had not been an easy one. The doctor had forbidden Molly to leave her bed and go downstairs, even for Rachel's wedding.

Rachel pirouetted in a slow circle, letting her skirt of soft white voile float outward over the ruffled petticoat beneath. Her veil of simple tulle, anchored to her upswept hair by a single fresh pink rose, drifted like a cloud around her radiant face.

"Do I look all right? Nothing unbuttoned or hanging out where it shouldn't?" she asked anxiously.

"You look perfect!" Molly said. "You're absolutely glowing. Ryan and I are so happy for you!"

Rachel bent over the bed, kissed Molly's cheek,

and brushed a fingertip over the baby's downy head. "Maybe by next summer there'll be a playmate for this little miracle of yours," she said.

"I hope so." Molly found Rachel's hand and squeezed it hard. Her lovely violet eyes were moist with tears.

A sharp rap at the door broke the stillness between them. "Rachel!" Her father's voice penetrated the thick planks. "Everyone's in place downstairs. Should I have your mother signal the fiddler?"

"In a moment!" Rachel called back. "I'll be right out!"

As she adjusted her veil in the tall looking glass, Rachel's mind flew back to the last time she had heard Morgan's voice through a door. It was a miracle that he and the other men had come when they did—and the miracle had been Josh. In the dark hours before dawn, her brother had awakened long enough to tell his father that he had seen Slade raise his rifle from behind the rocks, just before he'd been shot. Hurrying to tell Rachel the news, Ryan had found the note on her pillow.

By the time Morgan, Ryan, Jacob and Johnny Chang arrived at Luke's place, the Carmodys had heard them coming and scattered, leaving nothing but the wounded dog. Rachel had since lovingly nursed both the dog and Luke back to health.

Armed with evidence that included Bart's distinctive boot track, a posse from Sheridan had rounded up Lem, Bart, Slade, the Irishman and the other hands who had not already fled. They were now in jail, awaiting trial.

But Rachel would not allow herself to think about the Carmodys now, on the happiest day of her life. Blowing a kiss to Molly and the baby, she opened the door and stepped out onto the landing to take her father's arm. She smiled up at him and saw the unexpected glimmer of tears in his eyes as the music began.

As they started down the stairs, she looked down at the loved faces below them. Rachel had wanted a simple wedding with just the family and a few close friends. But by the time they included the longtime workers on the ranch, the entire Chang clan, Luke's two young herders and her own family, the guests filled the dining room, the parlor, the entry and part of the porch.

As they neared the bottom of the stairs, Rachel caught sight of her mother standing before the fireplace, wearing a blue dress and a tearful smile. Jacob and Josh stood beside her, dressed in identical brown suits.

Standing next to the preacher, she saw Luke—her love, her life. From this day forward they would share every happiness, every sorrow, every wonderful adventure that the future had to offer them.

His eyes shone with love as they met hers. Rachel felt her father's arm release her. Radiant with joy, she moved forward to stand at Luke's side.

* * * * * *

Harlequin Historicals®
Historical Romantic Adventure!

IMMERSE YOURSELF IN THE RUGGED
LANDSCAPE AND INTOXICATING
ROMANCE ON THE AMERICAN FRONTIER.

<u>**ON SALE NOVEMBER 2004**</u>

WYOMING WOMAN by Elizabeth Lane

After attending college back east, Rachel Tolliver
returns to her family's cattle ranch and falls for sheep
rancher Luke Vicente. Will their romance mean disaster
for their feuding families—or can love truly conquer all?

THE WEDDING CAKE WAR by Lynna Banning

Spinster Leora Mayfield answers an ad for a mail-order
bride, only to find she must compete with two other
ladies to wed Colonel Macready. Can baking the perfect
wedding cake win the contest—and the colonel?

<u>**ON SALE DECEMBER 2004**</u>

THE LAST HONEST LAWMAN by Carol Finch

After witnessing a shooting, Rozalie Matthews is
abducted by wounded outlaw Eli McCain. Framed
for a murder he didn't commit, Eli is desperate to
prove his innocence. Can Roz listen to her heart
and help him—before it's too late?

MONTANA WIFE by Jillian Hart

Rayna Ludgrin faces financial ruin after her
husband's death, until chivalrous neighbor
Daniel Lindsay offers his help—and his hand in
marriage. When their friendship deepens, Rayna
finds love is sweeter the second time around.

www.eHarlequin.com

HHWEST34

Harlequin Historicals®
Historical Romantic Adventure!

TRAVEL BACK TO THE FUTURE
FOR ROMANCE—WESTERN-STYLE!
ONLY WITH HARLEQUIN HISTORICALS.

ON SALE JANUARY 2005

TEXAS LAWMAN by Carolyn Davidson

Sarah Murphy will do whatever it takes to save her nephew
from dangerous fortune seekers—including marrying lawman
Blake Caulfield. Can the Lone Star lawman keep them
safe—without losing his heart to the feisty lady?

WHIRLWIND GROOM by Debra Cowan

Desperate to avenge the murder of her parents, all trails lead
Josie Webster to Whirlwind, Texas, much to the chagrin of
charming sheriff Davis Lee Holt. Let the games begin as
Davis Lee tries to ignore the beautiful seamstress who stirs
both his suspicions and his desires....

ON SALE FEBRUARY 2005

PRAIRIE WIFE by Cheryl St.John

Jesse and Amy Shelby find themselves drifting apart after
the devastating death of their young son. Can they put
their grief behind them and renew their deep and abiding
love—before it's too late?

THE UNLIKELY GROOM by Wendy Douglas

Stranded by her brother in a rough-and-rugged Alaskan
gold town, Ashlynne Mackenzie is forced to rely on the
kindness of saloon owner Lucas Templeton. But kindness
has nothing to do with Lucas's urges to both protect the
innocent woman and to claim her for his own.